OUND

An EVERNEATH Novel

BRODI ASHTON

BALZER + BRAY
An Imprint of HarperCollins*Publishers*

Balzer + Bray is an imprint of HarperCollins Publishers.

Library of Congress Cataloging-in-Publication Data
Ashton, Brodi.
Everbound : an Everneath novel / Brodi Ashton. — 1st ed.
    p. cm. — (Everneath)
Summary: "Now that Nikki Beckett's boyfriend has been sucked into the
Tunnels of the Everneath, Nikki must journey down to the underworld to
bring him back before he is lost forever."—Provided by publisher.
    ISBN 978-0-06-207116-3
    [1. Supernatural—Fiction. 2. Future life—Fiction. 3. Love—Fiction.
4. Hell—Fiction.] I. Title.
PZ7.A8276Eum 2013   2012028327
[E]—dc23   CIP
                                                                  AC

Typography by Ray Shappell
Map illustration by Jordan Saia
13 14 15 16   LP/RRDH   10 9 8 7 6 5 4 3 2 1
❖
First Edition

To Sam
For always being sure,
even when I'm not

It is by going down into the abyss
that we recover the treasures of life.
Where you stumble, there lies your treasure.
—Joseph Campbell

THE EVERNEATH

PROLOGUE

Ancient Greeks called it the Underworld or Hades. Ancient Egyptians called it Aaru or the Duat. Both believed it was a place for the souls of the dead.

Both were wrong.

Those who know the truth call it the Everneath, and it's not an afterlife. It's a place for the Everliving and the Forfeits.

The Everliving are immortals who survive by feeding on the emotions of humans.

Forfeits are humans trapped in the Tunnels of the Everneath, being drained of all energy to supply the Everneath with power. The only escape from the Tunnels is death.

Jack—the boy who got me through hell, the boy I Returned for, the boy I love—is in the Tunnels. He is a Forfeit.

I know the truth. It should've been me.

ONE

AT NIGHT
My bedroom.

I see Jack every night. In my dreams.

He's lying next to me. Parallel worlds—the Surface for me, the Tunnels of the Everneath for him—that overlap at this one spot, and only for a moment. In my bedroom, while I dream.

His hair still curls in perfect waves past his ears. Tonight, the steel post that pierces his eyebrow shines in the dull moonlight through my window. It looks as if I could raise my finger and touch it.

But I have to remind myself that it doesn't really shine, because the post is a faint copy of the real object. Just like Jack is.

He is starting to forget little things. Things he never would have forgotten before.

"What do we talk about when I'm here?" he asks.

"All sorts of things," I say.

"Like what?"

"You always say you miss me."

He puts his hand over mine, and it slips right through. He has forgotten he is a ghost to me. Or maybe I am the ghost. "That's obvious," he says. "What else?"

"You talk about the time Jules told you I liked you."

"And?"

My words flow out as the memories wrap around my heart like a blanket. "You talk about your uncle's cabin. The Christmas Dance. How my hair hides my eyes. How my hand fits in yours. How you love me. How you'll never leave."

"And what do you say to me?"

"I say I'm sorry. And I ask you how I'm supposed to do this." My voice wavers. "How am I supposed to do this, Jack?"

"Do what?"

"Live this borrowed life. Without you. Knowing that you're there because of me."

He is quiet. The first rays of sunlight stream in and morning is upon us, always too fast, and I can't help but stir in my sleep.

He watches me. He knows I am about to wake up. "How do we say good-bye?"

I try not to let my face show my heartache at that word, or my anger at the Everneath for existing in the first place, or my resentment of Cole for taking me to the Feed just over a year ago. But mostly, I have to hide how angry I am with myself. Jack doesn't like to see me angry.

When I speak, I make sure my voice is calm. "We say 'See you tomorrow.'"

"See you tomorrow, Becks." He squeezes his eyes shut, as if he can't stand to watch me disappear.

I place my hand over his, helplessly grasping at air.

I am worried about the forgetting. Most nights he is lucid; his thoughts are clear. But then he has bad nights, like this one; and I wonder if he will eventually forget me, and then he won't visit me in my dreams anymore.

If that happens, will I be able to keep him alive?

The sun rises, I open my eyes, and Jack is gone. My bed is empty, and I'm left with only my guilt for a companion. I hug my pillow tight and wonder how long I will be able to survive with the crack in my heart.

Perhaps it will grow large enough to consume me.

If it does, will I find Jack in the next life?

NOW

The Surface. My bedroom.

The headline read THE DEADS POP UP IN AUSTIN.

I rolled my eyes. That made it sound like the beginning of a zombie apocalypse and not what it really was, which was a surprise concert given by the Dead Elvises in Austin, Texas.

A couple of months ago, a reporter from *Rolling Stone* magazine dubbed them the "next Grateful Deads." Ever since, the nickname the Deads had stuck. I wanted to punch that reporter.

But lately, I kind of wanted to punch everybody.

I printed the article, cut out the headline, and took it over to my desk. Probably most people would have kept things like this on their computer, but when it came to my search for Cole—and the rest of the Dead Elvises—I liked the tangible clues. The map I could spread out. The headlines I could fold and refold.

If it kept my hands busy, it kept my brain busy; and if it kept my brain busy, it was almost possible to keep the memories of my latest dreams of Jack tucked away.

Almost.

Who was I kidding? Most mornings it felt as if I had to glue the pieces of myself back together just to start the day. Because what Jack had done for me—when he jumped into the Tunnels and took my place in hell—it had fractured my soul.

I stole a glance at the shelf above my desk, where several pictures of Jack and me rested alongside a crumpled note with the words *Ever Yours* scrawled in Jack's messy boy handwriting. The ghost of his presence was everywhere—in the deck of cards set out on the desk, the quilt on my bed, the book he'd lent me years ago—but it was especially strong on this shelf. I didn't know how many times I'd tried to put the pictures away, in a drawer or under my bed, out of sight. But I couldn't.

I went to reach for one in the corner that showed half of my face and all of Jack's. It was one of those self-taken shots. Jack had turned the camera around on us at the top of the Alpine Slide, but all you could see was our faces and the blur of evergreens in the background.

The memory squeezed me like a vise around my heart, and just as my fingers touched the frame I yanked my hand back, sending the picture flying off the shelf. The glass in the frame shattered on the wood floor. The sound it made was more than glass shattering. It was the sound of old wounds reopening, and it echoed from deep inside of me. I put my hands over my head and squeezed. Sometimes it was the only way to keep the pieces inside from falling out.

It was thoughts like this that made me realize no amount of visualization exercises from Dr. Hill—my Dad-mandated therapist—could help me.

I heard the sound of footsteps in the hallway, and I held my breath. Maybe my father had heard the glass break. I kept waiting for a knock on the door, but it never came. Running my fingers through my hair, I tried to straighten up my desk and focus on the map. I couldn't let my dad see how broken I was. Not just the kind of broken warranted by the sudden disappearance of the boy I loved. The kind of broken where I knew I was the only one to blame.

My dad had been through enough.

The top middle drawer of my desk was large and flat, perfect for the map of the United States. I uncapped my red pen and put a shaky little red dot over Austin, then added the clipping to the pile of headlines next to the map.

DEAD ELVISES SAY "THANK YOU" TO CHICAGO FANS WITH SURPRISE CONCERT

DEAD ELVISES GIVE IMPROMPTU FREE CONCERT IN NYC

I was looking for the Deads too, but not because I was a fan. Cole Stockton, their lead guitarist, had disappeared on me three weeks ago without a trace, taking away my only chance to get to the Everneath.

My only chance to find Jack.

I closed my eyes.

Stay with me, Becks. Dream of me. I am ever yours.

Two months ago Jack said those words to me. They were the last words he spoke before the Tunnels of the Everneath sucked him away. The words haunted me, and I knew I wouldn't be able to live any kind of life until he was back with me. The problem was, how to get him back.

Not just anybody can go to the Everneath. In all the research I'd done over the past two months, I'd never come across a human who'd made it to the Everneath without the help of an Everliving. No one who'd made it there—and back—alone.

So it all came down to Cole. He and his band were the only Everlivings I knew.

Cole had visited me once, about a month after that horrible night. He'd stood in the yard outside my house, his swagger gone. He wanted me to become immortal like him.

I have ninety-nine years until I have to Feed again, he'd said. *What makes you think I'd ever give up?*

He'd seemed so smug. I'd placed my hand on his chest.

If you feel anything, *please leave me alone,* I'd said.

I didn't think he would, but he did. He'd disappeared. My only connection to the Everneath was gone. Now I regretted asking him to leave me alone.

I wrote the date next to Austin, Texas. *6/1.*

Running my finger eastward, I read the previous tour stops: Houston, 5/29; New Orleans, 5/27; Tampa, 5/24.

The Dead Elvises were heading west. For a little while, I had tried to guess which city they'd end up in next, pack up my car, and take off. But my dad could only take the sudden disappearances of his daughter so many times, and I was already in enough therapy now.

Besides, the spontaneous trips never helped my search, because I always guessed wrong. It was a pointless quest. As much as I thought I knew Cole, I was bad at anticipating his moves.

I ran my finger west of Austin, toward the possible cities for their next surprise stop. Fort Worth? Albuquerque? Phoenix? I bent the path northward until my finger rested on my hometown. Could I allow myself to hope that the Dead Elvises would return to Park City? That I would finally get my chance to grab a strand of Cole's hair and go to the Everneath?

I leaned back in my chair and looked at all the red dots. From farther away, they formed the shape of a backward *C*, starting in Chicago and swinging to the east before dipping to the south and now heading west. Yes. I could hope they were coming home, to Park City.

If there was one way I'd changed in the past few months, it was this: I always hoped.

But the fact was, until I found Cole, or a lock of his hair, I was stuck on the Surface. I'd seen a human sacrifice swallow a strand of Everliving hair once. A woman, in clothes that didn't fit right, with a face that had seen too much of the world, had sat in the back of the Shop-n-Go, on the spot that was the weak point between the Surface and the Everneath. Maxwell Bones, second guitarist of the Dead Elvises, had handed her a pill. She swallowed it and slipped downward beneath the floor.

At the time, the scene had made me sick. But I would do it now if it meant I could get to Jack.

Not that I had a plan for what I would do if I got to the Everneath. Cole once told me I wouldn't know where to start looking for the Tunnels that held Jack captive. But maybe the arbiters of energy—the Shades—would find me first. They were in charge of maximizing the energy stolen from humans to fuel the Everneath. They were the ones who took humans to the Tunnels. Two months ago I was running away from them; but maybe now the Shades would find me and take me to the Tunnels, and maybe then I could figure out a way to get to Jack. . . .

But I was getting ahead of myself, thinking of all the things I didn't know. I had to focus on the one thing I did know, and that was the fact that I couldn't save Jack without getting to the Everneath; and to do that I needed Cole.

Or at least a piece of his DNA.

Because as long as I was stuck on the Surface, Jack would be stuck in the Tunnels. Until the Tunnels drained every last drop of energy inside of him.

Until he died.

My hand went to my stomach, fighting against the sudden pain that always hit when I thought of Jack dying. I looked at the shards of glass on the floor. They would never be whole again.

Wasn't I just as irreparable?

Shaking my head, I closed my eyes and tilted back on my chair, imagining instead seeing Cole again. His dark eyes. Cheekbones that looked as if they'd been chiseled by a sculptor thousands of years ago. His blond hair, specifically the wispy hairs that always ran wild around his face.

If I could get close enough, I could pluck one of those hairs out of his head.

It was all I could think about. Especially considering the task ahead of me today. I opened my eyes and reached for the knitting basket lying at the side of my desk. This was going to be one of those days when I would be able to start and finish an entire sweater rather than let my mind go to the dark places.

As I completed the first row of stitches and looped the red yarn around the end of the needle, the knots in the pattern tightened and the knots in my stomach loosened. Knitting was survival.

A pungent aroma made me freeze midrow.

Bacon.

Something was wrong. Bacon cooking? Maybe no one else would've been alarmed by this, but I hadn't smelled fresh bacon in our house in almost two years.

Since before my mom died.

I flattened the headlines and closed the map drawer. As far as I knew, my dad didn't know about the drawer, and he never would.

As I opened my bedroom door, the bacon smell was joined by the clattering of pans coming from the kitchen. I didn't know if it was because of the smell and the sounds, but a sudden memory flashed through my brain—of my mom and me sitting at breakfast on a Sunday morning. I used to love bacon. Sometimes the smell and the promise of bacon was the only effective incentive for me to do my chores. Before she died, my mom had used the tactic several times. But no one else in my family liked bacon very much, which is why I couldn't figure out who would be cooking it.

I quickly dressed and then followed the scent of bacon to the kitchen, where my dad was bent over the stove, a spatula in hand. His freshly combed hair looked grayer than usual in the morning light that streamed through the window. His face was still too hollow in the cheeks, as it had been for a few months now.

The guilt weighed heavy in my stomach for a moment.

"What's the occasion?" I asked.

"Morning, sunshine." He infused his voice with exuberance. "No occasion. Just thought it's been a while since we've had a proper breakfast. You still love bacon, right?"

He was so . . . chipper. "Yes," I said warily.

"Excellent!" He grabbed a plate off the granite countertop and filled it with scrambled eggs and about half a pig's worth of bacon. "There's some juice on the table."

"Okay. Um . . . thanks."

I sat next to Tommy, my ten-year-old brother, who was making his way through a pile of eggs. He held up his fork and gave me a goofy grin. "Breakfast is awesome!"

Okay, maybe it had been longer than I'd thought since we'd done this.

"Yeah, it is."

I looked down at my own plate of protein and resisted the urge to vomit. Maybe eating bacon wasn't like riding a bike. My stomach was protesting just looking at it.

My dad clicked off the stove and brought his own plate over to the table.

"This is nice, isn't it?" he said.

"It's awesome!" Tommy said.

I suppressed a laugh. It was as if we'd never eaten before.

"You were up late last night," my dad said. He probably noticed the light on in my room. "Couldn't sleep?"

"I was reading." More like studying. Every myth I could get my hands on.

My dad hoisted his briefcase onto the table. "That reminds me. I have something for you."

I narrowed my eyes at the bacon suspiciously, thinking that it suddenly looked like a bribe. "What is it?"

"Hold on." He fished around deep inside the leather case.

"Ah. Here it is." He pulled out a large, worn book. "Sally at the office had it."

He handed it to me. The cover read *D'Aulaires' Book of Greek Myths*. I couldn't have been more surprised if he'd handed me a unicorn. I thumbed through the first few pages. They told the story of Gaia the Earth, who fell in love with the Sky. Accompanying the story was a series of beautiful artwork. "Okay, Dad. What's going on?"

He diverted his eyes. "Nothing. Can't a dad give his daughter gifts?"

"Yes. But not when that gift is a book about mythology and you've been trying to cure your daughter of her 'unhealthy obsession'"—I curled my fingers into air quotes—"with mythology." He didn't know that my obsession was really a desperate search to find a story that would hold the key to rescuing Jack. That there really was an Underworld, once ruled by Persephone. That myths were real. To him, it just looked like another red flag for a therapist to investigate.

"I never used the word *unhealthy*."

I held up the book so that the cover was facing him. "Dad. What's going on?" I demanded.

His smile faded. "I was hoping that if I gave you this, you might do something for me."

I eyed him suspiciously. "What?"

He looked sheepish. "Maybe you could spend today reading instead of . . . doing other things."

And there it was. The real reason for the bacon. And the book.

I put the book on the table and slid it toward him. "I'm going to graduation."

Any remnants of his earlier levity disappeared, and his expression shifted to a pained look. "Why? It's not *your* graduation. Why are you putting yourself through this? Dr. Hill is very concerned."

"I don't care what Dr. Hill thinks," I snapped. My dad winced. I hated that I couldn't talk to him without upsetting him anymore. I lowered my voice. "I'm going because the graduation ceremony is where *he* would be."

"But Jack's not here."

I flinched at his name. "I know—"

"And you going to graduation won't bring him back."

"I know that!" I said, more harshly than I'd intended.

Silence fell upon us. The only sound came from Tommy's fork scraping across his plate. He was used to this discussion.

"I'd feel better about it all if you'd at least talk about J . . . *him* to Dr. Hill. You know it would all be confidential."

Confidentiality wasn't what I was worried about. I was more worried about the fragile dam I'd constructed around my heart over the past two months. It had taken me this long just to find a way to function. To stand without falling. To breathe in and out without concentrating. To talk without sobbing. If I started to let those feelings out, I'd never stop; the broken dam would destroy everything around me, and I'd be back to where I was.

Dr. Hill couldn't help me face reality, because my reality was so unreal to humans. My dad always said honesty is the best policy; but when I imagined telling Dr. Hill the truth, it was almost comical.

"So, Nikki, what's really on your mind?" she'd say.

You see, Dr. Hill, there's this Everliving named Cole—an immortal—who feeds on the emotions of humans. He Fed on me in the Underworld for a hundred years; and when I survived the Feed without growing old, he became convinced I was destined to be the next queen. Then I Returned to the Surface, where I had six months to be with my family and make amends with my ex-boyfriend, Jack, before the Tunnels of the Everneath came for me.

And, oh yeah, Dr. Hill, Jack and I tried to kill Cole by smashing his guitar; but that didn't work, so Jack jumped into the Tunnels, taking my place in hell, and now he's being drained of everything—like a battery—until he wastes away and dies.

"I'm sorry, Dr. Hill. What was the question?"

I'd be taken away by the men in white coats. But the truth was, I didn't belong here, in this kitchen, in my bed, in my car. Breathing air. Free. I didn't belong in this life on the Surface. The life that should've been his.

I was going to the ceremony, and no amount of mythology books could convince me otherwise. Jack had taken my place in hell. The least I could do was take his place on Earth.

My eyes started to sting, and I tried to blink back the tears. I pushed the book toward my dad. "I'm going."

He watched me carefully, then put his arms around me. My dad isn't usually a hugger, and it didn't last long; but it told me what my face must've looked like.

"I know," he said, running his hand through his hair, messing up the perfect comb lines. "Will you be okay?"

I half smiled. Jack was gone. I didn't think I'd ever be okay again.

"I'll be fine."

TWO

NOW

The Surface. Graduation day.

As I drove to the school, clouds from an early-summer storm rolled over the mountains, sweeping everything away, leaving only clear blue sky in their wake. I wished the wind could do the same thing to my soul: sweep away all of the horrible things I'd done until there was a clean soul left, with no memories, no guilt.

Most of the horrible things, though, were just the fallout from one stupid decision: going with Cole to the Feed. He had taken me to the Everneath and fed on my emotions for a hundred years. I relived that decision a thousand times a day, adjusting the factors that led to it to see if I could mentally change the outcome. What if my mom hadn't been killed by a drunk driver the year before? Her death changed me. What if the driver of the car hadn't been acquitted? I didn't know I had it in me to be so angry after the verdict. What if I'd stayed home instead of driving up to Jack's football camp? What if

I hadn't seen Lacey Greene leaving his dorm room, in shorts that were barely there?

What if I had stayed and let Jack explain instead of peeling out of the parking lot and going straight to Cole?

I shook my head. That was the decision I was most ashamed of. Jack had never done anything to jeopardize my complete trust in him. It had been my own stupid insecurities that let doubt of his character in. If I had stayed . . .

If I had just stayed.

But I hadn't. I'd gone straight to Cole's condo. I'd begged him to take my pain away, and he did. Cole drained me of my emotions. I was his Forfeit. For a hundred years, he fed off my energy, leaving me a shell of my former self.

Brake lights ahead of me snapped me back to the present, and I made the final turn toward the school. A half hour before the start of the ceremony, the parking lot was already nearly full, but I found a place at the end of the farthest row, turned off the engine, and sat quietly for a moment.

Despite what I'd said to my dad, I still wasn't sure about my decision to be here. There would be more than a few people in the audience who blamed me for Jack's disappearance, even though nobody knew the truth about what had happened that night. It was an undisputed fact that I was the last one who had seen Park City's football hero. I couldn't go anywhere in this town without feeling the unspoken scorn directed at me. Thankfully, because I'd recovered all of my own emotions, I could no longer taste other people's like I could when I'd first

Returned to the Surface. I imagined that the scorn would've tasted bitter and would've stung as it traveled down my throat.

But I deserved it, because it was true. I had been the last one to see Jack the night the Tunnels came for me, and he had pushed me out of the way and taken my place. I had been the last one to touch his hand as the mark on my arm—the black Shade inside of me that led the Tunnels directly to me—had jumped from my skin to Jack's.

I had been the last one to scream his name. I had been the last one to stop crying over Jack.

The truth is, I never stopped.

I had no control over the tears. They fell even now as I sat in my car, wiping at them futilely. They fell even though I was sure there couldn't be any moisture left inside of me. They stained my pillow every night and greeted me in the mirror every morning.

When I'd first Returned from the Feed, I'd been drained so dry that I wondered if I would ever be able to feel anything again.

Now it felt as if I were made up of shards of glass and tears, and nothing else.

I grabbed two tissues from the box I kept in my car, emptying it out. Balling up one in each hand, I shoved the tissues against my eyes. Lately, I'd started to attack my tears as I would any other bleeding wound in my body. Apply pressure until the bleeding stops.

Despite the tears, I knew I would eventually get out of the

car. I would be at the ceremony, just like I'd watched spring football tryouts from the bleachers and the Park City soccer games from the parking lot. I couldn't help going to the places where Jack should've been.

But maybe my dad was right. What difference did it make if I was here or not? It wasn't as if Jack would know. I felt like a hypocrite. I leaned my head on the steering wheel and closed my eyes. Maybe I should just drive away.

A knock at my window made me jump. I raised my head to find Will's face staring back.

I smiled.

I'd seen Jack's older brother a few times since the night we'd tried to kill Cole. Will's eyes were clear. If there was one good thing that came out of this whole mess, it was that Will had stopped drinking the moment the Tunnels took Jack. Maybe, like me, he needed to feel the pain—not numb it—to be closer to his brother.

I rolled down the window.

"Hey, Becks," he said with a sympathetic smile. He leaned his elbows on the car door. "I thought I'd find you here. You weren't having second thoughts, were you?"

I shook my head. It was hard when Will was so nice to me, because I felt guiltiest around him. Two months ago he had watched the Tunnels of the Everneath come for me, and leave with his brother. How could he look at me without thinking that they'd taken the wrong person?

"I was just psyching myself up," I said.

He opened the door. "C'mon. We'll sit together." He tilted his head to the side, just enough to let a flash of sunlight blind me; and in that flash, with his profile against the light, Will looked like Jack. So much so that I held my breath and had to stop myself from reaching up to touch his face.

The moment passed.

We walked side by side, silent through the first few rows of cars, our feet crunching against the gravel. The sun shone especially bright and strong. As I stepped onto the sidewalk that led to the football field, Will stretched out his arm in front of me and pulled me back.

"What is it?" I asked. I followed his gaze to see Mrs. Caputo—Jack and Will's mom—a few yards ahead of us. "Oh."

Will shrugged and gave me a guilty look. "Sorry, Becks."

"No, it's fine." I forced a smile. "Of course she blames me."

Will's cheeks turned pink, and he shook his head. "It's not that she blames you. She just doesn't know anything about what happened, except that you were the last one to see him. If it wasn't for Jack's note . . ."

Jack's note. His mother found the note the day after Jack disappeared. In it, Jack had said that he was running away. He begged them not to look for him. I hadn't known about the note until after he was gone.

"Do you . . . do you think he knew what he was going to do?" My voice cracked at the end, and I took a deep breath. "I mean, how could he have known? How could he . . ." But he did know. The note proved it.

Will put his arms around me and held me tight as I focused on not causing a scene.

"I was as surprised as you were. He never said a word about taking your place. If anything, I thought he was planning on going *with* you."

"It's my fault."

"Don't say that. Jack knew what he was doing. Besides, if he were still here and he had lost you again . . . there'd be no living with him." Will's lips pulled up in a sad smile. "Trust me, I've seen it. There's a lot of moping, body piercing, bad poetry, tattoos. It's not pretty."

I smiled and thought about the tattoo on Jack's arm. It said *Ever Yours* in ancient Sanskrit symbols. The same words he had written to me after our first dance. His last words to me before the Tunnels took him.

"Nothing could have changed Jack's mind," Will said.

I didn't answer, but I knew Will was wrong. I was the reason Jack was getting the life sucked out of him. Some part of Will had to believe that too, even though he'd never say.

I shivered despite the warmth from the sun. He held me quietly for a few moments more until my regular breathing had resumed and his mom had made it a sufficient distance away.

We started walking again.

Will broke the silence first. "It's been two months. Do you think he's still alive?"

"I know he is." That was the truth. I'd told Will about my dreams countless times, but I could understand how difficult it was to believe. Or maybe it was comforting to hear me say it again and again.

"Tell me how you know," he said.

I smiled. "He'd told me that the symbols on his tattoo were ancient Sanskrit. I researched it, and it's true. How could my subconscious have known to look in ancient Sanskrit?"

He nodded.

I grabbed his arm. "I'm going after him, Will. You know that, don't you?"

Will shook his head and smiled faintly. "How, Becks?"

I hesitated to tell him about my map of the Dead Elvises sightings and my theory that they were getting closer to Park City. I didn't want to get his hopes up, but then I thought about our history. For a few of us there was no such thing as getting our hopes up too high. It wasn't possible.

"Cole's band was in Austin last night," I said. "He's getting closer. I think he's coming back."

Will's face changed so slightly, I almost didn't catch it. But there it was. In the tiny lines around his eyes, in the microscopic twitch of his mouth. Hope.

Not the beach sands of hope of someone who hadn't been through what we'd been through. Will's hope was like mine. A tiny kernel. One grain of sand coursing through our bodies, leaving traces of it in ways only the other could see.

I grabbed his arm. "And if Cole comes back, all I need is one little part of him. One strand of hair. One . . . I don't know . . . fingernail. Anything I can swallow in the Shop-n-Go."

We were at the bleachers now, the graduates and their families filing past us, but Will stopped.

"If Cole comes back," he said, "I'm gonna kill him."

I snorted despite the seriousness of the situation. "You can't kill him."

"Why not? We know where his heart is now. I can break his pick."

"But if you do, we lose our best chance to get back to the Everneath." He was quiet for a moment as he considered this. "Besides," I added. "We aren't even sure what would happen if we broke his pick."

It was true. We'd only been acting on a theory about breaking Cole's heart. Another Forfeit, named Meredith, had given me an ancient bracelet with Egyptian symbols on it. She was convinced that it held the key to killing an Everliving, but the Tunnels captured her before she could find out. Jack and I showed a picture of the bracelet to a professor of anthropology named Dr. Spears; after he studied the symbols, he'd theorized that breaking the heart would destroy the Everliving.

Because Everlivings such as Cole didn't have real hearts inside their chests. Their hearts had been transformed into objects they could carry around with them. It happened the instant they became immortals. The emptiness in their chests symbolized their unbreakable link to the Everneath, and also meant that they couldn't survive on the Surface unless they stole emotions from humans. There was a point when I thought I'd figured out that Cole's heart was in his guitar and that smashing it should've killed him. Or at least made him mortal. But Cole's heart was actually in his guitar pick, and the Tunnels came for me anyway.

It was still hypothetical. We didn't know what would really happen because we never got that far.

"A guy can't live without his heart," Will said, but I could tell he was reconsidering Cole's immediate demise.

"C'mon." I tugged on the sleeve of his shirt. "We can't miss this."

But he didn't move. "Becks."

"What?"

"I want you to know, here and now, that if we can't get Jack back . . . you won't be able to stop me from killing Cole. Whether I have to break his heart or tear him apart."

I let out a breath. "If it gets to that point, it's *you* who won't be able to stop *me*."

I didn't know if I could physically kill Cole. Breaking a guitar pick was one thing, but doing something more violent? Such as . . . stabbing someone? Strangling someone? That was another thing entirely.

Then again, wasn't it murder just the same? I didn't know. But I had plenty of time to contemplate it because the graduation speakers were boring. Jennifer Carpenter talked about how the future was theirs for the taking, and Dione Warnick—yes, that was her real name—gave a resounding speech that had something to do with the size of the graduates' shoes and their carbon footprint on the earth. She even had visual aids: a pair of her grandpa's old hiking boots.

The principal spoke last. He made a reference to "loved ones who are no longer with us." All eyes shifted to the empty seat between Farah Cannon and Noni Chatworth, where Jack would've been sitting.

A few people glanced back toward me, which meant I hadn't entered as stealthily as I'd thought. Looks that said, *You were the last one with him. You should know where he is.*

The commencement announcer got to the Cs and called Jack's name; and despite the number of times I'd imagined this moment, and thought I'd prepared myself for it, hearing his name felt like a hammer on my heart, threatening the dam that I'd built up there.

In the silence that followed, a woman near the front stood and walked toward the podium. Jack's mom. I sank a little lower in my chair, trying not to think of the times she had grilled me since his disappearance. My story never changed. I didn't know where he'd gone or when he'd be back.

Mrs. Caputo climbed the stairs to the stage and took the diploma, shaking the principal's hand. She turned away and wiped under her eyes, and the audience applauded. Scattered football players in the crowd jumped out of their seats, and soon it turned into a standing ovation. I was at once overcome by the outpouring of love for Jack and immobilized by the guilt in my chest. I stayed in my seat, my head lowered.

The rest of the ceremony was a blur, only partly because of

the fresh moisture in my eyes.

A series of hugs. Hats thrown in the air. Yearbooks signed.

I saw it all from the shadows of the old sycamore trees at the end of the field. Will was off to the side, his arm around his crying mother. I watched them for a long time, until I caught something out of the corner of my eye. The sun glinting off long, blond hair and shining in my eyes.

Jules.

My best friend. Former best friend. Still best friend?

She was talking to Dan Gregson, the head of the yearbook committee. Like me, Jules wouldn't graduate until next year, so I wondered why she was here today. Maybe it was for Jack. After all, she'd been friends with him too. When I left last year, she became his best friend. Maybe even more than friends.

I studied her face. Her cheeks were not as round as they had been just two months ago. She was smiling at Dan, but the smile didn't reach any other part of her face.

I was so focused on Jules's face that I didn't see Jack's mom coming. I heard her before I saw her.

"You have some nerve showing up here!"

I turned to find Mrs. Caputo marching toward me, flanked by Will, whose expression seemed to read *I tried to stop her.* Her hand trembled at her side, as if she wanted to slap me but didn't dare.

"You avoid my phone calls, your father won't let me on your property, and then you show up *here*?"

Avoided her phone calls? My dad wouldn't let her on our

property? I had no idea what she was talking about. All I knew was that she had backed off over the past couple of weeks. I thought she'd given up.

"What are you doing here?" she demanded.

She was right on top of me now, and I took a step back. "I . . . I just wanted to . . ."

"To what? Keep up this . . . *charade* you've been selling?"

"What charade?"

"The one where you act like you don't have the first clue where my son is when you know damn well it's a lie."

Will put a hand on her shoulder. "Mom—"

She shook him away. "She pretends to be a friend, pretends to love Jack, and she won't even answer one question about where he went." She was talking to Will but glaring at me. Her voice grew softer but still resonated with anger. "You don't know anything about love."

Her words stung. "I'm sorry, Mrs. Caputo. I didn't know you were trying to get hold of me—"

"Enough with the innocent act," she said. "I can't even stand to look at you anymore."

She whipped around and stalked off. It wasn't until that moment that I realized we had an audience. Several people had wandered over, obviously curious about all the shouting. Now that she and Will had left, I was alone, the center of a dozen accusatory stares.

I put on my sunglasses to hide my eyes and set off for the parking lot. It wasn't an act. I really didn't know she had been trying so hard to talk to me. Was my dad playing the buffer? If so, part of me wanted to thank him, but another part of me was angry that he didn't tell me about it.

Mrs. Caputo's car came around the corner, and I ducked behind a tree. Of course I could understand her anger. The only thing keeping her from killing me had to be Jack's note. She could never know exactly how much I was to blame for Jack being gone, but I silently made her the same promise I made to Will.

I will find your son. As soon as I find Cole.

The moment I thought the words, a strange feeling came over me. It was unsettling, like a pull at my back. A warning, almost. I crept farther behind the tree as Mrs. Caputo's car passed by and suddenly, from behind me, two hands grasped my shoulders.

I jumped. Whipped around. Found myself staring into two dark eyes. And then I tried to stifle a scream that was equal parts panic and excitement.

"Hi, Nik," Cole said.

THREE

NOW
The Surface. Park City High.

*C*ole. Standing in front of me. No matter how many times I'd imagined this moment, it didn't prepare me enough. I forgot what I was supposed to be feeling. It wasn't relief that my best chance to get Jack back was here now, even though that's what I should've been feeling.

Instead, my emotions were much more basic.

Hatred and anger. As long as Jack was dying, it was easy for me to hate.

A group of seniors in caps and gowns wandered by, loudly congratulating one another, so Cole pulled me farther behind a small grove of trees until we were safely separated from everyone else.

Cole took a step closer. His dark eyes searched my face. "You look good."

I lowered my hands, which had been covering my mouth. "You disappeared."

His lip twitched. "Yes, well, I thought it only appropriate considering that you tried to kill me. I knew it was only a matter of time before you'd get that urge again."

We were quiet. He seemed just as oblivious to the graduation hoopla going on as I was. He hadn't changed since the first time I had ever met him, at Harry O's club during the Sundance Film Festival. I'd just lost my mother, and unlike everyone else, Cole hadn't tried to make me forget my pain. Instead, he'd given me space to feel every last drop of it.

Now I know he was probably feeding off every last drop of it.

Today he wore his regular uniform of black jeans, black T-shirt, black jacket. His eyes were still dark. His hair still blond.

His hair. *His hair.* My ticket to the Everneath, right in front of me. I looked at his face, but all I could think about was the last time I'd seen him, and how he'd promised to never give up trying to make me an Everliving and take over the throne, together.

My head was spinning.

"Nik? You okay?"

I tried to take a step away, but it was more like a lurch, and Cole reached out a hand to steady me.

I shook my arm free. "Don't touch me."

He pulled his hand back, palm outward. "Fine." He raised his eyebrows in a question, which made me want to gouge out his eyes. As if he should question why I'm so upset.

"Do you know what I've been through?" I said. "I lost . . ." I wanted to say *Jack*, but somehow it felt wrong to utter his name in front of Cole. In fact, I never said it anymore. And why was I talking about this? Wasn't I supposed to be asking Cole how to get to the Tunnels? But now that he was here, I suddenly needed him to understand my pain. To *feel* it. Because he looked so fine, as if he had been through nothing, and I knew how I looked.

Broken.

"Yes," Cole said.

"Yes what?"

He frowned and inclined his head toward me. "Yes, I know what you've been through. I know loss."

I shook my head and looked away.

"You may not believe me, but I do," he said, his voice quiet.

I faced him. "Why are you back?"

"We have some unfinished business."

"You or the band?"

He gave a soft smile. "Both. Maybe. In fact, I learned a few things in my travels. Things that might interest you."

"Like what?"

"Like how you survived the Feed."

My whole body tensed. "What do you mean?"

"I mean I know that Jack saved you, through his undying love for you while you were in the Feed."

My face went blank. If Cole knew that Jack was my anchor, did he also know that now I was keeping Jack alive? I didn't want him to know about my connection to Jack, or anything else that he could use against us.

Cole studied my face. "I can see this is not brand-new information. You already know how you survived, don't you? You've known all along."

"Not all along." Not until Meredith made the connection for me. "A friend helped me figure out about the anchors."

"Yes, well, I couldn't stop there. I had to find out more, but I couldn't think of a mythological precedent to go with the *anchor* theory." His forehead wrinkled as if he was working out a math problem. "Which is strange, considering how much of our real history is hidden in the myths. I was frustrated until some friends pointed me to the most obvious source."

"Which is?"

"Morpheus. The god of dreams." He let the name hang in the air for a moment before he continued. "Do you remember how I told you that mortals are consistently exchanging energy? How a smile can be infectious? And a bad mood can spread? Well, the same is true in dreams. The *dreamer* can provide energy to . . ." He waved his hand as he seemed to search for the right word.

"The dream-*ee*?" I offered.

He quirked an eyebrow. "The *subject* of the dream. This happens all the time. The Greeks simply created a god who embodied the connection between dreamer and . . . dream-ee."

"Morpheus."

"Yes. It's an even stronger connection when one mortal is in the Everneath, because the Everneath is fueled by emotions and therefore is closer to an actual dream state than anything on the Surface. I think that's how Jack kept you young during the Feed." He said this triumphantly. When I didn't respond immediately, he added an exasperated "Ta-da."

"So he kept me alive through his dreams."

He nodded.

I waited for him to go on, but he remained silent. "I'm happy you found your answers, but what was the point?"

"Well, on the off chance things don't work out between the two of us—"

I couldn't help snorting, and he gave me a faux-offended look.

"May I continue? If we don't work out, I'm going to have to find another Forfeit in about ninety-nine years. And I'd like to find one who has the same sort of attachment to the Surface. Of course, it will be infinitely more difficult to convince a Forfeit who is still attached to someone to come to the Everneath with me."

I narrowed my eyes. "You can be very persuasive though."

"Quite." He gave me a mischievous grin, and my mind flashed to how easily he'd persuaded me to give up everything.

I hurried to change the subject. "So why are you telling me this?"

"Because, Nik." He seemed to choose his words deliberately. "Haven't you figured out why? Now I know it's your turn to keep Jack alive."

I could feel my eyes go wide, and he grinned, satisfied that he finally had my undivided attention.

"How do *you* know he's still alive?" I said.

"Because you're still standing." He tilted his head in a knowing sort of way. "You've been dreaming about him, haven't you?"

I shifted uncomfortably. "Not your business."

"Yes, but . . ." He tugged at the sleeve of his jacket. "This limbo state you and Jack are in, it can't go on indefinitely. And you'll know when it's over. Because . . ." He hesitated.

"Because he won't be in my dreams anymore."

"Has that happened yet?" he asked.

"No," I said, my hands squeezing into fists. "He's still alive."

"But not for long. And when that happens, maybe you'll reconsider. Being with me." He shifted his stance and looked away.

My mouth hung open for a moment. "You're saying, Hey, when the love of your life dies, give me a ring?"

He frowned, and his voice grew soft. "Jack's as good as gone." I started to protest, but he stepped forward and grabbed my hand. His eyes looked forlorn, as if it hurt him to say what he was saying. "That pain you're feeling, it will get worse. And you know there's only one way to escape it."

"Death."

"No. *Life.* Eternal life. With me."

I closed my eyes. Cole had a way of showing up at my most desperate moments with the easy way out.

"I'm not a bad person, Nik. You changed me."

"How?" I demanded, skeptical.

"You showed me that relationships are worth sacrifices. I used to think they were fleeting, but I know better now." He took a deep breath. "You made me a better person. I mean, a better immortal." He said the last part with a wink.

I didn't believe what he was saying, but I decided to use it. "If you're such a better immortal now, then help me."

He raised an eyebrow. "With what?"

"I need to get to the Tunnels."

He froze for a moment, then gave a sarcastic laugh. "You kill me."

"He's still alive. I have to find him."

He frowned, all evidence of laughter gone. "Don't be stupid."

"I can get to the Tunnels. You said that woman who took the pill in the Shop-n-Go would be taken there."

"Yeah, by the Shades. And they weren't taking her there as part of some Everneath bus tour. They were taking her there to bury her alive and drain her." He spoke as if he were scolding a child.

"But at least she made it there." I could hear the desperation in my own voice.

This stopped him short. He looked at me as if I'd lost my last marble.

"Please help me."

He grabbed my shoulders, digging his fingers in. "Jack is beyond help. Jack is as good as dead. And if you go there, you will be too."

"But at least I would've tried," I said stubbornly. "Because

I can't spend my whole life, let alone the eternity you want, like this."

He pulled me even closer, our faces inches apart, and I felt that familiar electricity between us, that unmistakable draw from one to the other. The feeling that we belonged next to each other, limb to limb. Skin to skin. The result of spending a century intertwined. My legs touched his, my hip was against his; and at the contact, my body breathed a sigh of relief, as if it were whole once more. That feeling of being complete with Cole reached my brain too. It was suddenly hard to think.

His dark eyes pierced mine. "If you go to the Tunnels, that wouldn't be trying. That would be giving up. Giving up your life. The one that Jack saved."

His words faded away, because when I was this near to his lips, he couldn't help but feed off my top layer of emotion, which was my guilt. Just by breathing in he could make me feel better.

But he knew what I was doing, and he released me, taking a step back. The look on his face told me he was surprised I'd let him feed off of me. "I would never help you go to the Tunnels." He glanced away and seemed to deliberate for a moment. When he turned back, his shoulders were set and his jaw was tight, as if he had just decided his next move, and it wasn't what he had expected. "I can't stay here. This was a mistake."

"What?"

He sighed and shook his head. "I'm leaving. I'll see you again when it's over."

He meant *when Jack is dead.* "Wait!" He couldn't just disappear on me again. "Where will you be?"

He paused and looked over his shoulder. "I'll leave town again. Go someplace where I can be alone for a while."

Alone? That meant I wouldn't even be able to track the band, not that I'd been successful at that.

"But you just got here." My voice sounded frantic.

He shrugged. "I came alone. Told the guys I needed a break. But you're obviously not in the right state of mind to talk. It'll be easier if I go someplace and wait it out so I won't have to see your face when it all goes down with Jack. Believe it or not, I can't watch you go through it."

If he disappeared on me now, I would lose Jack. I had no idea where the rest of the band was, and I didn't know any other Everlivings. "Wait!"

He started walking again. My chance to save Jack was walking away.

"Cole, wait!"

He didn't stop.

So I did the one thing I had control over. I sprinted for him, and when I caught him, I grabbed a handful of hair on the back of his head. And yanked.

Hard.

"Ow! What the hell, Nik?"

Then I ran.

Rain pelted my windshield as I tore through the streets and toward the Shop-n-Go.

There was nothing in my rearview mirror. Did Cole have any idea what I was doing? Even if he did, did he care?

I thought about the last time I'd had Cole's hair at the Shop-n-Go. How I'd been so close to swallowing it and letting the floor of the store swallow me. If I'd had the courage to do it then, Jack would be here. Alive.

I hadn't been brave enough.

But today I had something I didn't have then. Now Jack's life was on the line, and I had nothing to lose. When I first Returned to the Surface, I'd wasted so much time thinking there was nothing I could do to escape my fate. I'd waited too long to act. I wouldn't make the same mistake again.

I tried not to let thoughts of my dad and my brother convince me otherwise; and before I knew it, I was rushing past Ezra, the Shop-n-Go cashier, on the way to the back of the store—the same corner where, months ago, I'd seen a tired, worn-out woman give up on life and choose the slow decay of the Tunnels. The exact spot where the wall between the Surface and the Everneath was at its thinnest.

And before I could think about failing, I placed Cole's hair on my tongue and swallowed. Hard.

As the floor turned liquid and covered me in a clear, slimy film, I heard shouting. Probably from Ezra. It sounded as if he was screaming through water.

It was too late. I was going to the Everneath.

FOUR

The Everneath.

$\mathcal{T}$he only way to describe the next feeling was like being caught in a washing machine. On spin cycle. The sensation of falling and never touching the ground. No light.

I threw my arms out, trying to find some sort of balance, but there was nothing I could grab on to and no way to right myself. I began to think this *was* the Everneath, and I would spend the rest of my days churning and twisting, when suddenly it all stopped and I landed somewhere solid. I blinked my eyes open and took in a sharp breath.

I shouldn't have expected the Everneath to be as dark as the Feed caverns. Cole had always told me that most of the Everneath was a place of light, but I wasn't expecting the extraordinary brightness of the place I had landed in. But it wasn't a true light; it was more like a film that had been over-exposed.

At first I couldn't see because of the brightness. I thought about calling out for Jack, but there was so much blurry activity going on in front of me, I was scared to draw attention to myself before I knew what I was in the middle of. Before my eyes had a chance to adjust, a loud noise thundered in my ears. Like hundreds of people screaming. My heart jumped to my throat, and I instinctively backed away from the noise until I hit a solid object.

I blinked my eyes. And as the image in front of me came into focus, I panicked.

I was on the outskirts of what looked like a city square filled with so many people I couldn't even begin to guess at how many there were. Hundreds? At least. They stood shoulder to shoulder, jostling for position. But I couldn't get a good look since I was on the very edge, at what I presumed was the back because every person was faced away from me and toward the other end.

The object I'd backed into was a short, wide wall that ran along the perimeter of the plaza, separating it from the tall, ancient-looking buildings that surrounded it. Several people were standing on top of the wall, taking advantage of the extra three feet of height it gave them, so they could see better.

But what were they looking at?

I saw a space on the wall and scrambled up. The man next to me gave me a quick glance, then turned back toward whatever everyone was looking at. Another swell of cheers sounded just as I regained my balance and straightened up and got a better look.

The scene took my breath away. My initial estimate had been way off. There had to be thousands of people, at least.

But no, not people. Everlivings. Both men and women. I realized I'd never seen a female Everliving, but about half of the audience was made up of them. Dark shadows bobbed and wove through the crowd, and it took me a moment to realize they weren't normal shadows, because I couldn't see a source of light. There was no sun to make shadows.

The shadows were Shades.

My initial instinct was to dive behind the wall and hide. The first time I'd ever seen the Shades was in the Feed, when they'd wrapped around Cole and me, cocooning us for a hundred years. The last time I'd seen a Shade, it was inside my arm, acting as a homing device for the Tunnels to find me.

But I came here to find the Tunnels and rescue Jack. I couldn't waste my time hiding. I just had to figure out where to start, and right now nobody looked as if they were about to tear their attention away from whatever they were doing to give me the time of day. Staying put, I squinted toward the opposite side of the square, following the gazes of everyone else, and that's when I saw the platform.

More like a stage, at the far end of the plaza.

People stood on their tiptoes, shifted their lines of sight, climbed whatever they could to get a better view of it. Twenty or thirty of them had perched on a large fountain in the middle of the square. A few were in the direct line of spray from the fountain, but they stayed where they were.

I couldn't figure out where the entertainment was, but the spectators were as captivated as if it were the Super Bowl.

Then I saw a woman at the center of the stage, and instantly I knew why nobody had noticed me. She drew the attention of every being in attendance, the men and the women, and even though I was far away, her beauty captivated me. I couldn't look away.

Her white dress glowed as if it were made of beams of sunlight. Red hair fell in waves down her back. I couldn't see how long it was. She didn't seem human.

On either side of her were several Shades. I couldn't count how many because they resembled swirls of oil from the way they were moving. Off to the side of the stage was a line of people. Maybe ten of them. Men and women. The whole thing seemed ominous, but I couldn't figure out exactly why.

They were waiting their turn for . . . something. She raised a hand, and an instant hush fell over the crowd. The first person in line climbed the steps. Slowly. As if he'd rather be anywhere than where he was.

He hesitantly crossed the stage to the center, and once he reached the exact middle, the Shades on the stage began to swirl. His visible fear had me worried for him, but when I looked at a woman who was standing a few feet away from me, she was watching the whole thing with a slight smile on her lips, as if it were totally normal.

The Shades joined together and spun in a circle. It reminded me of the funnel cloud of the Tunnels that came for me. Only this funnel fashioned a sharp point at the end, and before I could guess at what was happening, they rose up into the sky, lengthening as a single unit until they were one long, straight rod of black.

The sight was overwhelming. I watched it with the same astonishment I would feel at being dropped into the middle of the ocean.

The mass lingered there for a hushed moment and then shot downward in one collective spear toward the man. The Shades impaled him through the chest, pinning him for an instant to the ground.

I gasped.

Then the Shades disappeared inside the man's body. And for a split second there was silence.

Then an explosion. From *inside* the man. He was blown apart. Into millions of pieces. Maybe billions. There weren't any visible pieces of him that I could see. There was only a fine red mist hanging in the air, hovering above the crowd.

The mist spread in a delicate layer over the entire square. I stumbled off the wall, afraid of what the mist would do if it touched me.

A great gong sounded from somewhere near the stage. It was a signal of some sort. There was a collective intake of breath—the sound of a thousand people gasping—and as the chests of the crowd inflated, the mist disappeared. The Everlivings literally inhaled what was left of the man.

He was gone.

I sank to the ground just as I heard the crowd let out their breath and cheer.

Pressing my back against the rock wall, I clutched my stomach. Bile rose to my mouth. The man had to have been human. They'd never do that to one of their kind. If the Shades found me now, would they do the same thing to me?

Even worse, if they were eviscerating humans, would they take them from the Tunnels? Would they come for Jack?

My heart split. I could feel it, a literal ripping at my chest. I clutched at it, trying to hold it together, but I couldn't. My broken heart seeped through my fingers. I watched it happen, and yet I couldn't believe what I was seeing. White mist escaped from me, and in the mist I could see pictures of Jack as if some unseen hand were flipping through photo prints, and the resulting movie played out in the cloud in front of me.

I tried to reach for the images, but it was like trying to grab air. The mist carried Jack's face, floating it up and away from me. Over the top of the wall I was hiding behind.

And that's when I noticed that the cheers of the crowd had died down to almost a whisper. Why the sudden silence?

I raised my head and peeked over the top of the wall to see what was happening. And nearly screamed.

Every face there, every Shade even, turned toward me at once.

I froze.

Their eyes dropped from the mist above me to my face.

And then the woman's voice, calm and clear, pierced the

air. It traveled to me without any need for amplification. She said, "Who are you?"

Was she talking to me? I looked from side to side to see if I could find any face that showed an ounce of sympathy, but there was only one emotion that played on the faces here.

Hunger.

The Shades, who had been gathered at the platform, started toward me. Their movements became synchronized, and soon they were swirling up into the sky as they had just done before; only this time they were pointed right at me.

I backed away as fast as I could, but I'd only made it a few yards when I collided with the front of a building.

I closed my eyes.

"It will be quick," I whispered. "It will be over."

I kept my eyes closed and felt the rush of cold air coming toward me. Alarmed shouts reached my ears. At the moment I anticipated that the Shades would stab me in the gut, I said my final word, one that I hadn't spoken in days and days. "Jack."

FIVE

NOW

The Everneath.

A single voice rang out from somewhere above me. "Nikki! Your hand!"

I didn't have time to think. I reached up my hand toward the voice and felt warm fingers wrap around it, and my feet left the ground. Darkness surrounded me.

In the next moment, my back hit something hard and flat, and the impact crushed my ribs. Coughing, I rolled over and felt rocks against my cheek. I was lying on an asphalt road. I couldn't see very well. It looked like the sun had just set.

"Dammit, Nikki!" Cole's voice from somewhere above me. "How many times do I have to explain? Do you know what you've done?! If you want to kill yourself, do it in a way that I won't be getting a phone call from Ezra about!"

It took me a few long minutes to figure out what he was talking about. I was back on the Surface, but not at the Shop-n-Go. I was on a road. No Shades on me. No Jack.

No Jack.

I turned onto my back and closed my eyes. Cole had come for me. Did Ezra really call him? He must have. Or Cole had already figured out where I was going. In between shallow gasps, I said, "Sorry about the phone call. If there was another entrance besides the Shop-n-Go, I would've used it."

Cole's shoes crunched on the loose asphalt as he came over to me. He crouched down, and I saw his face. His lips pressed together so hard they had turned white. He shook his head.

"There are other ways to kill yourself. Next time, try a gun. Or a knife." Maybe it was because of the pitiful state I was in, but as he looked at me, the hard edges of his face softened. "Or a length of rope. Or starvation. Or even old age." He sank fully to the ground and brought his knees up to his chest; his nostrils flared.

"I wasn't trying to kill myself." I pushed against the asphalt road and sat up, and immediately wished I hadn't. My head felt as if it were full of clouds. I closed my eyes. "Whoa."

Cole put an arm around me to steady me. "Yeah, that's what happens when you face down an army of Shades." As soon as I was balanced, he released me. Quickly. He breathed out of his nose, his jaw set. "What were you thinking? If you weren't trying to kill yourself, what the hell were you doing?"

"I was trying to get to Jack."

Cole grunted. Loudly. He straightened up and ran his hands roughly through his hair. His lips pulled back from his teeth, and his eyes closed. When he opened them, they looked wild. I'd never seen him so frustrated. "That's what this is about? Some suicide quest borne out of your own guilt? You have no idea what you've done!"

"What *have* I done?"

"You're different, Nik!" He took a deep breath and lowered his voice. "You survived the Feed. You're a threat to the queen. And here you are, parading yourself in front of her like the prized calf at the slaughterhouse. If anyone from today's fiasco realized what you are . . ."

"Then what?"

Cole leaned his head back and stared at the darkening sky.

"What, Cole?"

He looked at me. "Then you're dead. Or worse."

I didn't need to ask if he was serious. His eyes were blazing. "Well, I was only there for a few seconds."

"I was twenty minutes behind you. You were probably there for hours."

I'd forgotten about the time discrepancy between the Everneath and the Surface. A hundred years in the Feed had only equaled six months on the Surface. "So next time I go I'll be more careful. I'll avoid the . . ."—I searched for the word—". . . city square."

He raised his eyebrows. "You can't avoid it." He chuckled. "The Shop-n-Go entrance will dump you in the same place every time. And why are we even talking about you going back? Have you already forgotten about the exploding man?"

I could feel the blood drain from my face as I remembered.

"What was that whole thing?"

He sighed. "It was the weekly slaughter, where people who find themselves on the wrong side of the queen get skewered and fed to the masses. The queen oversees it herself." I tensed, remembering the beautiful woman in white, and Cole noticed. "Yes. That was the queen. Lovely, isn't she?"

My stomach turned at the explanation. "Were they humans? The people being killed?"

Cole shrugged. "Some, maybe. Some were probably Wanderers too." At my confused expression, he continued. "Wanderers. They're like skeletal forms of Everlivings, sentenced to live a life without nourishment. They're the law-breakers. The queen doesn't mind ripping a few apart to keep her subjects happy. And nothing makes us happier than feeding."

I leaned toward him. "Then I *have* to go back."

He furrowed his brow. "What part of what I just said makes you think that?"

"If she's taking humans from the Tunnels, I have to go now before Jack gets chosen for a slaughter."

He put his head in his hands, exasperated. "The Shades were seconds away from tearing you apart like a turkey wishbone."

"I would find a better hiding place this time."

He raised his voice. "There's no hiding your energy!" He paused. "They found you because your broken heart leaked, and they picked up on your human energy. If I hadn't saved you they'd have turned you into a Nikki-kabob."

"But my energy didn't leak until I got scared. If I could stay calm—"

"You can't hide your humanity!" He slid a little closer and spoke softly. "The point is, they found you tonight. They'll always find you. And take you to the Tunnels. You can't find Jack if you're buried alive too."

Buried alive too. I closed my eyes for a few long moments, trying not to flinch at Cole's casual reference to Jack being buried alive, and realizing how close I'd just been to joining him.

"Then how *am* I supposed to find him?"

"Well, I should've said you can't find Jack no matter what. It would just suck for you to be buried alive as well."

I tried to turn away, but he grabbed my hand and pulled me closer.

"You knew this, Nik. You saw that woman at the Shop-n-Go take the pill. I told you what would happen to her."

I thought back to the woman in the back of the store, desperate looking, sinking to the ground. Taking the pill that contained Max's hair and then slipping *through* the ground. All in a sacrifice to the Everneath. I remembered seeing them at Harry O's, punching information into their smartphones.

Something clicked for me. They used text messages to track the sacrifices they sent to the Tunnels. "But the Shades were expecting her, weren't they? They were waiting for her. At the square," I said.

Cole narrowed his eyes. "Why do you think that?"

"Because I saw how you and Max would send information

about your sacrifices through your phones. You did it the first night I met you, but I didn't know what it meant." I smiled. "You told me they were texts from your manager. Who you called 'the queen.'" I shook my head at how it all made sense now. Cole and Max would alert someone on the other end to expect a sacrifice.

Cole frowned at my deduction skills. "It's true; the Shades wouldn't be expecting you. But your energy would eventually give you away like it did today. And why would you be stupid enough to try it? So stupid," he muttered. Anger flashed across his face, but he seemed to will it away with a deep breath. "Why am I trying to convince you when you *saw* it happen?"

I turned away. From where we were, we could look out over the Park City valley. But my brain was too muddled to even try to figure out which mountain we were on.

"So, Nik. Here we are again. Stuck between a rock and a bigger, harder rock. How do we always end up like this?"

I glared at him. "There has to be a way around it. There has to be a way to hide. Maybe there's something we could do to . . . I don't know . . . *conceal* my energy."

Cole's eyes narrowed, and for a moment something in his expression made me think I was on to something. But too soon his face went blank, and I was left wondering if I had only imagined the flicker of recognition.

"Leave it alone, Nik. There's no way to cover you."

He pushed himself off the ground and brushed off his jeans. He was getting ready to leave.

I grabbed the hem of his pants. "Has anyone ever done it before?"

He didn't look at me, but he didn't walk away. "What do you mean?"

"Has a human ever gone to the Everneath and made it to the Tunnels without the Shades knowing?"

He finally met my gaze. "Maybe. But that's not the point. The question you should be asking yourself is, did anyone ever make it back out?"

His expression told me the answer to that question.

I wrenched the hem of his jeans tighter. "But they didn't have you. You know the Everneath. You know *me*. You told me today that I changed you. Prove it."

He pulled his leg free. "I'm tired, Nik. What I just did . . . you know, the whole saving thing . . . that took some energy. I'm done."

He turned and started to walk away, and that's when I remembered that I had no idea where we were. Somewhere in the mountains, but I was completely at a loss for directions or anything familiar.

"Why aren't we at the Shop-n-Go?"

He was still walking away when he answered. "Because I'm an Everliving. I can enter and exit anyplace I want. If anyone happened to follow us, they would've checked the Shop-n-Go first, so I brought us here."

"Oh."

Cole stopped by a motorcycle on the side of the road. I

hadn't seen it until now. He swung his leg over it and kicked it to life.

"You brought your bike?" I shouted over the roar of the engine. "How did you even—"

"I told the band where I'd be coming out. On the off chance I found you in time. They left it for me."

"The band's *here*?"

He ignored me. With a screech of tires against asphalt, he whipped his bike around.

"Wait!" I called out.

"You are *so* finding your own way home," he answered.

"But where are we?"

"Deer Valley."

It was the small ski resort town just above Park City on the mountain. "Which way do I go?"

He revved the engine. "When given the choice to go up or down, go down."

I ran over to his bike. "You said the band's here, right? You guys are staying?" Had he lied about coming alone?

He clicked his bike into gear and looked at me. "If you still want to talk, you know where to find me. *Tomorrow* night. Do you think you can wait? For one day? Before you do something stupid again?"

He didn't wait for me to answer. He just took off.

I started walking, all the while looking over my shoulder as if a tall woman with red hair would suddenly appear.

Cole said I was safe, I told myself over and over.

* * *

By the time I got home, it was dark. The lights in my dad's study were on. Apparently I'd only been gone a couple of hours, including the time it took me to walk from Deer Valley to my house. As I climbed the stairs, my knees wobbled and I grabbed on to the railing for support.

I was exhausted, but I knew I had to face my dad.

I stopped by the study. My dad looked up from the article he was reading in *The Economist.* "How'd it go?"

I thought of what I'd just been through. Traipsed through the Everneath; had my first encounter with the queen; watched a man get blown apart; faced hundreds of Shades intent on doing the same to me, or worse; headed toward the Tunnels until Cole—an immortal—pulled me out and dropped me in Deer Valley.

How'd it go? "Fine," I answered. It took me a moment to realize he was talking about the graduation ceremony. "I saw Mrs. Caputo. She said she's been trying to contact me."

My dad didn't deny it. "I wanted to give you some more time."

"She's not going to give up."

"I know." He took off his reading glasses and placed them on his desk. "That's why I agreed that her detective could interview you tomorrow afternoon. I was going to tell you in the morning, because I didn't want you to worry about it and lose sleep."

"It's good," I said, nodding my head and trying to convince myself. I had so many other things to worry about. "It's time."

"Do you want to talk about it first?"

"No. I'm tired."

"Okay, Nikki. Besides, you have nothing to worry about. All you have to do is tell the truth."

I smiled at how complicated the truth really was. "No problem. Good night, Dad."

"Good night. Get some rest."

SIX

NOW

The Surface. My bedroom.

I dream.

In my dream, I tell Jack of my attempt to find him.

"It didn't go quite as expected," I say.

"Why?"

"I almost got caught. By some . . . Shades."

"No," he says. "Why are you trying?"

His words slam my heart. "I'll never stop trying, Jack. You know this."

He closes his eyes. "Your hair used to fall in your eyes."

The abrupt topic change makes me pause. "What?"

He opens his eyes and looks into mine, and he is suddenly so aware. So with me. So different from the night before. He holds up his hand, palm toward me, and I mirror with my own. "Your hair used to fall in your eyes. I'd get so frustrated. I'd think, Why does she let it happen? Is it a matter of needing a clip or something? Why doesn't it bother her like it bothers me? I used to think I hated it. But then there came a time when all I could think about was how much I wanted to push it out of your eyes for you. I convinced myself that you needed me because otherwise your hair would blind you, and that wouldn't be good for your health."

I smile. "I remember the first time you brushed it out of my face. We were hiking the Fiery Furnace with our history class. We stopped on that rock—"

"The Loveseat," he interrupts.

"Yeah, the Loveseat. I was opening the string cheese, and my hair fell in my eyes, and you brushed my hair away and tucked it behind my ear."

He glances at my hair. "It was a milestone for me. It took me a year to get up the courage to do it."

"I'm glad you did," I say, surprised that the memory has stuck with him as it has with me.

He shrugs. "Well, it was either that or buy you a hair clip. And I didn't have any money."

I laugh. He curls his fingers around my hand in a move formed out of habit and then frowns as they only wrap around air. He looks at me with sad eyes.

"I'm trying not to give up," he says.

"Don't say that."

But he doesn't speak anymore.

He hasn't given up. I tell myself over and over, He hasn't given up. He will never give up. Even if I have to remind him.

But before I can say it out loud, the sun rises, and he's gone.

* * *

I jolted awake and fell out of bed. Scrambling to get up, I lurched to my desk. Ransacked it, opening every drawer until I found what I was looking for. A picture of the freshman and sophomore classes on our trip two years ago to Arches National Park. The picture was taken at the base of a rock formation known as the Fiery Furnace because of the way the red sandstone juts into the sky like the spires of a fire.

I ran my finger over the glass of the frame. There we were, in the far right-hand corner. Me and Jack, his arm slung casually around my neck.

"You are not giving up, Jack Caputo," I murmured. *And neither am I.*

I set the picture upright on my shelf and thought about last night. Cole was so adamant that it was impossible, but there had to be more to it. He was holding back something. I could feel it.

I did learn one good thing. Cole wasn't alone in Park City. The band was here. That meant that he wasn't going anywhere, at least for now.

Setting the Fiery Furnace picture upright next to my computer, I ran my finger over the mouse pad and woke up the sleeping screen.

WHERE ARE THE DEAD ELVISES PLAYING NEXT? the headline of the Looking for the Deads blog read.

I knew the answer to that one. Park City. Harry O's on Main Street, most likely. I had to see Cole again. Find out what he was hiding. But I couldn't go there unprepared. I had to talk to Mrs. Jenkins. She was the only other mortal who knew all about the Everneath, and I'd been talking to her about how to get back there. But we'd been so focused on that first step—finding Cole—that we hadn't discussed anything else. Maybe she would know what Cole was hiding.

If anything.

It was too early to go to Mrs. Jenkins's house now, so I closed the drawer and went into the kitchen to brew some coffee. Tommy was at the table. He still had school today. Three more days until he was done for the summer.

I looked over his shoulder. The top of the paper read HELP DOROTHY FIND HER WAY TO THE WIZARD. "Mazes? That's what the fourth grade considers homework?"

Tommy pressed his pencil into the paper so he wouldn't lose his spot and looked up at me. "It's the last week of school. I have, like, a stack of these to do." He lowered his head. "And they're harder than they look."

"Start from the end."

"Why?"

I paused, not really sure why. It was just how I'd always done them. "It's easier that way."

He lifted his pencil and placed the point deliberately at the end. "I'll try," he said.

I couldn't stop staring at the maze. Pencil lines twisted around corners and back on themselves where Tommy had run into a block.

I'd never understood the educational legitimacy of mazes.

They didn't necessarily test cognitive ability. Wasn't it really just an exercise in trial and error? Did anyone ever lose points for going the wrong way initially?

Not in a maze. And yet the exercise of putting pencil to paper and getting to the end of a maze never disappeared. Nobody lost points for going the wrong way at first in a maze. But they did in life. Every wrong turn had an effect on the rest of the maze. Every mistake affected the path, didn't it?

My wrong turn—choosing to go to the Everneath with Cole—had taken a life.

No. My choice hadn't taken a life yet. Jack wasn't dead yet.

Mazes. Why was I dwelling on them? Last night Cole had described the Everneath as a maze. I closed my eyes and rubbed my forehead. There was something there. It was as if seeing Tommy's maze had caused a flash inside my head. Not a big flash but more like the negative of a photograph. A little seedling deep in my mind, prompting me forward.

Grabbing the new mythology book that had been sitting on the table all day, I ruffed up Tommy's hair and then went to my room. I pushed aside the stacks of books next to my computer to make space. Where had I read about a maze before? Or a labyrinth?

I rifled through the scattered notes on my desk, a compilation of every myth and legend that I thought might have something to do with the Everneath. Cole used to tell me that myths and legends were rooted in truth. The problem was discovering which ones were specific to my case.

But none of my latest notes mentioned a maze. Leaning back in my chair, I grabbed the new book my dad had given me and skimmed the topics page.

There was nothing about mazes under the *M*s, so I tried *L* for *labyrinth*. There I found the reference for "Labyrinth, Minotaur."

I smacked my head. Of course I should've remembered the story about the Minotaur—the half-man, half-bull creature—who was trapped in the labyrinth. Every nine years, fourteen young Athenians were sent inside the maze as a sacrifice to ward off a plague. This happened until someone, a hero maybe, entered the maze and killed the Minotaur. And then found his way out. Who was it?

I had picked up the book to thumb through it to the page listed in the index when I heard the garage door open. My dad was home early. He never came home early. Then it hit me.

"Crap," I muttered. I'd forgotten about Mrs. Caputo's detective coming to interview me.

I threw the book on my bed and closed my eyes. Last night I hadn't been nervous about facing the detective, but maybe that was because I'd been exhausted and weakened by my encounter with the Shades.

Today it was daunting.

You can do this, I told myself.

A knock sounded at my door.

"Come in," I said.

My dad came in and sat on my bed, and I covered my notes

with my books. Why did I even try to hide it? It was stupid, really. My dad knew how much I was obsessed with myths.

He ignored the books. "You ready to get this over with?"

"Mrs. Caputo blames me." I picked at the quilt on top of my bed. "Even if I tell the truth, I don't think she'd let the detective she hired with her own money give up on what she considers her biggest lead."

"From everything I've heard, Detective Jackson is a reasonable man. I've checked him out. Just because Mrs. Caputo is paying his bills doesn't mean he can fabricate evidence against an innocent person where there is none."

I considered this. *Fabricating evidence. A nosy detective.* It all seemed so routine for a missing boy. But we were dealing with the extraordinary. An underworld that wasn't supposed to exist. Immortals who would never die. It seemed a little beyond what an earthly detective could do.

Detective Jackson smelled like smoke, and he had a wicked comb-over. It swept from the top of one ear and meandered up and over the slope of his head until it ended in a gelled curve behind his other ear. It gave the illusion that his face was on the side of his head.

I couldn't stop staring at it.

"Nikki," my dad said, nudging my knee.

"What?"

"Are you going to answer the question?" Detective Jackson said.

How long had I been staring at his hair? "Sorry, can you repeat it?"

"That last night you were with Jack—"

"March twenty-seventh," I interrupted.

"Yes, I know." He could've surprised me. It didn't seem to matter what he knew. He still asked the same questions over and over. "That night, was he acting different? Strange? Stressed out?"

Oh boy. That was an understatement. It was the night I was supposed to disappear forever.

"No," I said. "We were playing poker in the park, with his brother, Will. Jack was winning a lot."

"Poker in the park," he repeated.

"Yes." I'd told him this several times.

My dad interjected. "The kids did that a lot. It wasn't—"

The detective held up his hand. "Please, Mayor. Let her answer."

"He's right," I said. "We did that all the time. The guys had their own set of poker chips that their grandpa had given them. Red ones. And blue ones. And black ones." I stopped, realizing that was probably a little too much detail.

"Right. So, after the poker game you left to go home."

"Yes."

"And then Will left." He looked at his notes as if he really had to concentrate to get the next part right. "And he took Jack's car with him. And drove it home. So Jack was alone, in the park, not a friend in sight, and car-less."

I cast my eyes downward. It was closer to the truth than the detective knew. Jack ended up alone that night. Not a friend in sight.

My dad must have seen the discomfort in my face because he said, "We've been over this. Can we move on?"

"I'd love to move on," Detective Jackson answered. "To the point where Jack just disappears . . . 'runs away' according to his note . . . without a car."

My dad looked at me. Neither of us said anything.

"Maybe he took a bus," my dad said, and I cringed. Wouldn't there be some sort of paper trail? I stayed quiet.

"I thought that too. But there was no record of him buying a ticket," the detective said.

"There wouldn't be if he paid cash," my dad replied.

Good point, Dad!

"There was nothing on the security footage either," the detective countered.

"Cameras miss people all the time. I'm sure you know this."

The detective's steely demeanor broke for a moment. "We checked bus stops in surrounding cities as well."

My dad leaned forward, his elbows on his knees and his hands clasped together. It was about to get good. "You mean to tell me you checked every single direction a bus could've gone from here? Every stop? Every small town? Everywhere? You must have endless resources."

My dad gave Detective Jackson the same stare he'd used on Councilman Fred Graves during their first primary debate, when the councilman had argued against environmental protection in favor of government money.

The detective tore his gaze away and looked at me. "What do you think, Nikki? Is that what happened? Jack just took a bus and paid using all that extra cash he'd saved working as a delivery boy, and ducked beneath all of the cameras—"

"We're done here," my dad said, cutting him off. "Now you're asking Nikki to speculate as to Jack's motives and actions only he could know. We've just crossed the line from interview to waste of time."

I had to make an effort not to cheer. My dad stood up, and I did the same. He put a hand on my shoulder. "Nikki, go to your room. I'll show the detective out."

Thank you, Dad. My dad came through for me at the most surprising times.

"I have some errands to run," I said, and my dad waved me away, keeping his eyes on the detective.

I ran to my room, gathered up my notes, and headed out the door, hoping Mrs. Jenkins would know what to tell me.

On the way to Mrs. Jenkins's house, I called Will. I'd promised to tell him everything, and I hadn't been very good about keeping that promise over the last twenty-four hours.

When he answered, I took a deep breath and told him about my trip to the Everneath, my encounter with the queen, and how Cole had said that the Shades would track my energy if I tried it again.

When I'd finished, he was quiet for a moment. "You went to the Everneath. And came back again."

"Yeah."

"Last night. After graduation."

"Yeah."

He breathed loudly into the phone. "Are you crazy?"

"I saw Cole, and I had to take my chance."

"So, what are we going to do?"

"I'm on my way to talk to Mrs. Jenkins. Maybe she knows a way to hide my energy. Maybe there's some trick to avoiding the Shades."

I heard what sounded like a door closing in the background. When he spoke again, his voice was low. "You're talking about going again?"

I didn't answer right away, as I turned off the highway and onto the frontage road.

"Becks, you still there?" Will said.

"Yes. And yes, I have to go again if we're going to save Jack." He was quiet. I rounded the last corner before Mrs. Jenkins's house. "Look, I'm here. I'll call you when I'm done, okay?"

"Okay."

Mrs. Jenkins and I had a strange relationship. It was her daughter, Meredith, who'd given me the ancient bracelet that had led us to the theory about Cole's heart. Mrs. Jenkins was a member of the group known as the Daughters of Persephone, which was dedicated to finding the next queen of the Everneath. She raised Meredith to be a Forfeit in the Feed in the hopes that the power would fall to her daughter. Meredith was Max's Forfeit, but she hadn't survived like I had. She'd emerged from the Feed as an old woman suffering from dementia. After six months on the Surface, the Tunnels had come for her.

She didn't have someone like Jack to take her place.

At the time, Mrs. Jenkins had seemed so unfeeling, but I think Meredith's fate wore on her mother's soul. When I lost Jack, I had come to Mrs. Jenkins, searching for a way to get back to the Everneath; but she only told me what I already knew: I would need a piece of Cole.

Still, we'd talked a few times since then. I was always hoping some spark of intuition would hit her and she'd have answers, but it never happened. I wouldn't have called us friends. More like two people who shared a similar sense of loss. The Everneath had taken someone I loved, and it had taken someone she didn't know she loved.

In that way her pain was greater than mine.

I knocked on the door, and when she opened it, she raised her eyebrows. "Nikki."

"Mrs. Jenkins. Cole's back."

She nodded and ushered me inside. While she stayed in the kitchen to brew tea—a mainstay in her home—I brought her up to speed on Cole's return to Park City and my spontaneous trip to the Everneath.

She emerged carrying a tray with two teacups and a kettle. It struck me at that moment how alone she was. I couldn't imagine she had an excuse to use the tea tray very much these days.

"So, Jack is still alive?" she asked. She had always been amazed to learn about the dream connection, even though it was her own daughter who had figured out that the Forfeits who survived the Feed were the ones who had anchors on the Surface.

"Yes. Meredith's theory is still true. I'm Jack's anchor now, like he was for me. But I don't know how much longer he can survive."

I told her about him forgetting things. She got a faraway look in her eyes and stared at her fireplace. "Meredith was so smart to figure it out. I always thought she would be the next one to survive," she said, inclining her head toward the jar on her mantelpiece. I knew what was inside that jar. The ashes of a Forfeit named Adonia. The last person in Meredith's family line to have survived the Feed.

Adonia didn't last long. Apparently, she didn't want to fight the current queen and try to take over the throne, so—according to Mrs. Jenkins—Adonia's Everliving betrayed her. Told the queen where she could find her. And the queen sucked out all of her energy until there was nothing left.

I guess that was one reason I had to be grateful to Cole. He never turned me over to the queen.

"Meredith had the numbers," Mrs. Jenkins went on. "She was the thirty-third female born from the descendants of Adonia's mother."

I frowned. "What does that have to do with it?"

"The number three is important with the Everlivings. Symbolic. I thought it would mean something for Meredith. Make her special."

Her voice had taken on a dreamlike quality. Mrs. Jenkins believed the queen had the power to immortalize entire ancestral lines at her discretion. If Meredith had survived the Feed and taken over the throne, it would've meant eternal life for Mrs. Jenkins.

She had a way of drifting off like this, as if her thoughts always revolved around Meredith's failure and her own missed opportunity. I tore my gaze away from the jar and tried to focus her. "Mrs. Jenkins, I'm going to the Everneath again. With Cole back, I know I can steal another piece of his hair, and—"

"You'd try it again without an escort? Do you *want* to die?"

This stopped me short. *Escort?* In all of our talks, she had never mentioned an escort to me. Before I could say anything, though, she went on. "You can't just go to the Everneath without an escort. The Shades will find you and take you to the Tunnels. I thought you knew this."

"Wait," I said, interrupting her. "Did you say *escort?*"

"Well, yes. I mean, without an escort, your energy will attract—"

"By escort, do you mean an Everliving?"

"Of course. No human who wants to live would venture into the Everneath without an Everliving. Their energy void masks your energy abundance. They absorb what you give off. And then the Shades aren't so attracted. To go alone is suicide.

You knew this. That's why you needed to find Cole."

I sigh, exasperated. "I thought I needed him for his hair!"

"Don't you know your mythology?" she said in a *tsk-tsk* kind of way. "You need the entire ferryman to escort you to the Underworld. That's your Everliving. Otherwise, the Shades come circling like sharks who smell blood."

I bit the inside of my cheek. Part of me wanted to jump up and down at the news that I might be able to hide, and the other part wanted to smack Cole for not telling me. Was it possible that he didn't know? I only considered it for a moment. Cole was hundreds, maybe thousands of years old. Of course he knew.

He just didn't want *me* to know.

"So an escort is the key."

"Yes."

"Does the Everliving escort have to be willing?"

She cocked her head as if I were crazy.

"Never mind. I have to go. I have someone I need to talk to."

She walked me to the door; and as she opened it, she said, "Just remember, if you do go to the Everneath, don't eat anything."

I didn't need to ask her why not. Persephone had eaten six pomegranate seeds, and that was why she'd been forced to become queen of the Underworld.

"Don't worry. I won't eat a bite."

When I got inside the car, I slammed the door shut, fuming. Cole had told me it was impossible to mask my energy, because he didn't think I'd ever find out the truth. But he didn't know I had Mrs. Jenkins.

"You lied to me, Cole." I said it out loud. I was going to kill him. Then I was going to take his lifeless body, drag it to the Everneath with me, and use it as my "escort."

Deep breaths.

Twenty minutes later, after several calming exercises Dr. Hill had taught me, I was in my room getting dressed for Harry O's. I was pretty sure that's where the Dead Elvises would be playing tonight, and now that I knew the truth, I wasn't about to miss my chance to confront Cole.

SEVEN

NOW

The Surface. Harry O's.

There were rumblings on the internet about Deads sightings in Park City. According to eyewitnesses on the scene, fans were already starting to line up at Harry O's.

I pulled off my yoga pants and changed into some dark jeans. I even put on my black leather boots, which Cole had complimented once. Anything I could do to encourage him to give up information. But after our encounter yesterday and then that whole fiasco with the queen, I didn't know if I was ready to face him again. Every meeting with him brimmed with intensity. It didn't matter how sure I was of my intentions when I was alone. When I was with him, I couldn't trust myself. I knew it when he showed up at the graduation ceremony. My reaction was beyond the reasoning mechanism inside my head. It was down to an elemental level. My brain knew to stay away, but every cell in my body reached out to him. A reflex reaction.

I wondered if he could sense it too. I hoped he couldn't.

I needed him to think I wasn't susceptible to his influence. It would make saving Jack harder if he knew the truth.

My dad had gone back to work after the detective left. Despite his protectiveness today, some of the discrepancies surrounding Jack's disappearance had to be bothering him as well. But I couldn't think about that now. I realized how selfish it sounded, but repairing my damaged family would have to wait. Would there ever be a time when my strained relationship with my father and brother wouldn't be overshadowed by the fallout from my mistakes?

I hoped so.

I got to Harry O's a few minutes before the band was scheduled to take the stage. The air in the club dripped with sweat and an alcoholic mist. There was no way I'd avoid coming home smelling like beer. One step inside and my clothes had already soaked it up. Hundreds of fans crammed the dance floor and overflowed onto the viewing platforms near the bar at the back. There was a lot more skin showing than the last time I was here, evidence of the summer weather.

Because I was alone, I easily slipped through the congested areas and settled into a spot on the edge of the first riser. The Dead Elvises' popularity had grown in the past few months. They'd released a couple of new songs, and rumor was they were going to debut one tonight. Since the concert was technically a secret, there was no guest list at the entrance. People would file in until the crowd threatened the fire ordinance.

I couldn't believe I was here again. I'd met Cole at this

very club. Jules had talked me into going with her. She'd been worried about me because the trial of the drunk driver who'd killed my mom was about to start.

I thought I'd been good at hiding my grief, but Cole could see it.

C'mon, sad girl, he'd said. *Dancing makes everything better.*

It was the first time I'd realized there was something about him . . . something more than human. Something irresistible.

It was also the first time I'd acknowledged the strange connection between us.

That connection only grew during our hundred years together in the Feed. It was still there at Jack's graduation ceremony, when I'd felt him behind me before I saw him.

Even now I could sense his presence. His nearness. The band wasn't out onstage yet, but I knew he was close. I stared at the stage. Past it. If the curtains suddenly disappeared, I knew I would find Cole in my direct line of sight. My tingling skin knew it as well. The connection would never break.

The lights dimmed, and the MP3s faded out. The anticipation was palpable. I glimpsed movement on the stage, but it was too dark to be sure. Then, in one sudden moment, the stage lit up, reflective light bouncing off chrome instruments, and there was the band.

Max on second guitar, his black hair longer than I remembered. Oliver on bass. Gavin on drums.

And there was Cole. Fierce and beautiful and seizing all the attention in the room with one sure strum of his guitar.

His onstage glory hit me fresh, as if I'd been in a rainstorm for the past few months and the sun had finally come out.

I wondered if the other people in the crowd had that same reaction to him when he was playing, or if it was because of our distinct history—our literal tie to each other. The faces of the people around me showed that they felt it too. At least to some degree.

For me it was overpowering. I had to look away. Staying in one place became difficult, because my natural instinct right now was to storm the stage.

But when I felt Cole's gaze on me, I chanced a look up.

In the sea of faces, his eyes somehow found mine, his face a strange mixture of surprise and something else I couldn't pinpoint. It had taken him seconds to spot me.

As he played, I could feel a change inside me. The black pit of guilt—the constant ache that had defined me since Jack disappeared—began to ease up. The viselike grip it had on my soul relaxed slightly.

For a split second the relief from my pain felt good. So good, I didn't think I ever wanted it to end. But something wasn't right; and, in the back of my mind, I realized Cole was feeding on my guilt.

Feeding on my emotions. Again. It's what Everlivings did best. Cole was so good at it, he could focus on me from across the room and skim off my uppermost layers of emotions. The worst ones, like my guilt right now, were always at the top.

Cole was draining my guilt, and for a moment I let him.

I angled my shoulders toward him to make it easier. The pressure, the weight of my pain—not just Jack, but also the pain of missing my mother, of disappointing my father, of abandoning my brother—began to ease away, releasing its constricting hold on my heart. I closed my eyes, and for a moment I let myself believe that nothing mattered.

I was alone. Surrounded by his music, all the tension in my body assuaged by the melody, each strum of his guitar pressing against the aches. Because that's what Cole could do. He could make everything that mattered disappear. In a room full of people, he could make me feel as if I was the only one and that I had nothing to worry about.

Someone bumped into my shoulder, jolting me out of the daze.

"Sorry," the boy dancing beside me said.

I blinked a few times at him, then turned toward the stage. Cole smirked and lifted his head up in a *welcome back* sort of way.

Ashamed, I tore my eyes away from him; and, with all the strength I could muster, I made my way to the exit, his music following me, reaching for me almost like the Shades in the Everneath had done.

I paused outside the club doors with a hand over my heart. The light feeling left and the full weight of my guilt returned. My guilt must've been a powerful emotion for it to come back so quickly. It was my constant reminder of Jack. The pain of missing him was such a part of me now that if I didn't hold on to it, I felt as if I would disappear. I couldn't let anyone ever take it away. The guilt was my strongest reminder of what I needed to do.

I pushed off against the wall I'd been leaning on and ran into someone coming into the club. "Sorry—"

"Nikki?"

I glanced up. It was Jules. Looking pretty and light. I almost turned and ran back inside.

Everywhere Jules went, it was as if she brought the sunshine with her. She was with Tara Bolton and Kaylee . . . somebody. I couldn't remember her last name. They were girls in our grade.

"Hey," I said.

Jules looked at the other girls. "You guys go ahead."

Tara shot me a curious glance, then went inside with Kaylee trailing behind.

When I didn't say anything, Jules said, "You know, I'm not really in the mood for a concert. You wanna grab a coffee? I've been wanting to ask you something."

Ask me something? I was almost more scared of her questions than I had been of the interrogation by the detective. Jules could always tell when I was lying.

We crossed the street and went into the coffee parlor at Grounds&Ink. Half of the place was dedicated to pool tables and the other half to cozy booths and comfy chairs. We ducked into a booth near the entrance that gave me a good view of Harry O's and flagged down a waitress.

"Coffee?" Jules said.

She nodded and returned moments later with two mugs.

We sipped in silence. It was hard for me to look Jules in the face. If I had never come back, Jack would probably be with her, and they would be happy.

Jules was so close to both of us, yet she had no idea what had really happened last March. In her mind, Jack had come back to me and then disappeared. How could she not blame me?

She broke the silence first. "Detective Jackson keeps asking me questions about you."

"Like what?"

She gave a faint smile. "They're not very flattering questions. He wants to know if you're mentally stable. If you've been seeing a shrink. If you've been acting weird. If I knew where you went when you disappeared before. Stuff like that."

I grimaced. "What did you tell him?"

"That I don't know anything. Because I *don't* know anything."

I stared at my coffee mug and took a long sip. I could feel her eyes on me. "Jules, I'm really sorry. About everything."

She nodded. "Will you answer me one question?"

"Yes."

"Do you know where he is?"

How I wanted to tell her the truth. Last year, there wasn't anything I would've kept from her. But the instant I imagined saying yes, I also imagined what I would have to explain, starting with the fact that there is an underworld called the Everneath.

I looked her in the eye and answered without any further hesitation. "I don't know where he is."

"I believe you."

I felt my shoulders relax. "You do?"

She smiled. "If I know one thing about you, it's this. You would never do anything to purposely hurt Jack. And if you knew where he was, you'd do whatever it took to find him."

I wanted to leap across the table and hug her.

Jules ran her finger over the rim of her mug. "Do you remember when the Caputo boys and their little gang of thugs used to ride past our houses?"

My fingertips broke out in a sweat at the mention of the name Caputo. We were walking into dangerous territory. Memories. It was the memories of Jack that hurt the most. When I'd first come back from the Feed, I lived inside of those memories with him, because I knew he'd be okay. They were safe spots. But now, memories were just reminders that Jack was beyond my reach. That he'd never be safe again.

Memories were part of what I kept secured in the dam around my heart.

Jules watched me expectantly.

"I remember," I whispered, hoping that would be the end of it.

"And you and I would store those spiky chestnuts, and we'd throw—"

I slammed my hand down on the table, startling her. "Sorry. I . . . don't remember as much as I used to."

She shook her head. "You're lying. You just don't want to remember." She could still read me so well. But she wasn't sympathizing. By cutting her off, I could see I'd crossed some sort of line. She frowned. "And I can only think of two reasons you don't want to remember. Either you don't know how to face what happened . . . or you feel guilty."

It was as if I were sitting in front of her completely transparent. I looked away, out the window. A lot of time had passed, and people were now trickling out of Harry O's.

I couldn't face her anymore. "I have to go."

Suddenly she latched on to my hand. "Becks. If you know where he is . . . you have to do something."

"But—"

"Just promise me. If you know what's happened to him, even if it's bad, you have to tell someone. Do you hear me?" Her voice shook with emotion. "No more lies."

I opened my mouth but couldn't answer. So much for thinking Jules believed me. She knew I was hiding the truth from everyone. She knew I was responsible for Jack's disappearance. She knew I was lying.

She lowered her eyes, slapped some bills on the table, and left without another word. Everything she said had added weight in my chest. I sat in the booth for a long time, staring at the checkered pattern on the plastic tablecloth, willing myself to get up.

When I finally stood, I crossed the street as the last few stragglers trickled out of the club. Cole was inside. And he held my only chance for getting Jack back.

Please, Cole. Please give me hope.

EIGHT

NOW

The Surface. Harry O's.

As I walked in, the lingering smell of sweat and beer hit me in the face. A tall guy behind the bar eyed me. "Are you Nikki?"

I looked from side to side. "Um . . . yes."

"Follow me. Cole's in the back."

Cole must have known I'd be here. I took a deep breath and followed the bartender back behind the stage and through a small hallway that led to a beat-up wooden door marked GREEN ROOM.

The bartender knocked three times. I read some of the messages carved into the door.

LB + TK + FR = AWESOME TRIFECTA

Before I could decipher what it meant, the door opened and Gavin's face appeared. The last time I'd seen the Dead Elvises' drummer was when I was sneaking around trying to figure out what was so special about the Shop-n-Go. He'd almost caught me there. "What?" he demanded.

Then he recognized me.

"Oh."

He closed the door, and a few seconds later it opened again and Gavin walked out, followed by Oliver and lastly Max. I watched them, quiet.

Max paused as he passed by. He leaned down to talk to me, and I remembered how much taller he was than Cole. "Nik, be gentle. Cole was doing so much better until that stunt you pulled last night. Don't screw him up again."

I looked at him incredulously. "Me screw *him* up?"

Max just walked away. Cole had destroyed six months of my life, most of my soul, and the boy I love, and Max was worried about me hurting him?

Okay, so maybe some of that had been my own doing, but still.

I went inside and shut the door behind me, feeling more riled up by the second. Before I turned around, I heard an intake of breath.

"Nik," Cole said. "Those boots. You *do* care."

Turn around, Becks. Turn around. Why was it so hard to be in the same room with him? I took a deep breath and faced him. He was sitting on the corner of an old brown leather couch. It was worn in the center seat, where a large chunk of leather was missing. His guitar sat beside him like a constant, faithful companion; and he flipped a guitar pick over the knuckles of his fingers, passing it from finger to finger like he always did.

I must have been staring at the pick, because Cole froze it

midflip, then tossed it into the palm of his other hand and held it out to me. "It's not what you think it is."

"I think it's a pick," I said, even though I knew what he was talking about. I'd never look at a pick again without wondering if it was Cole's heart.

He cocked an eyebrow. "But the look in your eyes was murderous. Do you have a thing against guitar picks, or were you hoping I'd be stupid enough to still carry my heart around with me?"

Cole watched my reaction carefully, deliberately taking a sip from a water bottle. The last thing I wanted to talk about was my feeble attempt to kill him moments before Jack disappeared.

"Yes," I said.

He leaned back in the sofa and put his hands behind his head. "There's the old Nik. No 'How do you do,' no talk of the weather. Just a good swift kick to the balls."

"A kick to your balls is an option?"

He frowned. "Now, that doesn't sound like you."

"People change."

"Not you. Not that much."

"You don't know me."

He scoffed. "It always amazes me when you so easily dismiss the fact that we were together—from cheek to toes, literally together—for a hundred years."

"I don't want to talk about that," I said, my voice cracking.

"I know." He took a breath and flipped his guitar pick

again. "I chased you for six months, and now suddenly I can't get rid of you. Please sit."

I crossed the room and sat on the farthest corner of the couch.

He shifted to face me. "What can I do for you?"

"You lied to me, Cole."

He frowned and didn't answer. But he didn't seem surprised.

"Why didn't you tell me it was possible?" I said. "That an Everliving *escort* can help mask the energy from a human."

He shrugged. "It wasn't pertinent information."

"Not pertinent?" I gave a deranged little laugh. "How is it not pertinent?"

"Even if you could hide from the Shades, there are other creatures in the Everneath that would like nothing more than to drain a human. We don't even know where the Tunnels are hidden. And that still wouldn't be our biggest problem." I was about to protest, but he held up a finger. "Let me finish." He shifted on the couch so he was facing me. "What do you think is keeping Jack alive right now?"

"That's easy. Me."

"It's not just you." He leaned over and pressed his finger to my forehead. "It's what's inside your head. It's because you are intact that you have the strength to keep him alive. In the Everneath, the longer you're there, the more you'll begin to lose your mind. You won't dream, you'll forget why you went there in the first place, and no amount of words from me will help you remember."

"I'd never forget Jack. I was with you for a hundred years, and his face never left me."

"Yes, but you forgot everything else. I bet you even forgot his name."

I didn't disagree.

"That's why I didn't tell you about the escort. I would never be able to convince you how quickly you'll forget."

I looked down at the woven rug at our feet. He was right. During the Feed, I'd only remembered Jack's face. It wasn't until I'd reached the Surface again that I remembered all of him. "But this time you won't be Feeding on me. It will be easier for me to remember."

"Nik, it doesn't work that way. *I* won't be Feeding on you, but the entire Everneath will be. It's a place of imbalance, constantly draining those with hearts"—he gestured toward me—"and constantly Feeding those of us without hearts. If you aren't an Everliving, my world will drain you. And the first thing to go will be your memories."

"I don't care."

He cocked his head at this.

"I don't care, Cole. I don't even want my memories now. And at least then I could say I tried. At least I wouldn't be sitting here, helpless on the Surface, trying to find comfort in *memories*, while the boy I love is dying a slow death all for me."

At the word *love*, Cole looked away.

"And if I lose my memory, and it's so far gone that it will never come back . . . well . . ."

"Don't tell me you think that's okay." His voice was gruff. "You do realize that if you forget him completely, he *will* die. Tell me you know this."

I blinked a few times, trying to block the coming tears. "He's dying anyway. I have to go to the Everneath. Nothing will stop me."

He ran a hand through his hair, making it stick out in a couple of places. "Well then, Nik, you aren't factoring in one very important thing."

"What's that?"

"That I'm not going with you."

NINE

NOW

The Surface. Harry O's.

*C*ole's words hit me like a fist to the chest, but I was stupid to have expected a different reaction.

His face had become blank, without emotion. "I'd never do it."

I stood up. "Why? It's nothing to you. It's just a trip to your own world. You wouldn't have to do anything. You just have to come with me."

"You're partly right."

"About what?"

"It's nothing to me."

I could feel my face crashing. I sat down on the couch again, speechless.

"Jack is nothing to me. Saving him is nothing to me."

"But—"

"And it's not just another trip to the Everneath, because *you* are a liability. Just because you decided you're not going to become an Everliving doesn't mean you're not still a threat to the queen. You survived the Feed. That changed you, even though we don't know exactly how. The change was permanent. If the queen knew you existed . . ."

"She's already seen me."

"Yes, but she doesn't know who you are." He leaned forward and put his elbows on his legs. "She doesn't know a Forfeit survived the Feed. If she knew, she wouldn't waste time with the Tunnels. She'd rip you apart."

I tensed. Cole saw it.

"Don't worry," he said. "You're safe here. But I'm not about to parade you around under her nose. Why would I risk angering the Shades *and* the queen to help you?" He grimaced. "What do I get for a grand prize on the tiny chance we do succeed? You and Jack, together. There's nothing in it for me, Nik."

I watched his face closely. And it cracked. Only a little, but I knew he was holding something back. Something strong. But just as I noticed, the crack disappeared again. Maybe I had imagined it, but I pounced anyway.

"You're a better person than this. You're a better person than you think you are." I grabbed his hand. "You told me that I had changed you. But it's not just me. You have a good heart."

He frowned, a wary look in his eyes. "I don't have a heart."

"You *do* have a heart. Maybe not one that beats, but you have one that defines your soul. And so what if up until now your soul's been a bit on the darker side? This is your chance to redefine your soul."

He took his hand away and rolled his guitar pick over his fingers, averting his gaze. "I told you a long time ago, I'm not a hero."

"But—"

"You should go, Nik." He stood up, walked over to the door, and opened it wide. "Go somewhere and wait it out. That's your only choice."

I stayed where I was.

"Nik, I said go."

"No."

In a quick move, he stomped over to me, grabbed me by the shoulders, hoisted me off the couch, and nearly threw me toward the door. "It's not a request."

He didn't give me a chance to recover my balance. With one hand around my waist, he lifted me off the ground, careful not to hurt me but tight enough that I couldn't put up a fight.

Before I knew it I was out the door and he was slamming it in my face. I tried to open it again, but he had already locked it.

I pounded on the door. "Cole! Please!" But there was no sound from the other side. I put my ear against the door, hoping to hear any sign that Cole would open the door back up.

But there was nothing. So much for Cole claiming I had too much control over him.

I had no influence over him at all. I raised my fist to pound again, but the bartender suddenly appeared in the hallway. He folded his arms across his chest and leaned against the wall, watching me.

I dropped my hand and walked away. How had things

turned upside down so quickly? I was tracking down Cole, and he was throwing me out of his room. A few months ago I would've considered my behavior reckless.

As I crossed the now-empty club floor, I heard the metal click of a lighter from the corner of the room. Max was there, leaning against the wall.

Waiting for me.

I walked over to him. "What?" I said.

He clicked his lighter open, and a flame appeared. "Leave him be."

My shoulders sank. "I need his help. I'm not trying to hurt him."

"You hurt him by existing." He snapped the lighter shut. "He's not himself anymore. He suddenly has this weird . . . empathy for humans." He shuddered.

"If you're so worried about him being near me, why'd the band come to Park City?"

Max pushed away from the wall and came toward me. "Have you ever tried to tell him what to do?" He shook his head as if he already knew the answer, then he walked right past me and out the exit.

I looked at the ceiling and sighed. First Cole threw me out, then Max—who I would've thought wanted me to be the next queen just as much as Cole did—was warning me to stay away.

The world was officially backward.

I walked out of the club, still reeling from Cole's rejection. I don't know why I expected a different reaction from him. In his eyes, I had ruined his chance to rule the Everneath.

I was the accidental almost-queen who had denied him everything he had ever wanted. And now I was asking for his help to save the boy I loved.

The night air had a bite to it. In the mountains, even the hottest nights always had a chill. I walked down the dark street to where I'd left my car. A black sedan was parked behind me. I wouldn't have noticed it except that I could see a tiny red glow coming from the driver's seat. It looked like the lit end of a cigarette.

Fumbling with the keys, I got into my car as fast as I could and locked the door.

When I pulled out, the sedan pulled out too, keeping its lights off. Was it following me? Detective Jackson had smelled like smoke. Did he drive a town car?

Or was I just being paranoid? I shook my head. It probably wasn't him. And even if it was, I wasn't doing anything wrong.

I thought about calling my dad to complain, but I didn't want to worry him; and as far as I knew, it wasn't against the law to follow someone. Besides, complaining or trying to lose him might make me look even guiltier. If Detective Jackson was following me in the hope that I'd lead him to Jack, he was taking the wrong road.

I couldn't lead him to Jack even if I wanted to.

Before I went to bed, I glanced at the mythology book I'd thrown down yesterday. It had fallen to the floor open-faced. A black-and-white drawing of a Minotaur took up the entire page on the right.

The myth of the Minotaur and the labyrinth. I picked up the book and read from the passage.

It was a story of war.

It told the account of Minos, king of Crete, who kept a Minotaur at the heart of an impenetrable labyrinth. Every nine years, Minos forced their enemies, the Athenians, to send fourteen young men and women, in a black-sailed ship, as food for the beast.

Theseus, a prince in Athens, volunteered to be fed to the Minotaur. But he really planned to slay the monster.

King Minos's daughter, Ariadne, fell in love with Theseus. She vowed to help him by giving him a ball of twine so he wouldn't get lost in the maze.

Theseus succeeded in killing the Minotaur and used the twine to find his way out of the labyrinth.

A simple ball of twine had saved his life. I could do what Ariadne did. If I could just hold Jack's hand again . . . and give him a ball of twine, he could use it to lead himself out.

If I could just hold his hand in mine again, I would pull him out.

I turned back to the story of the Minotaur. The celebration of slaying the monster was short-lived. Theseus abandoned Ariadne. And his own father—believing his son was dead—committed suicide.

Damn myths.

TEN

Tonight, in my dream, I wait alone on my side of the bed for a long time. There is an empty space next to me where Jack usually is. I don't move. I don't want to rustle the atmosphere and create any disturbance that would prevent him from coming to me.

I don't know how much time passes or how long I am alone. Finally, Jack appears by my side. His eyes are open only to slits.

"Becks," he whispers. "Are you there?"

"Shhh," I say, holding the air that is his hand. "I'm here. Don't waste your energy."

He struggles to raise his eyelids, and I am reminded of those dreams I have when I am so exhausted that I can't keep my eyes open, even in my dream.

The effort tires him, and he shuts his eyes. "I can't see. Tell me you're here."

"I'm here. I'm not going anywhere."

"I think if I could just touch you again, I could come home."

"Then touch me," I say, holding out my hand.

Instead of reaching for it, he leans toward me as if he would kiss me. I do the same, mirroring him, still hoping beyond all reason that if I wanted it badly enough, our lips would touch. But just as we should have made contact if we were real to each other, morning is here. I wake up.

It's not enough time.

LATER THAT MORNING
The Surface. The Java Hut.

I ran my fingers over my head so many times, I was surprised there wasn't a huge pile of hair on the floor next to my booth. Jack was barely there last night. Barely there! I knew the dreams kept him alive, but it only worked when he was actually there, didn't it? If I was losing him even with entire nights of dreaming about him, how much faster would he slip away with only a few minutes together?

The waitress at the Java Hut noticed my agitation and slipped over to top off my coffee mug. As if more caffeine would help. But I didn't stop her. The crowd was sparse today, probably because of the record-high temperatures and the fact that the Java Hut didn't do iced beverages. Or air conditioning.

I checked my watch. If Will was any later, I'd slip into a caffeine coma. That didn't make any sense, I know, but nothing in my life was right side up. And last night . . . last night Jack and

I had only seconds together, during which he couldn't even see. I couldn't keep him alive in such a short time. I couldn't keep him alive. Tears welled up in my eyes and began to spill over onto my cheeks.

I was losing him. Every second put him further and further out of my reach.

An ache on my scalp brought me back to the present. If I wasn't careful, I'd be bald soon. I sipped my Kona Roast coffee, closing my eyes as I inhaled the scent. Jack and I used to wonder if the Java Hut put some sort of drug in it to make it smell so good. One whiff and you had to have it.

I put my mug down, leaned back on the bench, and waited. The front door squeaked, and Will walked in, a pair of dark sunglasses perched on the bridge of his nose. The glasses couldn't hide the red beneath his eyes.

"How'd it go with Cole?" he mumbled, sliding into the spot across from me and keeping his glasses in place even though we were inside.

I reached toward his face and tugged on the sunglasses until I could see his bloodshot eyes. He pulled back and pushed them up. "Will," I said.

"You can't exactly blame me, considering everything."

I pressed my lips together, worried that my impulsive dash to the Everneath had caused the relapse. "But . . . you were doing so well—"

"Stop, Becks. Let's take inventory of our priorities. First, go to the Underworld and save my brother. Second, don't die while doing it. Third, start a grassroots campaign to add diversity to the state's conservative legislature. Fourth, then maybe tackle my excessive drinking." I frowned, and he leaned forward. "Thank you for caring. But you know we don't have time for it. Tell me how it went with Cole."

I took a deep breath, wondering how to describe my conversation with Cole, when really it was very simple. "He says he won't come with me. And I don't know what to do."

At this, Will was quiet. It was hard to read his expression with those sunglasses on. I reached over and gently removed them, and this time he let me.

He folded his arms and rested his elbows on the table. "So there's no way to do this without Cole."

I shook my head. "Unless you can find me another Everliving I can charm to the point where he'll help me save my boyfriend. No, Cole is the only one I ever imagined I had any influence over, and apparently it's not as strong a pull as I thought."

"I wouldn't discount your control over him. He spent six months trying to convince you he loved you. I don't think it was all a lie."

"I wouldn't bet on it. He's thrown me out twice now."

The waitress set a mug of coffee in front of Will. "So let's think about it. What do you have to bargain with? What does he want more than anything else?"

I paused even though I knew without a doubt what he wanted more than anything. Jack had asked me the same thing months ago. Will knew it too. He knew it before he even asked the question. It was as true now as it was before. "Me," I said. "He wants me to become an Everliving and overthrow the queen. But what am I supposed to do? Promise him I'll become his queen if we save Jack?"

Will shook his head. "You and Jack can't keep going back and forth sacrificing yourselves for each other. You know what it would do to him if you saved him at the cost of your own life."

I looked down at the table, at the ring of liquid my coffee mug had made there. I knew exactly how that would feel. I was feeling it right now. It didn't solve anything.

Will leaned forward, placing his elbows on the table. "What if we discarded the carrot approach and went with the whip instead?"

"Huh?"

"What if instead of dangling a carrot—you—in front of him to get him to move, we push him from behind. Threaten him somehow."

"How? He's hidden the real pick. We'll never find it. And, come to think of it, we still don't know if breaking his pick would destroy him. What do we have?"

He looked down sheepishly. "Let's threaten to take away—permanently—the one thing he wants most." He raised his eyes. "Despite everything that's happened, you're still his best chance for the throne. We don't have to give him you. We just have to make him think he's going to lose you for good. We make him think you're going to the Everneath no matter what. If he believes you might disappear forever . . . he'll fold."

I thought about the night before at the club, how Cole had thrown me out. "I don't think he'd go just to save me."

"He did it two days ago."

"But that was because I didn't know what I was doing. If I went again, knowing exactly what would happen . . . I think he'd say good riddance."

"Becks, how long has he been searching for someone who could survive the Feed?"

I shrugged. "He said thousands of years. But I don't know how literal that was."

"And now he's finally found you. Do you think he'd really let you go? Sit back and watch his one chance for the throne disappear and never come back?" He shook his head. "No way. If we let him think you're going to the Everneath tonight . . . with or without him . . ." He paused. "He'd cave."

I thought about it. "But I don't have his hair or his finger-nail or anything."

"He doesn't know that. Weren't you in his dressing room?"

"Yes."

"Would it be so crazy to tell him you grabbed a hair there?"

We both leaned back and thought for a few minutes. The ceiling fans circled above, providing just enough breeze to keep us from sweating. Soft ukulele music played in the background.

And we were contemplating a bluff against an Everliving.

"He flat-out told me he'd never save me again."

"Let's see if he was serious."

I leaned toward Will, taking in his bloodshot eyes. "How are you thinking so clearly?"

His lips twitched. "I'm not. But I thought about it last night. Before I started drinking."

"Okay," I said.

"Okay what?"

"Okay, I'll do it."

He frowned, as if my finally agreeing to the plan made him question what we were doing. But he didn't say anything other than "Okay."

Lunchtime brought a steady stream of people, definitely locals who were particular about their coffee. Will and I sat in the same booth all morning, talking it out.

We decided a phone call to Cole would be the best way to start the ball rolling.

"How much time are you going to give him?" Will asked.

I thought about my dream last night. My eyes met his. "Six hours."

"What?!"

"You said tonight. I'll give him six hours." I looked at my phone. "Till tonight at seven o'clock."

"I was using it as an example. That doesn't give you very much time."

"Time for what?"

He looked at me as if I wasn't getting something obvious. "Time to figure out what you're gonna tell your family. Time to . . . prepare . . . everything . . ."

"Jack's slipping away. I don't have time for preparations. I can feel it. I did the math. One day on the Surface equals six months in the Everneath."

"That was during the Feed. You said time went slower in the Feed."

"Still . . . if I wait another day, it will be months for him. Or weeks at least. And he won't make it. What if one more Surface day kills him?" My voice began to waver. I couldn't look Will in the eyes, so I stared hard out the window.

Will's hand closed around mine. Another tear slipped down my cheek; and without acknowledging it, Will used his thumb to wipe it away.

"It has to be tonight," I said. "Time goes really fast in the Everneath. If all goes well, I can be back before my dad even notices I'm gone."

Will squeezed my hand. "Six hours, Becks. We'll give him six hours. I'll take care of the rest."

I nodded and grabbed a napkin, sniffing.

He waited in silence for a few moments, typing and retyping Cole's phone number into his cell phone, watching for signs that I had composed myself.

Finally, he pressed in the last number and said, "Ready?"

I nodded. He handed the phone to me.

After two rings, Cole picked up. "Hello?"

"Cole, it's Nikki."

Pause.

"Nik," he said.

". . ."

". . ."

I looked to Will for strength. "Listen, because I'm only going to say this once. I'm going to the Everneath. I'm leaving at seven o'clock."

"I doubt that very much, Nik." Cole chuckled.

I ignored him. "I'll be at the Shop-n-Go at seven. And then I'm gone."

He scoffed through the receiver. "And how do you plan on getting there?"

"I have your hair."

Cole's end of the conversation went quiet. I met Will's gaze, and he nodded in encouragement.

"Three strands to be exact," I said, staring at my hand as if the hairs were actually there.

"How did you—"

"Why do you think I went to your dressing room last night?" I steadied my voice. "The entire band sheds in there. It wasn't hard at all."

He was quiet again. "If you're so sure, why bother telling me?"

I looked at Will, who waved his hand in a circular motion to keep going. "I'm giving you one more chance to come with me. You know what my odds are without you." I took a deep breath. "So that's it. You have six hours, or I'm gone from your life for good."

"Nik—" His voice was strained, but I snapped the phone shut before I could hear what he was going to say and handed it back to Will. "Do you think he bought it?" he said.

I nodded. "Without a doubt. But I still don't know if he'll come."

I left Will at the Java Hut and went home to get ready, even though I had no idea what *getting ready* would entail. What do you pack for the Underworld?

When I walked into the house, my dad was sitting in his study, door open.

"Nikki! Come in here, please." He didn't sound happy, but I couldn't think of anything I'd done lately that would make him feel that way.

I stood in the doorway. "What's up, Dad?"

He looked at his watch. "Did you forget something today?"

I racked my brain. It was Wednesday, wasn't it? About one thirty. Come to think of it, my dad shouldn't have been home. And then it hit me.

"Crap. Dr. Hill."

"Yes. She called to see if you were okay, because you didn't show up for your appointment. So I rushed home from the office to find you missing."

I sighed. "I'm sorry. I met a friend this morning, and I totally lost track of time."

"And didn't keep your phone with you?"

I drew in a breath and rummaged through my bag. My phone was at the bottom, completely dead. I had been gone until late last night and then had left early this morning without plugging it in.

"Sorry. Battery's dead." I waved the phone in front of him so he knew I was telling the truth.

My dad put his elbows on his desk and pressed his fingertips together. "I rescheduled your appointment for tomorrow. Same time."

Tomorrow. I was hopefully leaving with Cole *tonight*.

"I'm not sure that's going to work—"

I stopped short when I saw his face. It fell. Crumbled. Within the space of a moment, he'd gone from strong mayor to weak, tired old man. "Nikki," he said softly. "Please." He was not demanding. He was pleading. "I can't lose you again. Do you know what it did to me last time? To lose your mother . . . and then to lose you? Can you possibly fathom?"

I stared down at his desk, my eyes burning.

"I know I've made mistakes," he said, "but I can't go through it again. I can't."

I had no words. No expressions of comfort. No promises I could make in good conscience. For a moment I doubted my current course. How could I leave him again? How could I put him through it all again?

But Surface time was slow. I could be back before he knew it.

Unless I failed.

Was there a right answer? Yeah, right. There hadn't been a right answer since I went to the Everneath in the first place.

I walked around his desk, put my arms around him, and kissed the top of his head. And then I made another promise I wasn't sure I could keep.

"I know it's been difficult. And I know it's not over yet. But I promise you we'll get through it."

He didn't answer. He only nodded.

I went to my room. And waited.

ELEVEN

NOW

The Surface. The Shop-n-Go.

At six fifty-five I walked through the doorway of the Shop-n-Go, my heart drumming in my chest. I gave a quick wave to Ezra at the counter.

"Don't bother calling him," I said. "He already knows I'm here."

Yes, Cole knew I was here, but would he come now? I walked to the back, squeezing past the other two customers in the place. The kind of customers who never seemed to see what was really going on here. I sat on the floor. Ezra had changed out the snacks. Powdered doughnuts now lined the bottom shelf where the chocolate-covered raisins used to be.

Involuntarily, I thought of that day a few months ago when Jack had confronted me inside the Shop-n-Go.

"You don't like raisins," Jack had said.

"They're not so bad now," I'd lied.

"But I don't change, Jack," I whispered now. "I won't change."

A knock at the window broke me from the memory. Will

was on the other side, gesturing to the back of the store to let me know he'd be waiting.

I smiled and nodded, then checked my watch. Six fifty-nine. No sign of Cole.

I took out the blond hair I had in my pocket. Will had to steal it from the new bartender at Mulligan's on Main Street. There was a shocking lack of blond people in my life, except for Jules, and I couldn't very well nonchalantly ask her for a strand of her hair. Bartender Jimmy let Will get away with a lot more than the previous owner did, but I think even he was a little surprised about the hair thing.

I checked my phone. Time was up. But there was still no sign of Cole. My heart was no longer drumming. It now felt as if it were lodged in my throat. I shook my head. Maybe I was stupid to think I meant anything to him. Maybe he'd finally had enough, and the possibility that he'd found his queen was no longer worth it.

I still brought the strand to my mouth, trying not to think about the fact that I was about to eat the hair of a bartender named Jimmy. Will and I had already planned to go through with the eating of the hair in case Cole was watching from somewhere else.

If Cole caught me in this bluff, I'd probably be blowing my last chance to get him to come with me. Then again, I'd already run out of chances.

The hair was light and roughly Cole's length. It could've been his hair. I wondered for a moment, if I really had a strand of his hair, would I go through with it again?

"Here goes," I said softly.

Just as I opened my mouth, a hand grabbed my wrist hard.

I whirled around, expecting to see Cole but it wasn't him. It was Max.

With his hand clenched around my wrist, he took the hair out of my fingers, held it up to his eyes, and examined it.

"This isn't Cole's." His hair looked black under the fluorescent lights, and his eyes looked even blacker.

"How do you know?"

He flicked the hair aside, ignoring my question. Turning his tall, lanky body to the window, he made a motion, and then he watched me silently, leather-clad arms folded across his chest. The muscles around his mouth were tight, making him look hard and detached at the same time. Like a bodyguard.

I looked out the window, to where he'd signaled, but I didn't see anything. "What, did you alert the authorities or something?" I mumbled. "Unauthorized attempt to eat hair at the Shop-n-Go?"

He looked unimpressed but stayed quiet. The doors to the store opened and shut, and moments later Cole joined us.

"Pay up," Max said to him, holding out his hand.

Cole sighed and pulled a ten-dollar bill from his pocket. Max wadded it up and wandered toward the front of the store, leaving Cole and me alone.

"What was that about?" I asked.

"Ah, Nik." He ran his fingers through his blond hair, and

my gaze darted to his hand to see if he had any loose strands. "You're always losing me bets. You see, Max bet that you were bluffing. *Lying.* About having a hair of mine. As usual, I was blinded by my high expectations of you. I didn't think you had it in you to pull that kind of bluff."

"Jack and I played poker once a week for years. I can lie."

"An admirable trait, to be sure."

My eyes involuntarily went up to his head. His hair. Maybe if I—

"Stop thinking about it, Nik!"

"What?"

He grinned and shook his head. "You *know* what. You're looking at my hair like an addict at a crack carnival. Enough already." He took a step closer. "Look. You may have bluffed, but I know enough about you to know you won't stop until you get my hair; and at the risk of you taking my scalp with you, I'll go."

His words didn't quite reach my brain. "You'll go where?"

He rolled his eyes and then spoke slowly. "I'll go with you."

"You'll go with me?" I said, incredulous.

"Yes. But not because I have any feelings for you or I'm attached to you in any way. I'm just attached to my hair. Quite literally."

I didn't know what to say. "You'll go with me?"

He gave a sideways glance. "Oh boy. It's like your brain is on a ten-second delay. Just do what you have to do and then meet me at my condo. We need to prepare."

"Prepare how?"

"Look, the Everneath is not a place you go to lightly. If you land in the wrong spot, if you make a wrong turn, you'll die. And if you die, I'll lose everything I've been working toward."

The air was heavy with a sudden ominous feeling until Cole clapped his hands together loudly. "Right then. See you later!"

"What do I pack?"

His lips turned up. "Pack light. You can't really bring much to the Everneath. But one thing you will need is a token of Jack's."

"A token?"

His face grew serious. "Yes. A token. Look, Nik, there are scary things that go bump in the Everneath, and the terrain is hard to navigate, but our biggest challenge will be you." He took his pointer finger and poked my forehead. "More specifically, your memory. Find something that reminds you of Jack. Something that connects your brain to him, and only him."

"Like what?"

"The two of you were lovey-dovey. Didn't he ever give you . . . I don't know . . . a heart-shaped locket necklace?"

"No."

"A teddy? With a T-shirt that says I LOVE YOU BEARY MUCH?"

I rolled my eyes. "*No.* He wasn't like that."

"Whatever. Just find some object that makes you think of Jack and no one else, and bring it with you." He started to turn away.

"So you're going with me?" I said.

He paused for a moment, shook his head in an exasperated

sort of way, and then continued out of the store. Max followed closely behind, shooting me a disgusted glance before storming out the doorway.

I heard motorcycles rev up and pull away, and then Will came rushing in.

"What happened? Did he say no?" He looked at my face when I didn't answer. "Becks, are you okay?"

I shook my head.

"You're not okay?"

"No. Yes, I'm okay. But no, he didn't say no." I threw my arms around Will. "I'm going to get Jack."

I knew what object I needed. Something small enough to carry. Something that made me instantly think of Jack the moment I saw it. Something tangible and tactile that I could press into the palm of my hand and identify without even seeing it.

The feel of it gave me an instant connection to Jack. I always kept it nearby, always at hand. Even after I'd Returned and things were so different between us, this object was my tether to the life I'd given up. The life I had before. The life with Jack.

I found it in my bedroom, under my bed. A note. Jack's note.

Ever Yours

He had given it to me after the Christmas Dance last year. No amount of Everneath brain-suck could take away the meaning behind those two words. The same ones he had on his tattoo. I was sure of it.

I decided not to see my father and Tommy again. I didn't leave a note or anything. If I didn't make it back by tomorrow morning, that would mean I'd been in the Everneath for weeks. And I probably wasn't ever coming back.

Will drove me to Cole's condo. When we got there, we sat there in silence for a minute or two, then Will grabbed my hand. Squeezed it tight.

"I want to come with you," he said.

"Absolutely not."

"But I can help." His eyes were pleading.

I couldn't believe he was bringing this up *now*. "Will. You know you can't come."

"Why not?"

I watched him for a moment. He knew why. But maybe he needed me to tell him it was impossible so he could take comfort in the fact that he'd done everything he could. I listed the reasons.

"Number one, I doubt Cole would take you. Number two, your mother needs you, and I need you to take care of everything here. Number three, there is no way in hell I will be responsible for losing both of the Caputo brothers."

He frowned and brought my hand to his lips. "I know you're right." He sighed. "I want my brother back," he said. "But I don't know if this is the right way."

I brought his hand to my own lips. "This is the only way."

"But you're putting your trust in Cole. The same Cole who did everything he could to keep you and Jack apart."

I sighed. "I'd be more worried about Cole's motives if Max wasn't so intent on keeping me away from him. If Cole had some evil plan, Max would be in on it. Not objecting to it."

He looked forward, a helpless expression on his face. I opened my door. "I'll see you soon. Maybe even tonight."

Will only nodded.

"Watch after my family."

He nodded again.

I slipped out, and before I was halfway up the staircase outside Cole's condo, Will drove away. I put my hand in my pocket and pressed my fingertips against Jack's note, feeling closer to him already.

TWELVE

Cole swung open the door and gestured for me to come inside. A clicking sound made me turn toward the living room, where Max was lounging on the couch. He fiddled with a silver lighter in his hand.

"What's he doing here?" I asked.

"He's coming with us." At my expression, Cole added, "More specifically, he's coming to keep me in line. I tend to make galactically stupid decisions when it comes to you, and the Everneath is not a place where you want to make stupid decisions. Besides, two of us will hide your energy better than just one."

I held up my hands in a *fine by me* gesture. Cole was taking me to the Everneath. I wasn't about to argue with anything, although I was pretty sure Max was also going to keep me from messing up Cole again.

Cole took off the guitar that had been strapped over his

shoulder and placed the instrument gently in its case in the corner of the room.

"I'm going to miss you," he said tenderly, his mouth turned up in a half smile.

"You're not bringing your guitar?" I said. I rarely saw him without it.

Max and Cole both looked at me with alarmed expressions. "No," Cole said. "I don't want to die."

"What do you mean?" I said warily.

"Music. It's forbidden. Like the penalty-of-death kind of forbidden."

"Why?"

Max clicked his lighter closed. "Because music is a powerful manipulator of emotions, and the Shades can't control it," he said.

"And the Shades don't like things they can't control." Cole snapped the case shut and straightened up. "Speaking of things you can't control, did you bring your token?"

I pulled the note out of my pocket. "Yes, but I don't think I'm going to need it."

"That's because you're currently standing on the Surface. Your brain is still intact."

I sighed and slipped the paper back into my pocket. "When we get there . . . well, how will we avoid getting caught?"

Cole frowned and ran a hand through his hair. "Last time you dropped down in the New York City of the Everneath. I'm going to take us to . . . Oklahoma." I must've looked lost, because he raced to the kitchen and came back with a piece of blank paper and a pencil in hand. With a sweeping gesture, he cleared the coffee table of everything on it, sending a few books, sheets of music, and a dirty coffee mug to the carpet. Then he put the paper down on top.

"Watch carefully." He proceeded to draw a large circle, then a slightly smaller one inside it, and another and another until he had drawn five concentric circles leading to a bull's-eye in the middle. "The Everneath is made up of elemental rings. The outermost one"—he pointed his pencil to the largest ring—"is the Ring of Earth. The five Common areas—cities, so to speak—are spread out evenly in this Ring of Earth." He drew smaller circles evenly spaced within the Ring of Earth. "When you took off with a tuft of my hair in your hands, you landed in one of these Commons." He pointed to one of the smaller circles in the outer ring. "This particular Common you went to is called Ouros. It means 'mountain.' It's named that because the entrance—at the Shop-n-Go—is located in a mountain. Each Common has several entrances, or 'rivers' as your mythology books call them."

I remembered reading about one of these, called the River Styx. I couldn't remember the names of the others, although, if each Common had more than one entrance, then there were a lot of them. More than the mythology books knew about.

He moved his finger inward to the second-largest ring. "This one is the Ring of Water, then the Ring of Wind, then the Ring of Fire. There are no cities in these rings."

I pointed to the middle circle, the bull's-eye of his map. "What's there?"

He looked up from his map. "Two things. The Feed caverns and the High Court, where the queen lives."

I'd been to the Feed caverns. I hadn't realized how close they were to the High Court. "So who exactly is in the High Court?"

"The queen, her chosen companion, and anyone else she wants." He took the pencil and drew an X over the bull's-eye. "We do not want to go there."

"Why?"

"Well, besides the fact that it's where the Shades and the queen live? Because the three rings that separate the High Court from the Commons—the Water, Wind, and Fire—are deadly. They're the queen's security system. They're there to keep Everlivings out."

"But then where are the Tunnels?"

He grimaced. "That's the question. They're hidden so nobody will mess with them. Only the Shades know where they are. But I've spent the last few weeks tracking down older Everlivings who might know something about their location. One of them believed the Tunnels were hidden in the void." He pointed on his map to the space outside the largest ring. "We're hoping he's right. The void is made up of all the unstable areas, the places of unformed energy. But that also means it's relatively uninhabited. It would be the perfect place to hide the Tunnels. So, my plan is to land us in the outer ring, between Commons"—he put his finger in the middle between two Commons, one of which was Ouros—"and see which way your tether to Jack leads us."

"My tether to Jack?"

He stood up and put the tip of his finger over my heart. "You're connected to him, and that bond is strong. It's what's keeping him alive. And when we're down there, it will point us in the right direction."

For some reason, the way he spoke of the tether made me think of Ariadne and the ball of twine she'd given to Theseus so he could find his way out of the labyrinth. I took in a few deep breaths, wondering if my connection to Jack could ever be so tangible.

"Are you sure?"

"Yes." He removed his finger from my chest. "At least that's what I learned from my search. Hopefully it's true. Or we'll get lost and the Shades will track you down and we'll both die via Shade impalement."

I narrowed my eyes at him.

He gave me an innocent look as if he hadn't just said the word *impalement*. "Don't worry. I don't think that's going to happen. Ready to go?" He stepped closer, and I flinched back. I guess I had trained myself a little too well to pull away from him.

His lips twitched. "Um, Nikki, if we're going to do this, we're going to have to touch."

"I know. Sorry. It was a reflex."

"I'll try not to be offended." He stepped closer again and took my hand. He smirked. "Your hand is clammy."

"It is not." But it was, and I knew why. I was being forced to trust the person in whom I had the least faith. I had no choice.

He squeezed my fingers. "Ready?"

Max stood up and came near us, ready to follow.

I closed my eyes for a moment. "Cole?"

"Yes?"

"Is it really . . ."—I pointed downward—". . . *underneath* us?"

A faint smile touched his lips. "No more than hell is. But to get there we go . . ." He tilted his head toward the floor. "Ready?"

"Ready." *I'm coming, Jack.*

The walls of his condo began to swirl right before my eyes; and just before everything went dark, Cole said, "The touchdown might be a little rougher than last time since we're aiming for outside the Commons."

I was in the washing machine again, but this time Cole's hand kept me oriented.

It was a hard landing. I ended up facedown, and as I gasped for breath, I inhaled whatever it was I was lying in and immediately choked. I coughed into my hand and saw dust land there.

Cole was next to me, breathing hard. "You okay, Nik?"

I nodded. He helped me up to a sitting position, and I got my first look at our surroundings. My mouth dropped open.

We were on hard ground—covered in a light-brown

dust—that seemed to stretch infinitely in all directions. The entire place had that too-white look, as if it were part of a filmstrip that had been overdeveloped. I turned in a complete circle, but the landscape never changed. The sky above shone blue, but again there was no source of light. No sun. The air even shimmered in the distance, as if heat were rising from the ground and distorting the image.

Max stood up and brushed himself off and then pulled a small metal object out of his pocket. He held it flat in his hand.

"So, it looks like Ouros is that way." He pointed behind me, and I turned, squinting at the horizon. Now that I focused on that point, I could see a faint gray line, and I wondered if it could be the wall that surrounded the Common.

"Which means that Limneo is that way." Maxwell pointed in the exact opposite direction.

"Limneo?" I said.

Max ignored me, but Cole answered. "Another Common. It's the Greek word for *lake*."

Max consulted the metal object in his hand again. "So we're in between Ouros and Limneo. Which means that the void is out there." He faced toward Limneo and pointed left. "And the High Court and the other three rings are that way." He jerked his head to the right.

I searched the horizon. The only things I could make out were the faint gray lines in the directions of Ouros and Limneo. Could the Everneath be that big? So big that I couldn't see the perimeter of the next ring?

I was about to ask Cole, but he spoke first. "We need Nikki's tether so we know which way to go." He was looking in the direction of the void as if he was planning on my tether pointing that way.

I'd forgotten all about the tether. I looked down at my chest, right where Cole said it was supposedly connected. "Should we be seeing it right now?" I said.

"We have to draw it out of you. Right now your energy will leak out at random times, probably when you least expect it, like your broken heart at the Ouros square. You have to learn to control it, focus on your connection with Jack. Once you do, it should take the form of a line to Jack. Maybe a rope, or an arrow."

"How?"

He put his hands on my shoulders and urged me to sit on the ground. "Close your eyes."

I obeyed.

"Now, share a memory about Jack."

I opened my eyes as my heart sped up. "A memory?" My dangerous territory. If it was hard to talk about him to my dad or Jules, it would be nearly impossible to talk about him with Cole. "Um, see, I have this dam. . . ." My hands made a frantic circular motion in front of my chest, as if that should explain it all.

He raised an eyebrow. "A dam?"

"Yeah, it's . . ." I didn't want to say *around my heart*, because it sounded so stupid now that I was putting it into words. How could I explain that for so long I'd fortified the dam because it was the only way I'd known how to keep all the pieces of me together? But that didn't matter. We were here for Jack. "Never mind."

The corner of his mouth twitched. "No, I want to hear about the dam."

"Drop it." I closed my eyes again. "What should I think about?"

"Well, we're trying to reach your connection to him. So maybe you could tell me exactly what it is that draws you to him."

His voice sounded strained, and I wondered how difficult this was for Cole. If his feelings for me were real, it couldn't have been easy. But how genuine were those feelings? I still didn't know.

But he was here with me, wasn't he?

"His smile," I said.

Cole was quiet for a moment. "Uh, we're going to need a little bit more than that, Nik."

I opened my eyes. "It's been a while since I've talked about him." I felt the dam in my chest bursting at the edges. I wasn't sure I was ready to cut it loose.

"You have to. We need your tether."

"But what if I don't have one?"

"There's only one way to find out."

I closed my eyes, forcing a fresh teardrop to roll down my cheek. I pictured Jack on my driveway, shooting hoops with

Will. The image came easily; they'd done it so many times. "Jack could palm a basketball with one hand. His hands were dry and always covered in calluses." I wiped at the tear on my face. "But when he held my hand, he was so gentle, as if I were extremely breakable." I paused.

"Keep going, Nik. You're getting it."

The dam around my heart started to crack. "At my mom's funeral, he didn't really say anything, but he stayed by my side throughout the entire day. And I could feel him there. Even when I wasn't facing him, I knew he was there. And when they lowered her casket into the ground . . . " I took in a shaky breath, and it was as if everything around me—Cole, Max, the Everneath—drowned out. "He held me up. Literally. He stopped me from climbing in with her. I know it sounds crazy, but I *was* crazy. I thought I would only ever be happy again if I were with her, and I didn't understand why that wouldn't work."

The dam burst, and everything I'd been holding in, all my feelings about Jack that I'd been scared to remember, exploded out. Muffled sounds reached me, but I didn't listen. I just kept talking faster and faster, the words pouring through the shattered barriers. "Jack put his arms around me and pulled me back from the hole, and we weren't even together then. He picked me up, and my feet were no longer touching the ground, and I knew I was safe. He saw every side of me—the good and the bad—and he never went away. My dad pulled away, and my brother was too young to really understand what was going on; but Jack, he was my constant. He was my lodestar. He was my fixed point in space. And now . . ."

I felt my face crumble.

The muffled voices were yelling now, and someone was shaking me by the shoulders. I tried to swat whoever it was away, but then I remembered Cole. Max. The Everneath.

I opened my eyes, and their voices came back into focus. "Stop, Nik!" Cole was yelling.

"What? Didn't it work?" I said.

Frowning, he gestured around him. "Take a look for yourself."

On either side of us, shooting high into the sky, were red-rock walls. The path we were on webbed out into at least ten different directions, many disappearing behind sharp hairpin turns in the canyon walls. Several natural arches formed in the walls, especially near the top where a blue sky shone through.

I touched the rock wall next to me, its surface rough beneath my fingers. A sprinkle of red sand fell to the ground as I drew my hand across.

Something here was so familiar.

"What. The. *Hell.*" It was Max's voice, and he sounded freaked. The sound echoed, reverberating between the two canyon walls.

Max and Cole turned in circles, open-mouthed.

Max spoke again. "What the hell, Cole? You said it was supposed to look like a rope. What the *hell is this*?" He turned his head and caught sight of red sand on the shoulder of his shirt, and he frantically brushed it off as if it were poisonous.

His frenetic actions caused Cole to whip around in the other direction, as if someone were about to ambush us.

I looked at the sand on my fingertips. It was red like the film on Max's shoulder, and right then I knew. "It's the Fiery Furnace."

They just looked at me as if I'd said "It's a puppy driving a tractor."

"I mean, I know it can't be real, but it looks like a place in Arches National Park called the Fiery Furnace. Look," I said, pointing to the largest arch in the rock at the top of one of the walls. It was very distinctive, with a post down the middle making it look like two large eyes. "That's Skull Arch."

Cole stepped toward me and grabbed my arm. "You know this place?"

I nodded. "I hiked it once."

"By yourself?"

"No. Nobody would ever hike the Fiery Furnace without a guide. It's like a maze. Narrow sandstone canyons. Dead ends. I came with my school." The memory was fresh in my mind, because I had just been looking at the framed picture from our trip there. It was the place where Jack brushed my hair from my eyes. I paused, watching Cole's face grow tenser by the second. But I was having the opposite reaction. From the moment I let my feelings go, every part of me, including the inside of my head, felt lighter. "We had a guide. But why would the Fiery Furnace be here? We're still in the Everneath, aren't we?"

Cole pressed his lips together in a tight line and looked at Max. "This is coming from her."

"From me?" I shook my head. "That's impossible."

"No. It's entirely possible from someone who survived the Feed."

Cole had always said that the fact that I hadn't aged during the hundred-year Feed meant that I was different. Strong somehow. Strong enough to take down a queen, he had told me. But how was the ability to project an image like the Fiery Furnace any sort of unique gift?

Cole frowned. "We have a problem."

"No shit," Max said.

"What's wrong?" I asked.

"When I asked you to let your feelings for Jack loose, I wasn't quite prepared for just how much you had stored up behind the floodgates. And it's a problem, because this much energy will attract attention we don't want."

I was about to ask what sort of attention when I saw someone. Just a flash of brown hair as someone disappeared around a bend in the rock. But a flash was all I needed to know who it was.

Jack. "Jack!" I screamed. It felt like forever since I'd seen him. "Jack!" I shouted again, sprinting in the direction he'd gone.

Faint voices called to me from behind, but I couldn't understand what they were saying. It was as if there were cotton balls in my ears. As I ran, I glanced up at the sky to let the sun warm my face.

But there was no sun. Not anywhere.

I stopped running. My own shadow stretched before me, taller than me. The sun was coming from behind. But when I whipped around, it wasn't there.

Why was I looking for the sun? There was something else I should look for first. Wasn't there?

I put my head in my hands and rubbed my scalp, frantically trying to remember what I'd been running to but my head felt like a leaking balloon. Everything was slipping out.

Turning in hectic circles, I started to pant until I caught sight of a face. Big brown eyes. Floppy hair. Wide grin. I knew this face. It was Jack's face.

"Jack!" I shouted, and took off running again. I stumbled around a sharp turn and scrambled up a large boulder that blocked the path, and when I reached the top, I saw him. Lying on the ground.

I sprang off the rock and landed next to his head. I knelt to the ground and put my hands on his cheeks. "Jack," I said, my voice barely reaching my ears.

"Nik!" It was a voice from the top of a boulder. Not Jack's.

"Shhhh!" I put up my hand, waving off whoever was there. "It's Jack! I found him."

"No, Nik. You didn't."

Was Cole blind? "What do you mean? He's right here!"

"Look at yourself. You're on the ground."

"I'm on the ground because Jack's on the ground," I answered forcefully. Then I had to think about it. Jack was on the ground.

I grabbed on to Jack's cheek and came up with a handful of red dirt.

"What the . . . ?" I relaxed my clenched fist, and dirt seeped through my fingers. I looked back at the ground, and there was Jack's face still, only this time he was maybe twelve years old, and he was playing in a baseball game.

It was as if I were watching home videos of Jack projected onto the dirt.

"What is this?" I held out the clump of dirt to Cole. "What's happening?"

Cole crouched down in front of me and closed his hands around mine.

Max appeared at the top of the boulder. "We're so screwed."

THIRTEEN

NOW
The Everneath. The Ring of Earth.

Cole put his hand under my chin and forced my gaze away from the images and movies of Jack that plastered every surface around us. "Nik, you're in the Everneath. You're projecting this scene onto the Everneath. It's not real. I told you how your feelings—your memories, emotions—affect your surroundings here. You're making this."

I looked back down at the movie of Jack. Now he was smiling toward the camera, holding a stick with a marshmallow on the end of it. The marshmallow was on fire, and he blew on it. I hated burned marshmallows.

How could I be making this? I tried to sort out what was happening, but it was as if my brain wasn't working at full power. I knew everything here was wrong—a different version of the Fiery Furnace, the moving pictures of Jack—but I couldn't make it right inside my head.

"Can you see him too?" I asked.

Cole nodded. "Yes, but I shouldn't be able to. You've got some strong memories. Usually the human projections look like . . . an aura, almost, around the person. I knew yours would be stronger because you survived the Feed, but I thought that meant you would project a more focused object, like a rope. You, however, are projecting an entire national park."

Max kicked the dirt. "We should leave."

"If we leave now and then come back, we'll be in the same predicament," Cole growled, but I could see he was just as frustrated.

"Why is it so dangerous?"

"Because there are Everlivings out here called Wanderers, and they are starving for energy, and they can sniff it out, and all of this"—he threw his arm around—"is basically a flashing neon sign that says EAT AT JOE'S." His voice grew. "And unlike normal humans, your subconscious projection is tangible, and *concrete*, and also happens to resemble a *maze!*" He jumped up and pounded his fist into the rock wall with a frustrated grunt. His voice echoed, bouncing from wall to wall. It lasted longer than seemed possible, his anger reverberating all around us.

As the last sounds died out, he shook his hand, a tiny drop of blood splattering on the sandstone at his feet. My projection was strong enough to break his skin. How was it possible that something coming from my mind was real enough to hurt him? What if I had projected us inside one of the caverns of the Fiery Furnace? Would we be trapped? Could it suffocate us? Could the rocks perched on the precipice of the canyon tumble down and crush us?

Even though I was freaking out, I couldn't let Cole and Max know. Max said he wanted to give up. Cole looked like he was thinking about it. I didn't want to add to the panic, because, if we left now and went back to the Surface, I might never get the chance to save Jack again.

Actually, if we left now, Jack would die. I knew it.

The silence was heavy in the air. I took a couple of deep breaths and then walked slowly over to Cole. The veins in his neck protruded. I couldn't let him change his mind about being here. I definitely didn't trust him, but right now he was the only person who could help me. It was a bad position to be in. But I took his injured hand in mine and brought it close to my face to get a good look at it. The lines around his eyes softened, making him look more like a wounded animal. Scared almost. Not because the cut was deep, but because I had taken his hand, I thought. He was vulnerable to my touch. I could see it.

Back on the Surface, he'd worked so hard to conceal it. Yes, he'd told me he wanted me to be with him, but those were just words. Right now I could see an involuntary physical reaction. The muscles on his arms tensed because of my nearness. His cheeks flushed because I was close.

I pulled the sleeve of my shirt forward and wiped away the blood on his knuckles. Then I looked into his eyes. "It'll be okay." I didn't mean his hand, and I thought he understood. Cole's face tightened.

"I can do this," I said. "When I first got here, I had no projection. There has to be a way for me to control it. Find some middle ground between nothing and the broken dam."

Cole sniffed and took his hand back. He nodded and frowned in a determined way.

Then he and Max walked in slow circles around me, and for the first time I noticed how the scenery they walked through rippled as they went, as if it were an oil painting that hadn't dried.

I guess they were soaking up some of the energy of the projection as they circled around me, but I could tell there was no way they could position themselves to hide me completely. The scenery in their wake simply recovered as they went.

Cole came to a stop in front of me. "Okay, Nik." He grabbed my hands in his. "Close your eyes. Focus. Bring it in. Imagine a tether, pointing from you to Jack. Like a compass needle."

"Okay." I squeezed my eyes shut and pictured the imagery: the rock walls, Skull Arch, the blue sky. And then I sucked in. And held my breath.

I heard Max snort and then a sound like Cole punching Max in the arm.

"Did it work?" I asked. Nobody answered. I opened my eyes, and the only thing that had changed in the projection was that the path was narrower. The entire thing looked . . . skinnier. But as I stood there, breathing regularly, it popped wider and back into position.

I could see why Max was trying not to laugh.

"It's all right," Cole said, and I was struck with how patient he was being. Cole on the Surface would have made some wiseass remark, but now he was determined to get me through this. Maybe it was because we weren't working against each other this time. "Okay, Nik. Try it again, only make it smaller. Not skinnier."

I closed my eyes and pictured everything again, then tried to imagine it growing smaller. But the more I tried, the more it felt as if I were pressing inward on an unbreakable balloon, one that refused to pop.

With my eyes closed and my teeth gritted, I asked, "Is it working?"

"Keep trying, Nik."

I mentally pressed and pressed on the balloon that was my projection, but nothing happened. I focused even harder, squeezing the image inside my head. I could feel a cold sweat break out on my forehead.

"That's enough, Nik."

"But I think I'm doing it!"

"No you're not. But you're sweating through your clothes."

I opened my eyes. He was right.

"Okay, let's try a different approach," Cole said. "I think this all happened because you were letting every single feeling you've ever had about Jack out at the same time. Maybe if we focus on one specific memory." He glanced around at all of the pictures of Jack that were plastered over the rocks. He gestured toward a nearby boulder, the face of which was covered with a moving picture: two hands, one small and delicate, one large and boyish. The hands would start out palm to palm, measuring against each other. Then they would clasp together. And then the little movie snippet would start over again.

"This hand thing shows up a lot," Cole said. "Why don't you focus on it? Sit down, close your eyes, and tell me about the memory behind it."

The memory behind it. The night I wondered if Jack would ever see me as anything other than a little sister. The night another boy got in our way.

"Okay."

FRESHMAN YEAR
The Surface. My house.

"How are you going to answer the Boze?" Jack asked.

We were sitting on my front porch after an evening jog took Jack right by my house. He had stopped midrun to find out if I'd been asked to Junior Prom. He'd heard a rumor.

I rolled my eyes. "I have no idea. My dad is still getting used to the fact that a boy known simply as Bozeman asked his only daughter to her first dance." I shrugged. "I think my mom is helping him warm up to the idea."

Jack gave me a playful shove with his shoulder. "Maybe he's worried because of the age difference."

I smiled, but Jack had a point. I was pretty sure I'd be one of the few freshmen there.

"It's not so much that he's *older*," I said. "It would help if the Boze weren't so dang big."

"He's the perfect size when I'm on the line." Jack was quarterback, and Bozeman was often the only thing standing between him and a sack.

"I know, but have you seen his hands?" I said. I held my hand flat out in the air. Compared to other girls my age I was average height, but my hands were small. My mom always cursed this fact when she was trying to teach me to play the piano.

Jack held his hand out and put it palm to palm against mine. My fingers almost ended before his even began.

He laughed and bent his fingers over mine.

"Exactly!" I said. "And Bozeman's hands are bigger than yours. Can you imagine them holding mine?" I shook my head, and Jack went quiet. I was suddenly very aware that he was still holding my hand.

When I looked up at him, he was frowning. I thought maybe it was because he was trying to figure out a way to let go of my hand, so I pulled mine away.

"Anyway . . . ," I said. "You want to help me answer the Boze?"

Finally, an easy smile.

At the store, we wandered the candy aisles, brainstorming ridiculous ways to say yes.

Jack pointed to the rack with the candy bars. "'People would *snicker* if I didn't say yes.'"

"Brilliant. Or how about, 'My face would go *red hot* if I couldn't go with you.'"

He grinned. "I'm not sure that conveys the solemnity of the occasion. At least, not as much as . . ." With a flare, he presented a box of Nerds. "'Everyone is a *nerd* compared to you, Boze.'"

I giggled. "Or we could go for simple and straightforward. Something that needs no other words. The answer is all in the name."

I pulled a Skor candy bar from behind my back. Jack registered the name, but he didn't laugh like I thought he would. His cheeks went red, and he turned away.

His reaction surprised me, but I was pretty sure I knew why. Jack had always thought of me as a kid. Instead of looking at me, he held up a package of Red Vines and studied the list of ingredients as if it were a treasure map.

"I'm only six months younger than you, you know," I said.

He shrugged, then put down the Red Vines and grabbed a Baby Ruth. "'Even though I'm practically a baby, I'll go with you,'" he said, not a trace of playfulness in his voice.

It was my turn to blush. He always joked about being so much older than me because he was twice my size and a grade ahead. It shouldn't have bugged me.

But it did.

I threw the Skor bar at his head, a little harder than I'd meant to.

"Ow."

"At least I don't throw like a baby." I took a step closer. "I'm not a little girl anymore, Jack Caputo."

I spun around and stomped down the aisle, acting more like a little girl than I had in a long time.

Jack answered me softly. "I know, Becks. I know."

We finally settled on a two-liter bottle of Coke with a note attached. "I'd pop to go to the dance with you."

It made the least sense out of all of our ideas, but Jack said if the Boze didn't get the picture, then he didn't deserve to go to the dance with me. He drove us to Bozeman's neighborhood; and as we turned onto his street, he flipped off his headlights, parking a few houses down from our target.

He reached toward me, and I froze until I realized he was going for the glove compartment. My cheeks went pink, and I was glad to be hidden in shadows.

He pulled out something dark and slammed the compartment door shut.

"Here." He threw the dark thing in my lap. I held it up near the window to get a good look at it. It was a black knit ski mask.

"Isn't that going a little overboard?"

I looked at him and choked on a laugh. Jack had pulled a nylon stocking over his head, and his facial features were smushed together and flattened out. He smiled, and the tightness of the stocking made him look deranged.

"I borrowed this from my mom."

I struggled to compose myself. "It totally suits you."

There was no way I'd look dorkier than him, so I pulled the ski mask down over my face and we got out of the car, Jack carrying the soda bottle.

We crept up to Bozeman's porch, me a few steps behind Jack. He set down the bottle. The porch light went on, and we both froze. No one opened the door, and we realized it was on a motion sensor.

Jack looked at me and nodded as if to say *Ready?*

I nodded back.

He rang the doorbell, and we took off running as if our lives depended on it. Jack went to the passenger side and opened my door for me.

"Now's not the time for chivalry!" I whisper-yelled.

He ran around the car, got in, turned the key, and floored the gas pedal down the street. It wasn't until we were out of Bozeman's neighborhood that he finally let up and turned on his headlights. When he did, I stared with dread at a piece of paper on the seat next to Jack. It was the note that was supposed to go with the soda.

"You forgot the note!" I said.

Jack looked down at it, but he didn't look surprised. "Well, if the Boze can't figure it out, he doesn't deserve to go."

"Figure it out? He's going to open the door and find a bottle of Coke sitting there with no explanation!"

"If the Boze can't use his imagination to figure out that

you're saying yes . . ."

I punched him in the arm, not too hard, and we both laughed.

The next morning at school, I slipped the note that was supposed to accompany the drink into Bozeman's locker.

He figured it out.

FOURTEEN

NOW

The Everneath. The Ring of Earth.

How touching," Max said.

"Shut up, it worked," Cole said.

"It worked?" I said.

I opened my eyes. At my feet, hovering about an inch above the ground, was what looked like a long metal rod. The end nearest me was thicker; and it tapered off toward the end pointing away, making it look as if I were the center of a dial.

I took a step forward, and the needle moved with me. I stepped back again, and it resumed its original position. I stooped down next to it and held my finger out. "Is it real?"

Cole crouched down next to me. "You mean, is it tangible like the Fiery Furnace was? I hope not. It could do some real damage if you tripped on it or something."

I raised my finger and swiped right through the tether as if it were a hologram.

"Good," Cole said. He smiled wryly. "So, now we've learned

our lesson. No more letting the dam free all at once, okay? In fact, keep focused. I'd prefer not to have the tether suddenly turn into another one of your childhood memories, like the Grand Canyon, or the cliffs of Dover or something."

"I'll stay focused," I promised.

"As long as you do, it should be there."

"Is it pointing to Jack?"

Cole stood back up, and Max held out the device that he had used earlier to figure out where we were. He and Cole exchanged glances, and then Cole said, "I think so. But there's a problem."

"What's the problem?" I asked.

Cole sighed. "It's not pointing into the void. It's pointing into the dead center of the rings. It's pointing straight to the High Court."

Straight to the High Court?

"But you said the Tunnels were hidden in the void," I said.

He frowned. "No, I said I *hoped* they were hidden in the void." His voice sounded rough and tired.

Max held the small, circular object in his hand, and I saw the face of it, which looked like a minirendering of the layout of the Everneath. "We're here," he said, pointing to the edge of the outermost circle between two Commons. "Your tether is pointing this way." He made a little line going toward the center.

"But what if the Tunnels are in the void on the exact opposite side of the outer ring?" I asked. I put my finger on the farthest spot away from us on the circular map. "And maybe it's only pointing to the High Court because the High Court happens to be on the direct line between us and the Tunnels?"

Max couldn't conceal an eye roll. "Yes, out of the million points on which we could've chosen to land, I guess there's a chance that we just happened to land on the exact opposite side of the Tunnels."

"There's only one way to find out," Cole said.

We both looked at him.

"We walk to Ouros. When we get there, if the compass is still pointed to the exact center . . ."

His face was grim.

"Why Ouros?" I asked.

"Because I have a friend there. A friend who owes me. And if it turns out that your tether is really pointing to the center of the maze, we're going to need help."

I knew even before we reached Ouros that my tether would still point to the bull's-eye. Nobody said anything, but I could see the subtle shift in the direction as if I were holding on to one end of a length of twine, the other end of which was secured in place in the middle. I'd asked Cole why he just couldn't zap us all there, and he said to do more than one trip at a time would be a waste of his energy. He needed to rest in between trips to replenish and refuel.

As we got closer to the great gray wall that surrounded Ouros, my blood started pounding. The last time I'd been here the queen and her Shades had vaporized a man, and now I was going back. I wondered how we would get through the wall, but then I saw a dark archway carved out of the base of the stone. The wall had to be incredibly thick, because I couldn't see any light coming from the other side.

"Is it guarded?" I asked.

Cole smiled. "In a way. Only those of us who have hearts can get through. That's how it keeps the Wanderers out. They've had their hearts taken away."

When we were a couple of yards away, Cole pulled an object out of his pocket. It was a black guitar pick. I knew his heart was stored inside of it. It was the first time I'd seen the pick since that night at the condo when we'd failed to guess where Cole's heart was.

Max pulled a dark strand from his pocket. It was tangled in knots.

"What is that?" I asked.

"It's a string from my first guitar."

"And that's your heart?"

He looked at me as if the answer should be obvious. As we reached the doorway, I wondered if it would really be able to sense my heart since it was actually in my chest and not in an object I could flash. What kind of defense mechanisms would it have? Spears that shot out of the ceiling? My imagination went wild with each step deeper into the tunneled entrance. I didn't want to talk for fear of setting off some sort of alarm.

But we emerged from the tunnel unscathed. I let out a sigh of relief, but my reprieve was short-lived. We were on the outskirts of the city. The structures closest to us were smaller than the buildings I remembered in the square. Single levels. Thick, dusty canopies jutted out from the entrances. Underneath the canopies were counters displaying rows and rows of glass jars.

It looked like an Old World marketplace, complete with shops and booths covered by canopies. I stepped closer to the nearest booth to get a look at the goods being exchanged, but what I saw didn't make sense. The glass jars lining the shelves were empty. Each jar was labeled with numbers and letters— 8h, 3d, 24h—but before I could even try to figure out what they meant, a poster hanging over the closest shop caught my eye, and I froze.

Cole saw it too. "Damn."

It was a black-and-white rendering of a girl with dark hair and pale skin.

Me.

Underneath the picture were the words DO YOU KNOW THIS HUMAN?

I pulled my hoodie up over my head. Cole and Max flanked me closely on either side. Cole held my elbow, guiding me quickly, but not too quickly, down an adjacent road and then down an alley. With both of the boys so near to me, my tether almost disappeared completely, absorbed by them. I could still feel it, that tug on my heart. It felt as if my projection should've come straight from my heart, out of my chest; but it didn't. I was grateful. It was less noticeable on the ground. But I knew it must have originated from deep inside of me, and only when it reached outside of my body did it get absorbed by Cole and Max.

I wondered what my energy tasted like to them. Was it full of my love for Jack? Or was it made up of the negative emotions—such as guilt or heartache—that Cole said always rose to the top?

I wasn't about to ask.

Cole and Max were quiet. I got the feeling we were taking back roads, although we did pass several Everlivings, some of them staring for longer than they needed to.

The buildings we passed looked ancient, but I didn't look hard enough to figure out why. The way Cole was racing, it felt as if we were being chased, even though I was pretty sure I hadn't been spotted by anyone yet. When we reached a building with two intricate columns at the doorway, Cole turned in. We'd been through enough twists and turns that I was completely lost.

Cole knocked.

"Who lives here?" I whispered.

"Ashe. The oldest Everliving I know. And the only person I know who's ever seen the maze."

He knocked again, more urgently. A strange-looking man swung open the door. When I saw him, the first word that came to my mind was *smoke*. His skin was a pale gray color, and it looked spongy, as if it were partly made up of mist. His gray hair stood straight up on his head. Even the irises of his eyes were gray.

Cole looked confused. "Ashe?"

Recognition flickered across the man's face. "Cole!" He seemed surprised, but Cole didn't give him a chance to ask questions.

"Can we take this inside?" he asked with a quick glance behind us.

Ashe reacted immediately, ushering us in and shutting the door.

Once we were safely inside, Cole and Ashe embraced in a sort of man hug, with a slap on the back. When they parted, Cole studied Ashe's face.

"What happened to you?" he said.

So apparently Ashe hadn't always looked like smoke.

He was about to answer, but he caught sight of something at my feet. My tether. Max and Cole had given me just enough space so that it reappeared fully.

Then his eyes traveled to my face, and he froze. He looked me up and down, and I could feel my cheeks go red under the scrutiny.

"Well, that's quite the defined energy projection. What have you got here?" He raised his eyebrows expectantly.

Cole answered his questioning look. "She survived the Feed."

Ashe backed up a few steps. "You're making a push for the throne, and you came here?!"

"No, no!" Cole held out his hands, palms down, in a

reassuring manner. And then as he seemed to think of how Ashe would interpret his next words, a disbelieving grin appeared on his lips. "We're going to the Tunnels."

We sat down at a table in the center of Ashe's home, and over the next few minutes, Cole told him everything. How I'd been his Forfeit and how I'd survived the Feed. How Jack had taken my place in the Tunnels and how I was keeping him alive in my dreams.

When he'd finished, the room went quiet. Ashe placed his elbows on the tabletop and clasped his hands.

"So you're going to the Tunnels. To save the boy," Ashe said incredulously.

Cole nodded.

"You always did enjoy the impossible tasks." Ashe chuckled.

Cole nodded again, acknowledging some history between them that I didn't know about.

"Why did you come here?"

Cole pointed to my tether. "Because her projection is directing us to Jack. And if you can tell where it's pointed . . ."

The answer dawned on Ashe's face. He looked from the tether to Cole. "Bullshit."

Cole leaned forward across the table. "We need your help."

Ashe mirrored Cole's position. "That's not all you're gonna need. Last I heard that place was full of Wanderers."

"So, maybe some weapons would be nice too."

The corner of Ashe's mouth pulled up as he looked at Cole's deadpan expression. I got the feeling that these boys liked danger.

FIFTEEN

NOW

The Everneath. Ashe's house.

Cole decided he and Max needed to go to the market and stock up on extra energy—which was the main commodity being sold at the market we'd passed. Since my face was plastered everywhere, they decided to leave me here, under Ashe's watch. Cole went around the room and closed the wooden shutters over the windows.

"Don't go outside," he said.

"I wasn't about to," I replied. "But do you really need more energy?"

"It's just a boost. But we need everything we can get."

Max came over. "Let's go," he said to Cole.

Cole looked pointedly at Ashe. "Nobody gets in here," he said. Ashe nodded, and then Cole and Max were out the door, leaving me alone with him.

Ashe took a seat on a wooden stool near a small crack in the window and gestured to a similar stool for me. I sat down, and he stared out into the street.

"You don't think anyone really saw me, do you?" I asked.

Ashe shrugged. "Even without your energy, humans look a little bit different. Not noticeable at first, but after a while, you can see an almost imperceptible . . . radiance. Maybe it's the light of mortality." He said it very matter-of-factly, without any censure. He didn't take his eyes off the street while he spoke. "You'd have to be looking for it, though."

"Even if someone did see my . . . *radiance*, would they really turn me in?"

"The queen's offered quite the bounty on you."

"Money?"

Finally he turned. "Even better. The queen is offering time in the Elysian Fields."

Elysian Fields. Cole had told me about them before. I thought back to the time in my bedroom when he'd placed his hands on either side of my face, and then, like a dream, I was standing in a field with the most incredible feeling of lightness, as if I could float away and never touch the ground again.

I thought about those jars I'd seen in the marketplace, and how the numbers on the labels suddenly made sense. "Was that what they were selling at one of the booths? Those jars marked eight D and twenty-four H. Did those represent time in the Fields?"

Ashe nodded. "The Fields are like a psychedelic coma for us. The best high. If they were more accessible, we'd probably become addicted. But the queen's the only one who has access to the Fields. She can sell her access. Or offer it up as a bounty." He looked out the window again.

I glanced around Ashe's home, finally able to get a feel for it. It consisted of one giant rectangular room, with stone walls at either end that entered into the street and what looked like a back courtyard of some sort, and wooden walls on the sides that I assumed separated this residence from the two adjacent ones. It had a strange mix of the old and the new about it. The structure and the table and chairs seemed ancient, made out of thick oak with intricate designs. But then a bookcase on one wall held not only older books but also more modern books with colorful spines.

One corner of the room was filled with stacks of old blankets and Persian-looking carpets, reminding me of the inside of a Bedouin tent or something. In the opposite corner was a contraption that looked like an old-fashioned telescope.

"What do you use the telescope for?" I said.

Ashe glanced briefly at the corner that held the contraption. "I don't use it. It has a . . . sentimental value."

Tokens and telescopes, guitar picks and hearts. Everlivings had a way of infusing ordinary objects with deeper meaning.

As if the telescope sparked something in Ashe, he said, "This person we're looking for. What's his name?"

"Jack," I said. "Jack Caputo."

"And you love him."

"Yes."

"And Cole's helping you save him."

"Yes."

"Even though he's in love with you too."

I frowned. Why did Everlivings talk about love when they had no hearts? "No. He's not."

Ashe raised his eyebrows skeptically.

"It's not love," I said. "It's a need. He needs me because he thinks I can become the next queen. He doesn't love me."

He tilted his head. "You really can't see it, can you?"

"See what?"

"He has a tether too. And it points right at you."

I opened my mouth but couldn't get any words out. Did he mean a literal tether? Ashe was wrong. Cole wasn't capable of love.

Right then the door swung open, and Cole and Max stepped in. Cole stopped when he saw my face, then he looked to Ashe with a curious expression. "What were you talking about?"

"Nothing," I said, too quickly.

Cole looked at me with narrowed eyes but didn't say anything. There was a tense, silent moment when Cole's gaze shifted from me to Ashe and back again. Then Max cleared his throat and nudged Cole with his shoulder. "Time."

Cole nodded.

Minutes later, Ashe, Cole, and I were huddled around an old parchment map that looked like it had been drawn at the same time as the Declaration of Independence, while Max stood guard at the window. The images on the map looked similar to what Cole had drawn for me, with the High Court and the Feed caverns inside a center bull's-eye and then three rings surrounding it, expanding in size as they went. The fourth ring showed the Commons.

Ashe placed a round piece of red wood that he used as a marker in one of the Commons that I assumed had to be Ouros. "We're here. And you're talking about going through the labyrinth."

"The labyrinth?" I asked.

"The labyrinth. Like a maze."

"I know what a labyrinth is," I said, flashing back to the story I'd read about the Minotaur.

"The inner three rings—Water, Wind, and Fire—make up a labyrinth whose sole purpose is to keep people out. The place is filled with physical obstacles, and those are tough enough; but it's the psychological obstacles that eat people alive."

My pulse increased. "What do you mean 'psychological obstacles'?"

"The first ring, the Ring of Water, messes with your emotions. The second ring, Wind, attacks your mind. And the third ring, Fire, brings out your despair. You can fight the physical threats. But you can't protect your mind. That's why nobody makes it very far. I never made it beyond the Ring of Water." He looked up, his face grim. "I've never heard of anyone who has."

I wanted to ask Ashe why he'd tried going through the

maze in the first place, but a look from Cole made me hesitate. "Is it even possible to get to the center?"

"The queen holds the blueprint to the maze for the people she invites to the High Court," Ashe said. "We just don't have the map."

"We do, though," Cole said, looking at me pointedly. They both stared at my tether, and I realized they intended to use it as a makeshift map.

Ashe frowned. "Let's hope she doesn't lose it."

Max, who had been quiet until now, spoke up from his position at the window. "What are we going to do about the time discrepancy?"

At my questioning expression, Cole said, "Time in the labyrinth runs parallel to time on the Surface. Ancient Egyptians believed their sun god stored all of the hours of the day and night in the Underworld. Specifically, they're kept in the maze."

I gave him what I was sure was a blank expression.

Cole sighed. "It means that when we are in the labyrinth, time will pass just as quickly as it does in Park City. Which means you'll be gone for longer than you realized."

I thought about the repercussions of this revelation. Every minute I was in the maze would be another minute I was away from my family. It would be impossible to get back without anyone knowing I'd been gone. Then another realization hit me, a worse one, and I saw in the faces of the others that they were one step ahead of me.

"I can't miss even one night of dreaming," I said. "Jack's

already out of time. If I miss a night of giving him energy . . . he'll die, won't he?"

Cole lowered his head and scratched the back of it like he always did when he was trying to work out a problem. When he raised it again, he said, "We'll kick her out. Every night, we'll kick her to the Surface so she can sleep. We'll stay in the maze, holding our place. Then in the morning, we'll reach up and bring her back."

I was sure my face looked like Cole had just spoken in ancient Latin. "I thought you said you couldn't land in the maze."

"We can't do a blind landing, which is what we'd have to do if we all went to the Surface. But if the rest of us stayed here and simply reached to the Surface to bring you under, that might work."

Ashe seemed to be working the scenario through his head. But I couldn't get over one specific word Cole had said.

"What did you mean by 'kicking' me out?"

Cole grinned. "Actually, it's exactly how it sounds."

Before I could ask him to elaborate, Max stood up. "Whatever we're going to do, we can't stay here long."

"Why?" I asked.

He slowly pulled the shutter a little tighter. "Four men. They've been standing at the corner for too long."

Cole looked to Ashe, who glanced at a pocket watch. "There's a scheduled blackout coming. We'll sneak out the back, but I don't think we can make it to the labyrinth entrance before it gets dark. I know a hideout not far from here. I think we can make it."

Everyone went into action. They each grabbed a weapon. Ashe strapped a small sword to his back. Max put on an iron contraption that slipped over four of his fingers; and when he made a fist, it became a weapon, like brass knuckles. Cole slung a knife sheath around his leg and tugged his jeans down over it.

Then Ashe drew the iron lock across the front door as Max cleared the table of the maps and markers we had been studying.

"What do you mean, blackout?" I asked.

"You'll see," Cole said. He grabbed my hand, and we ducked out the back door and into the courtyard.

The whole thing had taken maybe thirty seconds.

Ashe rushed us down dark alleys that were even narrower than the ones Cole had used to get us to Ashe's. As we ran, the daylight seemed to dim, throwing our path into dusk. Halfway down one of the passageways, Ashe stopped by a small, heavy, wooden door in the ground. It looked like a square lumber sewer lid. He heaved it open, and Cole dropped down it, then Max.

Ashe looked at me expectantly.

"Here goes," I said under my breath. I jumped in after Max and landed in a small cellar about the size of a living room. Ashe fell in beside me and used a rope on the door to shut it tight, but not before I realized that it was suddenly pitch-black outside.

"Make yourselves comfortable," he said. "When the blackout

lifts, we'll run for the labyrinth before anyone realizes where we went."

Using Max's lighter to see by, Cole and I settled into one corner of the room and the others spread out on the opposite side. There were a few blankets that had been left in there that we used as cushions against the cold cement floor.

Once everyone had stopped moving, Max flicked his lighter shut and we were thrown into darkness.

I could hear hushed voices talking, and from the direction in which they were coming, I assumed it was Max and Ashe. I was relieved that Cole sat next to me. In this sea of unfamiliar and scary things, Cole was definitely one thing: familiar. Comforting.

He draped a blanket over me. "It's only three hours," he whispered. "Try to relax."

"What is a blackout?" I whispered to Cole.

"It's just like it sounds. To conserve energy, the Shades periodically shut everything down. Everybody stays inside. It's better that it happens now than when we're in the maze."

He was quiet. I could still hear the murmurs from across the room, but I couldn't tell what they were saying.

"Cole?" I whispered.

"Yeah?"

"Will there be Shades in the maze?"

I heard him let out a breath. "I don't think so. They're focused on energy. It's all they care about, so they stick to the bull's-eye and the Commons, where they can manipulate the energy. They have no reason to be in the maze."

"Why do they do what they do?"

"It's like they're the embodiment of a devotion to the Everneath world. Some say that's all they are anymore. The last shade of an attachment. The last shadow of . . . love, without any of the reasons to back it up. All they know is to protect this world, and the energy inside of it."

"Where'd they come from?"

"I don't know."

There was so much Cole still didn't know about his own world. So much kept secret, even from the inhabitants. I turned toward him. "Do they die?"

"I don't know."

We were quiet for a few moments, and I could hear Cole settle further into the blankets.

"Are you going to sleep?" I asked.

Cole chuckled. "No. Sleep is purely a Surface thing, along with eating food. It's not something we need to do down here. That goes for you too while you're here."

Mrs. Jenkins had warned me not to eat down here. It sounded as if this was something I didn't need to worry about. It suddenly made sense why I hadn't seen a kitchen in Ashe's home.

I thought back to how Ashe was coming with us, no questions asked. "Is Ashe a regular Everliving?"

"A *regular* Everliving," Cole said with a smile in his voice.

"I mean, why does he look like . . . smoke?"

Cole sighed. "I don't know. His appearance is new to me. He didn't use to look like that. He said he missed the last Feed. Maybe that's why."

"What did you ever do for him that would make him agree to come with us?"

Cole paused. "He has an old debt to me. I once found something he had lost. Now he's paying me back."

"What did you find?"

He paused. "It's not important."

He didn't offer any more information. The other side of the room went quiet, and I felt as if they were listening, so I didn't press him.

Ashe was only coming because he owed Cole. But why was Cole here? In his view, he owed me nothing.

"Cole?"

"Yes, Nik?"

I let out a breath of air. I couldn't ask him why he'd finally decided to help me. I didn't want to give him an opportunity to reconsider what he'd gotten himself into. "Are you scared of getting killed?"

"No. I'm scared of something worse than death."

Worse than death? "Like what?"

"Everlivings can get trapped in a hell of their own minds." I felt him pick at a loose string on the sleeve of his jacket. "Do you ever notice how the punishments in mythology are always repetitive and continuous? Sisyphus rolling the boulder up the mountain, only to have it roll back at the end of the day? Souls being trapped in quicksand while carnivorous birds nip away at their intestines? The Everliving are afraid of eternal punishments, like the sentence of the Wanderers, who are always starving but will never die from it. We can fall prey to such destruction in our minds that death would actually be a release."

I remembered seeing pictures of these punishments and curses in the D'Aulaires' book. "Have you ever known someone who got trapped in something like that?" I asked.

"Yeah. Me." I turned toward him, and he felt the movement. "With you. Always trying, but never getting you. I have ninety-nine years of that to look forward to."

My cheeks grew hot. "You can't still be trying."

"I'll never stop."

"But . . . all this." I gestured around, even though I knew he couldn't see me. "You're doing all this when you know it's to save Jack."

"I know. And won't you owe me so bad when we succeed." There was a smile in his voice, but also something dead serious. I thought about what Ashe had said about his tether to me.

I shook my head. "Just what do you think I'll owe you?"

He leaned closer to me. "For saving the love of your life? Everything."

There was this incredibly tense moment, and I wished I could see Cole's face. But then I felt him relax against me.

"And then you'll just run away again, and I'll have to find another way to impress you; and that, Nikki Beckett, is the eternal loop."

I released a breath and at the same time tried to release the panic his words had brought on. He acted as if it were a joke, but did some part of him really believe it?

"I told you what I was afraid of, Nik. Now tell me what you're afraid of."

I answered as honestly as I could. "I'm afraid of how much I don't know about this world, and how I have to rely on everything you tell me."

"That *is* scary."

I couldn't hear a smile behind his voice.

SIXTEEN

NOW

The Everneath. Ouros.

As soon as the blackout lifted we hoisted ourselves out of the cellar and into the alley. Cole faced Ashe. "You know what we're up against. You owe me a debt, but it isn't fair for me to ask this as payment. If you want out, you can repay me another way."

There was a long moment of silence. I didn't say anything, no begging or pleading, because I was pretty sure Ashe's answer would have nothing to do with me and everything to do with his previous relationship with Cole.

Ashe stepped forward. "I'm in. I'm tired of owing you." He said it good-naturedly, though, not spitefully.

Cole smiled and smacked him on his shoulder, like a brother-in-arms.

Again we darted through alleys and back roads. We were quiet and quick. I was so turned around that if I had been left here alone, I'd never find my way out again. I kept my hood up. Any person we passed could be looking for me.

Cole moved directly in front of me, and Max stayed behind. "Follow me as close as you can, Nik."

"So you can . . ." I searched for the right words to describe his masking of my energy. "Suck it up better?"

I heard him let out a tiny laugh. "Exactly."

Ashe and Max flanked my sides, only farther away and less obviously than before.

Each Common had four entrances and exits. Two on opposite sides that led to the other Commons, one that led to the void, and one that served as the entrance to the maze. The way we were moving, the two Common exits were in the north and south points of the circle. The void was to the west, and the maze was to the east.

We ran. I couldn't see anyone following, and I was starting to believe we could leave unnoticed until Max said, "We've got company."

I turned my head just enough to catch a glimpse of two figures behind us at the end of the alley. "Maybe they're out for a walk?" I said hopefully.

"Let's check," Max said. He made a sudden turn down a side street and then took off running. We followed close behind. He made a series of quick, random turns in a row, then we all ducked into a particularly dark alley and waited.

For a minute nothing happened. After our mad dash, I couldn't imagine anyone being able to keep up.

But they did. The two figures appeared at the end of the alley from the way we'd come.

We all looked to Ashe, who had become the unofficial leader. He thought for a split second, then said, "We split up. Once you get to the entrance, go through immediately."

And just like that we scattered. Cole took my hand, and we ran.

I squeezed Jack's note in my hand. *Hang on, Jack,* I thought. *I'm coming.*

I had no idea if the men were following us or someone else in our group. We were going too fast for me to check. After a few minutes of flat-out sprinting, we reached an arched entryway, like the one we'd taken to enter Ouros; but this one looked as if it had rarely been used. It had distinct corners that hadn't been worn away from thousands of hands touching it. The dirt on the ground looked loose and unpacked.

We sprinted to it.

"Go! Go!" Cole said, urging me under the archway first. He followed, and then he flattened himself against the wall, in the shadow of the entrance, and watched the street we'd come on.

Nobody showed. I didn't know if the others were ahead of us or if they were still trying to get here. Cole finally tore his eyes away and looked ahead into the dark corridor. He went past me. "I'll go first."

As we made our way through the dark corridor, the sound of running water grew louder. The light at the end bounced off the walls, just like in an indoor swimming pool.

And then I got my first look at the Ring of Water.

I froze.

Up until this point I could tell myself that we were in some strange corner of the world but still on a planet I recognized. But looking at the Ring of Water, I'd never felt farther away from the Surface and all things familiar. The sight was so unearthly, it took my breath away.

Cole waited for me, his hand held out. His gaze met mine, and he recognized my sudden paralysis. "Are you ready for this?"

Without realizing it, I slowly shook my head back and forth. Cole smirked. "Sure you are, Nik. The only way out is through." He reached his hand farther toward me.

I took it, because I knew that if I didn't, I'd be stuck in the corridor for a long time. A light mist of water hit me in the face as I stepped out into the ring. It made sense, because the entire wall in front of me was made up of water, like a giant waterfall, only it didn't pool at the bottom and it seemed to come from nowhere.

It was a wall of running water, and it was forcing me to choose to go either right or left. The wall behind me looked exactly the same except for the small, dark opening of the corridor we'd just come through.

"Welcome to the maze," Ashe said. He was standing off to the side with Max. They'd beat us. "Try not to get too wet. The water here has certain . . . properties."

I remembered Ashe said that the water messed with emotions. "Like what?" I asked.

Cole pulled me toward the exact center of the pathway, I assumed so the least amount of water would splash me. "It can draw out your worst emotions. Get too wet, and you could drown in your own despair."

I looked at the giant wall in front of me, and the one behind me now, and wondered how in the world I was supposed to stay dry.

The others didn't look worried about the water, though. Right now they were all staring at my feet. I dropped my head and saw the problem. The tether was pointing straight toward the wall in front of me, still indicating the center of the maze.

"The tether's going to be no use if it's always pointing *through* the walls," I said.

Everyone looked to Cole, who was focused on the tether. "You were able to control your projection enough to focus it on this tether. Now we need you to tap into your connection with Jack even more so that your tether will tell us whether to go right or left."

"How?"

"Tell me a story."

Max rolled his eyes dramatically in the background.

Cole ignored him. "We know your focused memories are the best way to control your connection with Jack. Think of a decisive moment in your relationship with him."

I looked at the tether and the wall of water, and the sets of eyes on me waiting, and I couldn't think.

"Tell me when you first knew you loved him," Cole said.

His voice suddenly sounded tense, but his face remained a calm mask.

I glanced nervously around at our small group.

"Don't worry about them," Cole said. "Just tell me. Talk to me. When did you know?"

I knew exactly when it happened.

FRESHMAN YEAR

The Surface. My house.

A funeral is easy compared to the day after the funeral. The week after. The first Sunday morning after, when the silence in the kitchen—the sound of my mother not cooking French toast—hurts my ears. Getting dressed for school, when the fact that she isn't there to comment on my choice of shirts is like a palpable vacuum in my room.

It's the week after the funeral when the loneliness sucks the air out of my lungs.

I put my books in my schoolbag and checked my watch.

"Leaving early again?" my dad asked. He'd appeared in the doorway of my bedroom, wearing a gray suit with a red vest, the only reminder of last week's funeral in the dark circles under his eyes.

I tried my best to smile. "I wanted to pick up some coffee on the way."

He nodded, but I wasn't sure he believed me. He hesitated for a moment, then walked away. "Love you, Nikki."

"Love you too, Dad."

I slung the bag over my shoulder and headed out to my car, careful not to wake Tommy, whose school wouldn't start for another hour. The sunlight painted the tops of the evergreen trees, and I knew it would soon hit my mother's burial site too.

I didn't tell my dad the truth about where I was going because I didn't want him to worry about me. He had his own heartbreak to handle without having to deal with a daughter who had been spending most mornings sneaking off to the cemetery to talk to her dead mother.

It wasn't that I really thought I was talking to her or that I believed she was somewhere in the clouds listening to me. It was an outlet. A release. If I didn't let out some of the pain little by little, I would burst like an overfilled balloon.

It sounded crazy. I knew it. But I couldn't help it. My mom was gone. And any more mornings I spent in an empty house without her to mull over my choice in outfit, or to talk about my upcoming day while the coffee brewed, or to help twist my hair into a loose braid would just push her further away from me.

I pulled into the parking lot and let the car idle for a moment. *Was* I losing it? Did I really think I could keep her close by avoiding my morning routine? I didn't have any friends who'd lost a close relative, let alone one of their parents. Maybe if I had I'd know what a grieving daughter was supposed to look like, and then I could try to look like her.

I cut the ignition and got out of the car. Even though it was well into spring, the morning air seemed confused, as if the memory of winter was still fresh in its mind.

I made my way over to my mother's grave. The rectangular patch of grass was annoyingly fresh, and dark against the rest of the lawn, screaming to anyone who would listen about the newness of the tragedy in the Beckett family.

The *tragedy*. The casual word everyone else used to describe something remote from their own lives. But for me the loss went deep inside. And it was sharp, with serrated edges. It tore through me and settled into the darkest corners of my soul, dormant until the tiniest signs of healing spurred it into action again.

Was there a word for that? Tragedy didn't fit. It wasn't big enough.

I sank to the ground and as was often the case, couldn't think of a thing to say. We used to fly through the hours, talking without pausing. My dad would have to remind us of school, work, whatever we were missing.

And now I had no words. So I sat there silently.

A snap nearby startled me, and I turned toward the sound. Under the oak tree adjacent to the iron fence that provided the boundary for the cemetery, a figure sat down on the ground and opened a book.

Jack. Our eyes met. He didn't wave or say anything. He just smiled and nodded his head to let me know he saw me, then bent his head over his novel.

I don't know how he knew where to find me. Maybe he saw my car in the parking lot. Maybe my dad had called him. Maybe he just knew me.

However he'd found his way here, it didn't matter. I knew then that the boy under the tree had to be mine. That floppy hair should be mine to touch. That big, knuckly boy hand should be mine to hold. That gruff voice should be mine to hear, and those ears should be mine to tell all of my secrets to. Except for the biggest secret. That I loved him. More than the crush I'd been dealing with for years. More than I should've loved a best friend. More than he would ever love me back. I was gone for him.

I turned back to the grave, to where the marker would be once it arrived, and whispered, "Help me, Mom. What am I going to do about Jack?"

SEVENTEEN

NOW

The Everneath. The Ring of Water.

So he earns your undying love by reading a book under a tree?" Cole said dryly. "Why didn't I ever try that approach? I like books *and* trees."

I couldn't help but smile. "I'm not telling you these stories if you're going to make fun."

He held up his hands in surrender. "Hey. It's working. Look."

The tether had shifted position and was now pointing to the left.

"Let's move," Ashe said. "I'll take the lead; Max, you take the back; and, Cole, you stick with Nikki. Max, keep your eye out for Wanderers. They like to send single scouts. We can't afford to let even one of them know we're here." He looked at his watch. "It's midday. We've gotta make as much distance as we can before we kick Nikki out. Let's go."

"Wait a second. Midday?" My voice rose. "I left at night-time. Is it midday the next day?"

Ashe shrugged. "I only know the time of day. Not the date. Why?"

"The blackout may have sped up the time," Cole said. He turned toward me. "The time discrepancies in the Everneath aren't always consistent."

My shoulders sagged. "If it's the next day, then I've been missing overnight. That would mean I missed a dream with Jack." My breathing became accelerated. I was about to hyper-ventilate. "He's barely alive as it is. If I missed a night . . ."

Cole put a hand on my shoulder. "We can't do anything about it now, Nik," he said. "Except to get moving."

I nodded, hoping by some miracle that time had gone backward, and it was midday on the day I left.

I started speed-walking down the pathway. "Slow down," Cole said. "Make a mistake, and you'll get drenched."

I slowed down by a millisecond.

Ashe took the lead and scouted ahead, Cole walked beside me, and Max stayed far behind. Every time Ashe came to a decision point, where there were two or more possible routes, he would wait for us to catch up and see where my tether was pointing. He never got very far, because there were a lot of twists and turns, and forks in the road, and archways that seemed to be shortcuts to the next corridor over.

The sounds of the waterfalls adjusted in my ears so they became simply background noises.

No matter how centered we were on the pathway, the fine mist still covered my face. I tried to focus on not licking my lips or breathing in any of it, but it was difficult; and any time my mind wandered, I didn't know if it was normal or if it was the water seeping inside of me.

I thought back to the poster of my face. I turned to Cole. "Why is the queen so curious about me? Is it so weird that a human would come here?"

He kicked the dirt. "Humans only come to the Everneath for three reasons. To Feed an Everliving, to go to the Tunnels . . ." His voice trailed off.

"What's the third reason?"

"To *become* an Everliving. And you weren't doing any of those things."

I looked at Cole. "How does one become an Everliving?"

Cole hesitated for a moment. "It involves a series of rituals. It used to be between an Everliving and his human, but now the Shades like to oversee it. It's very rare."

"Why?"

"Because of our energy quota. If one of us decides to bring a human over, that Everliving host is then responsible for his own quota, plus the quota of the person brought over. So it's a big deal when we make the decision. And it doesn't involve—"

Cole's voice cut off as shouts from behind us sounded. We turned around just as Max ran into sight.

"Wanderers. Behind us," Max said.

"How many?" Cole asked.

"Ten, maybe. I only caught a glimpse because they were in another branch of the maze; but if they catch Nikki's scent—"

"My scent?" I said indignantly.

"He means, if they get a whiff of your energy, they can track you," Cole explained. "Which means we need to pick up the pace."

We resumed our original formation, except this time Max didn't fall as far behind and we walked quicker.

I started to pant a bit at our new pace. "They sound more like zombies than Everlivings," I said.

"That's how you should think of them. But zombies with brains," Cole replied. "Which means they're starving *and* cunning."

"Why are they even in the maze?"

"The queen sentences them to wander here. Another menace to intruders in the labyrinth."

I'd feel almost sorry for them if I wasn't so scared of them.

Ashe was waiting for us up ahead, which meant we were facing another fork in the road. By now I had completely lost my bearings in the maze, and I had no idea which way was inward and which way was out. The walls should've been convex or concave since the maze was circular; but the running water made it difficult to tell, and they didn't always curve the right way. Sometimes my tether seemed to lead us in one direction with one turn only to go in the opposite direction with the following three.

When we reached Ashe, I looked down at my tether and for the first time noticed it had faded a little bit.

Cole noticed too. "Keep your token in your hand and try

not to worry about the Wanderers."

"Does my stress level affect it?" I asked, my voice cracking.

"Everything inside you affects it," Cole said.

I pressed Jack's note into the palm of my hand, and the tether darkened a little bit. But we only made two more turns before we ran into our first Wanderer.

I knew something was wrong because Cole and I caught up with Ashe, who was backing up slowly. A few yards in front of him was a man whose clothes hung off of his stick-like limbs as if they were three sizes too big. His face glistened with sweat. He seemed just as surprised to see us as we were to see him.

"Hello, travelers," he said, his eyes suddenly alert.

"Stay calm," Cole whispered to me.

The man looked at Ashe, then at Cole, and finally at me. Cole pulled me tight against him; but the Wanderer had obviously caught a peek at my tether, because he was staring at where it had just been.

He didn't take his eyes off me, but he addressed Cole.

"Who are you hiding?"

With his arm across me, Cole gently urged me behind him so he was shielding me completely. "No one," he said. "We're just passing through."

"'Passing through'? In the labyrinth?" He smiled, giving his sunken face a crazy look. "Like for a summer stroll?" He spoke fast.

Cole took a step forward, and the move seemed offensive to me rather than defensive. "What about you, friend? Are you out here all alone?"

The Wanderer finally looked directly at Cole. "I'm never alone in the maze. And I always have stories in my head to keep me company. Like the one I heard recently about a human girl who showed up at the weekly slaughter in the Ouros square. Have you heard this one?"

Cole tensed. "Rumors."

I glanced down at his hands. He kept making fists.

The man eyed me carefully. "Whatever you say. I'd be willing to keep my mouth shut. In exchange for something."

Cole raised an eyebrow. "Like what?"

"Your Surface heart."

Surface heart? Did he mean Cole's pick?

I expected Cole to scoff, but he didn't. He shifted his stance, as if he were considering the offer. He wouldn't ever give up his heart, would he? And I didn't even know what this man could do with someone else's heart.

I kept my focus on the man. He had a desperate look in his eyes.

"Yes or no? Your heart for my silence?"

Cole's voice was even. "How do I know you'd keep your word?"

Suddenly two more Wanderers showed up, from the same place the first one had come from. One man and one woman. Both dressed in raggedy clothes. The woman's hair was knotted and sticking up from her head.

Three Wanderers. Three of us. Would they attack now?

Just then shouts came from behind us. Warning shouts. Probably from Max.

Ashe and Cole turned around, following the sound, and for a split second they had their eyes off of me. A split second was all the first Wanderer needed. He lurched forward and dived at me, catching me with his shoulder in my stomach.

I landed with a thud on the wet ground. The Wanderer pounced on top of me, his mouth open and his teeth bared. He used his knees to pin my arms. I struggled, but he was surprisingly strong. He dipped his face so it was within an inch of mine and inhaled deeply.

I felt the breath go out of me, and then I screamed at the sudden pain in my chest. A pain I hadn't felt since the Feed. That scraping inside of me.

Somebody ripped him off of me, and I caught a glimpse of Cole sailing through the air above me and colliding with the other two Wanderers. In one continuous movement, Max incapacitated the first Wanderer with a blow to the side of his head with his brass knuckles, then grabbed the woman's arm, wrenched it, and slipped behind her with a knife pointed at her throat.

I couldn't watch anymore. The pain in my chest made me squeeze my eyes shut. What had the Wanderer done to me? I rolled over onto my side and curled up in a ball, my hands pressing against my chest, trying to blunt the pain.

Everything inside of me was dark. It felt as if every bit of peace inside of me had been ripped out, every moment of light, every glimmer of hope, forced through my chest and away from me. There had to be a gaping hole right above my heart; but when I brought my hands to my face, they were dry. No blood.

Cole's face was over mine. "It's okay, Nik. We're taking care of them."

"What did he do to me?"

Cole frowned. "He fed on you. All the good stuff."

I heard a muffled scream, and despite the pain, I sat up. Ashe and Max each had a Wanderer by the neck, and they were holding their heads under the water of the wall. Two of them kicked their legs in protest. The third one—the one who received the blow from Max, I assumed—was still.

"What . . . what are they doing to them?"

"They're drowning them."

I felt weak and started to tip over, but Cole put his arm around me and righted me. "They won't die, though. Dead bodies will just attract attention. They'll just be filled to the brim with the water. They'll forget everything they've known and felt."

"For how long?"

He frowned. "Long enough for us either to finish, or fail."

Ashe and Max were doing their best to keep their faces turned away from the splashing water. They breathed hard.

A fresh wave of pain hit me in the chest, and I looked up at Cole as I tried to catch my breath and assuage the pain. "Why did he take the good emotions? I thought you said the bad ones always rose to the top."

"That's on the Surface. Here, all emotions carry the same weight. The Wanderers can pick and choose, so of course they pick the good ones."

Hope, joy, love, patience. It was as if the Wanderer had cut them all down to tiny stubs inside of me and replaced them with the black oil of despair, self-loathing. Hatred. The black hole tore through me, snaking through my veins, encasing my heart. I groaned.

"We're not going to make it," I said. My face twisted in despair. I could feel it, but I couldn't help it.

I caught blurry glimpses of the other two Wanderers as they relaxed their frantic kicking, and then they stopped moving altogether.

Ashe and Max pulled them out and laid them faceup on the ground. I rolled away and curved into a ball.

Max came over to us and held out a hand to me. "We have to move. I was on my way to warn you. There are more Wanderers on our trail."

More Wanderers. We were able to fight off three, but any more?

I didn't take his hand. I couldn't move. Without the lighter emotions to counteract the heavy ones, my guilt—at least, I think it was my guilt—had become crippling. It had turned my heart to cement. "I can't. It's never going to work. I'm never going to find him. If a Wanderer can take all that from me, what have the Tunnels already done to Jack? Do they take all of his hope first? All of his love?" I put my hand on my chest.

"How can anyone live with only what's left?"

Cole crouched down before me and grabbed my shoulders, shaking them a little. "Nik. Look at me. We did not come this far to have you lose hope now. Wanderers are after us, and we have to move."

His words made sense, but they weren't reaching my body. I didn't respond. Somewhere deep inside my brain I knew I had to get up and get moving. But I couldn't. Every cell of my body was filled with heavy guilt, and it was weighing me down like a lead balloon.

Cole shoved his hands under my arms. "Get up. We can't stay in one place. Jack needs you." He hoisted me up.

"Jack," I said. It wasn't that I had forgotten. It was just that I couldn't do anything.

"Yes, Jack. Of the *ever yours* Jack. Remember the boy who captured your heart by reading a book under a tree? Jack."

He put one of my arms around his shoulder and wrapped his own arm around my waist.

When I was upright, Max looked down at my tether. "Um, am I reading that right?"

I followed his gaze. Not one, but two tethers. One pointing to the right and one pointing straight ahead.

Ashe came running up. I guess he had gone back to check on the Wanderers.

"We're out of time," he said to Cole.

Cole grunted. "Which one is it, Nik? Which one is your tether to Jack?"

They looked exactly the same to me. I closed my eyes, but that clear connection to Jack had been wiped out. "I don't know."

Cole squeezed my arms. "Concentrate! We can't fight off a dozen Wanderers. Which way do we go?"

I stared at the tethers, looking for any sign that would show me which one led to Jack. The one pointing straight ahead seemed to be darker, or was that just my imagination?

"Which way?!"

"That way," I said, pointing straight ahead. We took off running, just as the first Wanderer appeared from around the corner behind us. I was still heavy from the attack. Each footstep felt as if I were running through quicksand.

I fought for breath. I knew they would be relentless.

As we ran, I looked down at both of my tethers and wondered if I had made the right decision.

I could feel us getting nearer to something. As if my tether were really an elastic band that was contracting as we went. The pain in my chest, however, was still strong, and tears continually ran down my face. If I didn't have a purpose, I would've probably curled up and cried for days.

I wasn't getting tired, though. The farther we went, the more the crippling cement in my veins dissipated. My legs felt as strong as when we'd first set foot in the maze. Cole started to fall back, but I kept running as fast as I could.

"Slow down, Nik!" he said in between pants.

"But I'm close to something. I can feel it." The harder I ran, the better the pain in my chest felt. I realized that maybe I was following that pain.

"Wait! Nik!" Cole called out. I could hear his footsteps behind me, but I was outrunning him. Whatever power it was that beckoned me forward, it was strong.

"Trust me. It's this way!" I called out to him over my shoulder.

I ran at a flat-out sprint. Cole shouted for Max to catch up to me, maybe because he had the longer legs of the two, but I was too far ahead. Even Jack wouldn't have been able to reach me.

Jack.

My feet faltered, but only for a moment, and I glanced down at my hand. I was clutching a piece of paper; but I didn't know what it was, and I couldn't think about that because I was so close to my destination. I made one more turn before the maze opened to a clearing and a large, beautiful lake.

There was one moment of warning, a split second when I knew that everything about that lake said *stay away*; but before I could pass that message along to my feet, I was running—sprinting—to the water.

EIGHTEEN

NOW

The Everneath. The Ring of Water.

$\mathscr{I}$ heard Cole shout my name, but it didn't make any sense. When I was a few yards away from the edge, I sprang off the ground and hovered above the surface for a moment before I descended.

As I hit the water, I had just enough brain power to notice that the lake didn't quite look right. But it was too late. I was underwater.

Only it didn't feel like water. It felt thicker.

I tried to open my eyes; but it was dark, and the liquid stung. Where was the surface? My arms and legs flailed about, but I couldn't figure out which way was up. I stretched my legs, trying to feel for the surface with my feet, but the lake seemed bottomless.

My lungs seized up, and I knew I needed air. Involuntarily, my mouth opened, and the liquid poured in.

It wasn't water. It was too rich. Too smooth. It had a metallic taste to it.

Blood.

Blood.

The realization triggered my gag reflex, but that just made me take in another deep breath.

Frantically I struggled to right myself, but I couldn't. The blood coagulated around my limbs. It was like trying to swim in a vat of cement. The more I fought for the surface, the more I sank.

So I held still. I let the blood settle between my fingers, my toes. I didn't sink or float, and then the blood didn't taste so bad.

I forgot how I'd gotten there, and then I forgot where I was. No more struggling.

Suddenly, something grabbed me around my waist. I was too tired to fight as the something dragged me farther under. Down to where I didn't need oxygen anymore. I'd never need it again.

At that moment we broke through the surface of the lake. "Nik!" Cole was yelling.

I was lying on the muddy beach. Someone was slapping my face.

"Nik! Can you hear me?"

I tried to speak, but only a gurgle came out.

"She drank it," I heard Max say to Cole.

"Shit."

I coughed some more and tried to open my eyes. There was a red film over them that cast a deeper scarlet glow over everything I could see.

Then there was Cole's face above mine, his eyes tight with worry. He was cradling my head in his lap. "You've got to kick her, Max." His voice sounded strained. Reluctant.

"Why me?" came Max's reply.

"Because I can't." Cole leaned down and put his lips to my ear. "Nik, remember when I told you the maze runs on Surface time and we would kick you to the Surface every night?"

I nodded but still couldn't speak.

"I'm going to do that right now. It's not quite time, but if you stay here, you'll drown."

I tried to open my mouth to tell him I wasn't in the lake anymore and that I couldn't drown, but my vocal cords had clamped shut. My body was acting as if I were still underwater. I started to panic. What if being on land didn't matter anymore? What if I never caught my breath again?

"It's okay. You'll be okay once you reach the Surface."

"You sure about that?" Max said.

"Yes," Cole growled. "If you do it now!" Then his lips were at my ear again. "Remember to sleep, and I'll find you in the morning."

He yanked me to my feet with Max's help, and the next seconds seemed to happen in slow motion. Max took a few steps backward and then ran full-out toward me, cocking his leg back and sending his foot flying into my stomach with such force that I left the ground. My lungs crushed together, and I didn't have any air left in me to scream. Everything around me disappeared.

There was no light. There was nothing. Until the moment my cheek hit something hard and cold.

"Mmph."

Footsteps neared my head.

"Nikki?"

I opened my eyes. A man's face was staring down at me. Ezra. The clerk at the Shop-n-Go. "Is that blood? Why are you covered in blood?"

I shut my eyes again. Max had kicked me back to the Surface.

NINETEEN

NOW

The Surface. Outside the Shop-n-Go.

$\mathcal{I}$ staggered out to the street, with Ezra's shouts following behind me, demanding to know who was going to clean up all the "red stuff" on the floor.

The natural sun was bright even though it was beginning to dip below the horizon, and I raised my hand to shield my eyes. That's when I saw how red my hand was. But not wet. The blood, or whatever it was, now looked like a dried powder. And it was all over me.

But at least I could breathe again.

I tried to brush it off my arm, but it was like a stain. People were staring. I must've looked like a giant raspberry walking down the street. Even my clothes were stained red. I was still clutching the *Ever Yours* note. How had I forgotten what it was?

I ducked down a side street and leaned against an abandoned brick building, trying to get my bearings.

I ticked off on my fingers what I knew:

I was in the Everneath.

A Wanderer fed off me, and two tethers appeared.

I took a swim in a lake of blood. Now that I thought about that one, I couldn't believe I'd jumped in.

Max kicked me.

I landed in the Shop-n-Go.

Why did he kick me? I rubbed my forehead, trying to remember what Max and Cole had said about it. The time in the maze ran concurrent with the time on the Surface, so they said they'd have to kick me out to sleep at night.

I looked at the stretching shadows along the ground. It was dusk now. But hadn't I left for the Everneath at night?

Two recycling bins stood at the end of the alley. With my head down, I walked over to read the dates on some of the papers scattered in front of them. Most of them were dated Wednesday, but then I found a couple of newer-looking ones. Thursday. I'd left on Wednesday night, and now it was Thursday night. I'd somehow missed a night of dreaming.

That also meant I had never gone home last night. My dad probably woke up to find me missing, which wasn't completely unusual; but then I missed my appointment with Dr. Hill too.

Where was I supposed to go now? Home, only to disappear again? How long before my dad called for a search party? I'd gone missing before, and it had taken him a while to figure out I wasn't coming back, and even longer to figure out what to do. If I disappeared again, would he assume I'd be back soon? Or would he call the authorities even quicker?

I sank down to the ground, pressing my back into the brick wall and breathing in and out for a few minutes; but I couldn't staunch the flow of tears. I wiped them away with the back of my hand. It was still red, but now it was smeared.

What was the deal with that lake? Was it really blood? I put my head in my hands. Crap. I just swam in blood.

But even worse, I had missed a night. An entire night. Had Jack looked for me?

As I sat back on the cement, I heard a scraping sound from my back pocket.

My phone.

I pulled it out and pressed the on button, but nothing happened. Maybe it needed to dry out from that swim in the lake.

I closed my eyes and let out a breath. There was really only one place I could go. Will's house was a couple of miles away, but I could make it there before it got too late. If I could crash with him tonight and dream of Jack, then I could leave a note for my dad in the morning saying that I needed to get away and I'd be back in a few days.

The porch lights were off at the Caputo home, but there were a few lights coming from the bedrooms. Will's room was in the basement, just below Jack's. Looking inside, I could see Will lying on his bed, eyes closed, earbuds in his ears. I crouched by the window and knocked softly.

Whatever he was listening to, it wasn't very loud, because he popped right up and put his face near the window to get a clear view. When he saw me, he ran out of his room.

I went around to the back, and Will opened the basement door.

"Becks! Where have you—"

He must've noticed my appearance, because his voice cut off completely. He motioned me inside and then threw his arms around me.

"What happened to you?"

I put my arms around him and buried my face in his shoulder. And sobbed.

Five minutes later, I was in the shower adjacent to Will's bedroom. I scrubbed and scrubbed until every bit of the red stuff disappeared down the drain.

LATER THAT NIGHT
The Surface. Will's bedroom.

I'm relieved when Jack appears, because that means my night away didn't kill him.

He is watching me expectantly.

"I'm coming for you. Do you know this?" I say.

Jack doesn't answer. He is watching my face, searching.

"What is it, Jack?" I say. "Are you in pain?"

His anguish is plain on his face. "I . . . I can't remember your name. I'm sorry. I'm so sorry." He closes his eyes and shakes his head.

He can't remember my name. We can't be to that point already, can we? I try not to show my worry, but all I want to do is scream my name loud enough to carry the sound from Will's bedroom on the Surface all the way to the Tunnels of the Everneath. Could one night away from him have done this much damage? I have to force myself to stay still. He can't know I'm falling apart. I reach out my hand to touch his cheek, but it slips through the air. "It's Becks," I say. "It's okay."

"Becks," he says. I know he is wrapping my name inside of him, folding it in the blanket of his heart. I know this because I used to do the same thing with his name when I was in the Feed.

"Becks," he says again.

"Yes," I say. Wrap it up tight, *I think.* You'll need something to hold on to.

The next morning, I shot out of bed, nearly stepping on Will, who was asleep on the floor.

"Wha??" Will jumped up and looked all around, trying to figure out where the threat was coming from. When he saw me, he sank to the floor and seemed to remember everything all at one. "Becks," he said. "Are you okay? Did you dream? Was he there?"

I nodded in a manic staccato sort of way. "I've got to get back."

"Cole said he'd bring you back down in the morning?"

I nodded again. I couldn't stop nodding.

"How?"

"I don't know. My leaving was . . . abrupt, and they didn't get a chance to explain it."

He tilted his head. "What if something happened to them?"

"I can't think about that."

The familiar buzz of my phone powering up sounded. I'd forgotten about it. Apparently it had dried enough to finally work. Pulling it from the pocket of the hoodie Will had loaned me, I groaned.

"Eight voice mails, twenty-two texts," I said, reading the screen. "All from my dad."

The most recent one simply read *CALL ME. NOW.*

I shut the phone off and put it back in my pocket. "Can you give me a ride home? I want to leave him a note before I go missing again." Especially since time was passing just as fast on the Surface as it was in the maze.

"But you're coming back every night. Can't you just . . . explain why you're gone during the day?"

I shook my head. "He wants me to go to Dr. Hill for some extra therapy, and I already missed my appointment yesterday. If I keep showing up at night, it will just be an endless confrontation. I think it's better if he thinks I'm going to be gone for the next few days but then I'll be back."

"You're sure?"

"I don't have a choice!" The words came out too sharp. "Sorry."

"It's okay," Will said. "I'll get the keys."

"Wait," I said as something occurred to me. "Maybe I

should walk. I have no idea how exactly Cole is going to find me, but I would imagine it will be harder in a moving car, don't you think?"

He shrugged but then nodded.

We quickly embraced. I had no idea when Cole would come for me, but I wanted to get the note to my dad before he did.

"I'll call you tonight," I said.

He nodded. "Stay safe."

As I walked away from his house, I realized my jeans were still covered in the red stuff. The Caputo household had absolutely no pants that would've stayed on me. I started to jog, and I'd made it two streets over when I heard the sound of a car's tires crunching against the gravel. It was coming from behind me, and I moved to the side so it could easily pass; but it skidded to a stop.

I turned around to see an official-looking dark sedan.

My dad's car.

TWENTY

NOW

The Surface. My dad's car.

$\mathcal{B}$efore I could figure out what to do, my dad jumped out of the passenger seat.

"Nikki!" He paused for a moment as he took in my red-caked pants, and then his arms were around me. "Where have you been?" he said into my hair. Then he pulled back to look at me. "What happened?"

My mind couldn't work fast enough to tell a believable lie. "I don't know."

"You don't *know*? Then where were you?"

"I . . . How did you find me?"

He pushed some of the hair from my eyes and then held my face in his hands. "Your phone."

I glanced down at the phone in my hand and then back to my dad. "What, like GPS?"

He didn't admit it, but he looked guilty. "What do you expect, Nikki? Your strange disappearances? Your missed appointments? And then last night your signal disappeared. I've been waiting for it to reappear every since."

I shook my head, still staring at my phone. My dad pulled on my elbow. "Come on. Get in the car. We'll discuss this on the way to Dr. Hill's."

"What?!"

"I called her on the way. She's squeezing you in, and you need it now more than ever."

I jerked my arm free and backed away. "No! Dad, I'm sorry; I can't explain right now, but I have to go."

"You're not going." He no longer had me in his grip, but there was nowhere for me to run. I looked at his eyes. His tired eyes. He didn't understand that this was life or death. Jack's life, or his death. I'd been hiding the truth for so long. Was this one of those times when only the truth would work? I don't know if it was my exhaustion or my desperation, but I blurted out the first honest thing I'd said in a long time.

"I know where Jack is! He's trapped, and I have to go or he's going to die." It was simple. And it was the truth, and yet the words still had the power to cut me to the core.

He froze. "Where is he?"

How to explain? "He's . . . not here. He's somewhere else. And I was on my way to find him last night—"

"When you got caught in a paint fight?" He was eyeing my red-covered pants, and his tone was more sarcastic than I'd ever heard from him. A sign that he was frustrated.

He didn't believe me. Of course he didn't believe me. But I

had to get rid of him before Cole came.

"Dad. Look at me." We were eye to eye. "Trust me. Believe in me. Jack will die if I don't get to him. And I'm the only one who can. He's in . . . sort of an alternate reality. I know it sounds crazy, but look at me. Do you see my pupils dilated? Do you see any other signs that I've lost it? You have to give me forty-eight hours. Alone. I can save Jack. But I need to go."

It was working. I could see it in his face. He believed me.

He turned toward his car and called to the driver. "James. Can you get me a bottle of water?"

Water. It sounded so good. James came around the car and handed it to my dad. My dad twisted it open.

"Here," he said, handing it to me. "Drink."

I gulped the entire thing down without pausing for a breath. My dad sat on the ground next to me and leaned his head against the wall. I handed him the empty bottle.

"I'm sorry I've been so crazy. But once I find Jack and bring him home, things will get better."

"Just relax, Nikki. You're back now."

I leaned my head against his shoulder. He needed to know I wasn't back for good, but the words to explain weren't there. I was tired.

So tired.

When I woke up I was on a couch. I rubbed my shoulder. "Ow."

I heard the squeak of someone shifting on leather. "Sorry,

Nikki. James accidentally bumped into the wall when he was carrying you in." Was that Dr. Hill's voice?

"I'm not supposed to be here." My mouth felt like cotton.

"Drink some water."

The water. My dad had given me water. "What was in it?"

Dr. Hill frowned and set a glass of water aside. "I'm afraid your father did something rash. He put Valium in your drink. He was worried about you, but he shouldn't have done that."

"My dad drugged me," I said, incredulous. "And here I was thinking he believed me."

"Believed you about what?"

I shook my head, trying to clear the cobwebs inside. I'd slept, but I hadn't dreamed. Was it because it was an artificially induced sleep? "I have to go."

"Of course. After we talk for a bit. After you start telling the truth."

The truth. If the past few hours had taught me anything, it was not to be honest.

She clicked her pen open and shut a couple of times and then held it again to the yellow legal pad resting on her lap.

"What happened to you?"

I shrugged, glancing at the windows in her office and wondering if I could maybe squeeze through one. But we were on the second floor.

She inhaled loudly. "Nikki, your father found you on the side of the road, your pants covered in . . . something, and talking incoherently about alternate dimensions. I know you don't feel safe with anyone; but if you want to get out of here, you've got to give me something."

I thought about it. "I don't know where to start."

"Close your eyes. Count backward from ten. Let your mind go."

Dr. Hill called this a guided imagery exercise. She had me do it at every appointment. It was supposed to get the conversation flowing. I nodded and then did as instructed.

"Now open your eyes."

I did, but it wasn't Dr. Hill's therapy face that caught my attention. It was something else, in the corner of the room. Behind Dr. Hill's rolling chair. A hand, pale and ghostly, coming out of the floor.

A phantom hand. *Crap.* Maybe I *am* crazy.

"Talk, Nikki." Dr. Hill was losing patience.

I tried to keep my eyes on her, but the hand was waving toward me, as if it was trying to get my attention.

"Nikki? You have to give me something."

The hand pointed to the side wall, opposite the entrance, where the bathroom was. I tried not to stare directly at it and risk Dr. Hill seeing it. Or maybe it really was a hallucination.

The hand made insistent gestures toward the bathroom.

"Um . . . may I please be excused?" I said.

"No more excuses."

"I can't help it if I need to use the restroom. I won't be able to think until I do."

She glanced at her watch. "Make it quick."

I stood from the couch and started walking toward the door, and the hand followed me, slinking along the floor and up the one step that led to the bathroom.

What the . . . ?

I went inside and shut the door, and the hand came through the wall. It reached out, fingers together, thumb up, as if it would shake my hand. I crouched down and noticed markings around each of the fingers on the hand. Tattoos.

I hadn't seen them before because the hand itself was practically translucent. There was only one person I knew with those tattoos.

"Cole?"

The hand went limp, as if exasperated, and then gave me an exaggerated thumbs-up signal.

I stood up to consider. Would I really be able to get to the Everneath from my doctor's office bathroom?

And how would my doctor explain it?

I was pretty sure there would be a manhunt after this; but Jack was down there, and Cole was waiting.

I had no choice but to grab the hand.

I took it as if I were shaking it; and within an instant I was gone again.

TWENTY-ONE

NOW
The Everneath. The Ring of Water.

$\mathscr{I}$ landed hard on the dirt pathway, my lungs compressed painfully. I coughed a few times.

"You okay, Nik?" Cole patted my back.

My eyes watered, and I sniffed. "No." I pushed myself up. "I am *not* okay. What happened? What did you do to me?"

"I told you we'd have to kick you to the Surface for the nights."

"But without warning?"

He pointed to the red lake. "You were covered in blood from the Lake of Blood and Guilt."

My chest constricted at the memory of that drowning feeling. "The Lake of what?"

He stared at the lake with a faraway look in his eyes. "The Lake of Blood and Guilt. It's an apt description, really, since it's made up of blood. And guilt."

"What are you talking about?"

Max interrupted. "We need to get moving, Cole. Considering how long it took us to get here."

"I know," Cole said. He went to grab my hand, but I yanked it away and he gave me an exasperated look. "I'll tell you what happened, but we need to keep moving."

Ashe was standing by one of the four entrances that led to the lake. He seemed to be pacing in his mind, throwing occasional anxious glances toward Cole.

The four entrances all looked alike. Even as I studied them, I couldn't be sure which one we had taken to get here.

"Did all of you stay here the whole time I was gone?" I asked Cole.

He nodded. "It was the safest place, because the Wanderers avoid the lake. But this place wears on us too, so everyone's pretty much ready to leave. Like now."

Ashe looked at his watch. "What time is it?" I said.

"One o'clock," Cole said.

One o'clock? My heart sank. So much time gone.

Cole nodded as if I'd spoken. "It took a long time to find you. Which means we need to go," he said. "Where's your token?"

I pulled the note from my pocket. It was stained red from the lake, but it didn't matter. Once it was in my hand, my tether appeared. The night on the Surface must have refilled the more positive emotions, because the tether glowed bright and true, and it pointed away from the lake, toward the leftmost entrance. But the night away didn't do anything for my energy level. I felt as if I was moving at half speed.

"This way," I said.

We started off in the same formation as before, with Ashe in front and Max in back. The walls were still running water, and I wondered if we would ever get to the Ring of Wind, let alone to the bull's-eye. A whole day had already passed, and we hadn't even gotten through one ring.

Cole walked beside me. His face looked worn, and there were dark circles under his eyes that I'd never seen before.

"You're tired," I said.

He gave a sad smile. "The Lake of Blood and Guilt will do that to a person."

"What was that? What happened?"

I hadn't realized I'd started to veer to the side, and Cole pulled me toward the center of the path again.

"When the Wanderer . . . fed on you"—he struggled to get the words out—"I'm guessing that the strongest emotion left in you was your guilt. It was even stronger than your connection to Jack, hence the second tether. Guilt's kind of a big thing around here. So big that all of the collective guilt from the sacrifices in the Everneath pooled together and formed a lake. The Lake of Blood and Guilt."

I thought about the symbolism and remembered something I'd read. "Wasn't there a Frozen Lake of Blood and Guilt in Dante's *Inferno*? It's made of blood, because blood symbolizes guilt so well."

He almost smiled. "You have been doing your research. In Dante's poem, it's the farthest place from warmth and light. The worst sinners are frozen there. Faces out. Mouths sealed shut."

"But my lake wasn't frozen."

"Dante always did like to romanticize everything. Besides, like most of our enduring myth makers, he was working off of a rumor of a rumor. But he did have one thing right."

"What's that?"

Cole smiled. "It's an eternal punishment. It's hard to escape it; and if you're not careful, every path leads back to it. We just have to hope your tether to Jack is stronger than our attraction to the lake."

I wouldn't have believed him if I hadn't experienced it myself.

Beside me, Cole yawned. He looked so exhausted, so sickly compared with the last time I'd seen him. "The lake hurts you too," I said.

He gave me a sad smile. "Everything in here will affect me. The lake draws out my guilt. Brings it to the surface."

"I thought one of your charms was that you never felt guilty for the things you've done."

"Not true. I just keep it buried as far as possible, down inside what you would probably refer to as the 'black hole that is my soul.'" He glanced at me sideways, and I feigned nonchalance and shrugged. He grinned. "The lake is like a magnet for the guilt. But your guilt was already strong. Your tether to Jack and your own guilt fought for your attention, hence two tethers. And you chose guilt. I didn't realize where you were leading us until you decided to take the world's most melodramatic swan dive."

I thought back to that moment when I jumped in. What was I thinking? "You could've given me a warning before Max kicked me."

"There was no time. Once you were immersed there was no bringing you back. You would have drowned from the inside out. You swallowed the blood. You were about to be swallowed by guilt."

I thought about it. How I'd drunk the blood. How I pictured myself disappearing in it. "If I drowned here, would I be dead?"

He frowned. "This isn't a dream, Nik. You're you here. If you die here, you're dead."

I took a deep breath. "So explain to me the kicking part again?"

"Kicking you out was the only way to save our place here, because we aren't allowed to land anywhere in the maze or in the bull's-eye. I can't go to the Surface with you because then we would have had to start all over at the beginning again. After you were clear of the lake, I had to try to locate you by making jumps to the Surface and following my connection to you. Max and Ashe had to stay here, grounding my connection to them so I could find my way back. But if my whole body had gone to the Surface, I wouldn't have been able to find Max again. It was a very delicate balancing act, and I would hope you'd appreciate the effort." He seemed to be growing impatient trying to explain it.

"I do, I do. But if you have the ability to reach to the

Surface, why don't you just grab people? Yank them down and force them to become sacrifices?"

"Nik, don't you know anything about the Everneath? They have to be *willing*. The Forfeits, the sacrifices, even you just now when you grabbed my hand. They all have to be willing. Can we walk faster, please?"

"One more question. Why did Max, and not you, kick me?"

He blushed. "It should be obvious."

Obvious? "It's not obvious."

He looked away, toward the waterfall wall. "I would prefer not to be the one who has to kick you in the stomach."

I stopped in my tracks. "Seriously? You Feed off of me for an entire century, take away any future I could possibly have, but you draw the line at a little aggravated assault?"

The words had poured out before I realized how they would sound. But then again, it was true, wasn't it?

He frowned. "Nik, when are you going to realize that I never hurt you? I never *will* hurt you. I only did what you asked."

"You 'never hurt me'?" I said, incredulous. Anger started to boil inside my chest, and it felt larger and more defined here, maybe because every emotion felt bigger in the Everneath. It was magnified; I knew this. But I couldn't stop myself. "You took away everything!"

His eyes were fierce. "Don't fool yourself. Yes, I wanted you to become an Everliving, but I left the choice up to you."

I scoffed. "I know it was my choice. But I didn't know what I was choosing. And you knew what it would do to me."

He grabbed my arm and yanked me back. His eyes searched my face. "Whatever you think of me, I was honest with you. Just because you want to live the mortal life doesn't mean that my path is any less moral."

"You feed off of people," I said.

"But it's their choice."

"You sacrifice humans."

"But it's *their choice*."

His face was so close to mine. His cheeks were bright with rushing blood underneath his skin. He was close enough that I imagined I could feel his connection to me. Feel the pull that was holding him fast to me. And for the first time, I realized that, for him, that connection would never break. Because I felt it.

I looked deep into his eyes. "If you tell yourself a lie enough times—that it's okay to steal other people's energy to stay alive—it becomes the truth. Even for you. They're only willing because they're weak. You're preying on the weak."

We stood face-to-face for a few tense moments. His dark eyes were tight, the circles under them more pronounced. "That's quite an indictment of the person you're trusting with your life right now."

My lower lip trembled. "I know." And I knew my culpability too. But I wasn't about to admit it.

He took a step forward, as if he wanted to grasp me, but he was trying to hold back. Was he worried he would hurt me? A large drop of water fell onto his cheek, and he flinched.

A few more drops fell hard on my head. Tilting my head

back, I looked into the sky. It was clear blue. But the walls of the maze were suddenly bulging.

Cole brought a finger to my cheek and then examined the drop of water with a curious expression. Right then, the rocks beneath our feet began to shake. Cole's eyes went wide. The walls swelled, expanding into the pathway.

Max appeared from around the corner, sprinting.

"Run!" Max yelled.

The sound of thunder crashed around our ears, and then the first waves of rapids erupted from behind him. Instantly, the white foam from the churning water exploded up the maze walls. It was an ocean, crashing toward us.

"Nik!" Cole grabbed my hand, and we were running. Full sprint. No time to care if we were heading in the right direction. We caught up with Ashe and pushed him forward. He stumbled.

"Go! Go!" Cole shouted, shoving him from behind. Ashe scrambled up. The path darted left. Then right. I was following behind Cole when he came to a screeching halt. I crashed into his back.

"Why'd you stop?!" I shouted, but then I saw the reason. My mouth fell open.

A giant waterfall blocked the pathway. It was a dead end.

We were trapped. We turned around. Max appeared. He caught sight of the dead end.

"Shit!" Max said.

The enormous white wall of water burst into view, a bullet train of power aimed directly at us.

"Cole!" I yelped.

Cole pulled me in front of him and wrapped both arms around me, putting his back toward the dead end. He didn't have to explain. He was putting a cushion of space between me and the impact of whatever lay behind the wall.

"Deep breath!" Cole shouted in my ear.

I had a moment when the faces of my brother and my father flashed through my head. Then a wall crashed into my back.

It threw us into the dead end. The jolt snapped my neck forward. There had to be something solid behind the dead-end waterfall.

Cole took the brunt of the impact. The water kept coming; the rapids closed over our heads, forcing us farther from the ground but not high enough to get our heads above the surface. My shoulder hit something jagged, and I opened my mouth to scream; but a gush of water rushed in and down my throat.

I kicked and waved my arms against the current, the force from millions of gallons pouring on top of me.

My lungs burned with the lack of oxygen. I saw a slice of light coming from what had to be the surface, and I kicked and kicked toward it.

Finally I broke the surface, only to discover that the flood had pushed us to the top of the dead-end wall. As I gasped in my first breath of air, we were thrown over the apex and surging toward the ground in a waterfall of flailing limbs and debris.

I landed on the ground, feet first, and then crumpled. The impact shook my bones. It probably would have shattered them if it hadn't been for the couple of feet of water that had accumulated at the bottom before we went over.

The current from the rushing water dragged me a few yards before it became too shallow. The sound of crashing waves subsided, and the sound of wind rushing through a canyon took its place.

I gulped in a few deep breaths until my brain stopped bouncing around in my head.

The tidal wave was gone, and the rest of the water turned into little streams, trickling down any declines it could find. A strong wind created ripples in the water, and then, before my eyes, the water dried up.

Someone coughed a few feet away. It was Max, sitting on the ground, his head between his knees as if he was trying to catch his breath. Ashe was in a similar state. Cole was flat on his back.

There was no rise and fall of his chest.

"Cole!" I shouted. I scrambled over to where he lay. Max weakly tried to follow me. Ashe couldn't move.

I shook Cole's shoulders. "Can you hear me? Cole?"

I lightly slapped his face, but there was no response. Mining the deep caverns of my mind for the CPR class I'd taken as a freshman, I put my ear next to his mouth.

"No breaths," I said.

I took my finger and traced his rib until it met his

sternum, put the heel of my hand against it, and interlocked my fingers together.

"One . . . two . . . three . . ." I started compressions. Was I supposed to do five or fifteen? I split the difference and stopped at ten. Then I tilted Cole's head back and plugged his nose. I covered his mouth with mine, and breathed. Twice.

Please, Cole. Breathe. If I lost Cole, I lost Jack.

I repeated the whole thing three times before he finally coughed.

"Cole!" Placing my hands behind his back, I helped him turn over so he could cough up the water.

Color rose to his cheeks again.

He opened his eyes to find me staring down at him. He mustered up a faint, lopsided grin and said, "Was it good for you too?"

We'd been drenched in the Everneath waters. I kept waiting for the emotional roller coaster that should've come from being covered in it, but it never happened. Maybe that was because, by the time Cole started to breathe again, all of the water had dried up. Even my hair was dry. Back on the Surface, it would take twenty minutes to dry my hair, but right now I couldn't have squeezed a drop from it.

The wind here was fierce, and that's when it hit me.

"The Ring of Wind!" I said.

We were here. One ring down. Two to go. One ring closer to Jack.

Cole coughed and nodded. The walls were no longer made up of water. They looked like minitornadoes made up of swirling dust and flying debris.

I blinked several times, trying to clear the thin film of dust that suddenly coated everything.

"How did that happen?" I asked.

Cole turned to Ashe, who was staring at the wind wall we'd just come flying over. A light mist hovered in the air at the top.

"It was a flash flood," Ashe said. "Probably from your fight."

I thought back to our tense words. Cole had told me the water was attracted to certain emotions. Maybe our anger had consolidated all around us, baiting the water, igniting a fire underneath it until it boiled over.

I was about to share my theory with Cole, but I caught a glimpse of his back. His T-shirt hung in tatters, and the skin beneath looked like raw meat.

"Your back," I said.

Cole turned his head and glanced behind him. "Yeah. It'll be fine. Apparently there were a few rocks behind the waterfall. I'm more worried about how to get your projection back, because right now it's gone."

I looked down. He was right; my tether had disappeared. "The water wiped it out."

Cole brought his knees to his chest and propped his arms on top. Some of the gashes on his back opened wider, but he didn't seem to notice. He was still recovering his breath.

I looked around for anything that could soothe the scrapes,

but there was nothing but dust. Grabbing the bottom of my T-shirt, I tried to rip off a piece, but it wouldn't budge. Wasn't that how they did it in the movies? Someone was bleeding, and the other person would just tear their shirt in a perfectly straight line?

Bunching a section of my shirt in my hand, I stretched the material away from my stomach.

"What are you doing?" Cole said.

"Something incredibly heroic," I said. I pressed the cloth against his wounds. Gingerly I tried to close the larger gashes, replacing some of the hanging skin and carefully cleaning out the dirt.

Not that long ago I had tended to the wound on his hand because I didn't want him to give up. But things were different now. I knew he wouldn't give up, and I tended to his scrapes simply because he was hurting. This small change in my motivation reflected a bigger change in my relationship with Cole. Shades of trust existed where they weren't before.

Ashe came over to us. "We're in the Ring of Wind now. Take heed. The wind has a way of tossing our brains, just like the water did our emotions. It's the most devious of the rings. Nikki, do you have your token?"

I held it out to show it to him.

"You have to be constantly aware, and remind yourself often of Jack."

I nodded, squeezing the paper in my fist. I'd held on to it during the flood.

"Good. While you're playing nurse to Cole, tell us another story about Jack. We need to get your tether back."

I'd told so many stories, and I was so tired. But then I remembered Jack, and where he was right now, and my cheeks went hot with shame. How could I complain? "What should I talk about?"

Cole looked at me with a suddenly hopeful face. "Was there ever a time when he didn't resemble a white knight? That'd be great right about now."

A memory instantly popped into my mind, and my face must've shown it, because Cole pressed. "It won't make a difference if it's an unpleasant memory. It's all part of your connection to him."

"Well, there was one time. . . ."

Suddenly Max was by my side. "Jack as the antihero? Dude, I'll bring the popcorn."

TWENTY-TWO

FRESHMAN YEAR
The Surface. Eating lunch with Jack and Jules.

The sun shone down on the school's courtyard tables. We liked to eat outside whenever the weather gave us the chance.

Jack took a bite of his sandwich, big enough to make half of it disappear. "You're coming to Paxton's party on Friday, right?" he said with a mouthful of turkey.

Brent Paxton's parties were legendary. His parents owned a house on the Deer Valley ski resort, and when they were out of town, the entire school could be found passed out on his floor or hanging from the rafters. Or making out in one of the eight bedrooms. I'd heard about the parties even when I was in middle school, and now that I was a freshman, I was officially invited.

Jules answered before I could. "I am. Ryan Maetani asked me to go with him."

I raised my eyebrows at her. "Finally Ryan succumbs to your spell. When did this happen?"

Jules explained how the magic happened over chemistry lab that morning. Jack was quiet, listening to Jules but watching me. At the first opportunity, he said, "What about you, Becks?"

I shrugged, and absentmindedly screwed the cap back on my Diet Coke bottle. "I would, but since Jules has a *date*"—I cut my eyes over to her—"I don't really have anyone to go with."

Jack opened his mouth to speak, but Jules beat him to it. "I know someone who would die to go with you."

"Who?" Jack and I said in unison.

Jules glanced around playfully before leaning in and saying, "Andrew Hanks."

I rolled my eyes. "Oh, please."

"I'm serious. Jack, you should see the way Andrew gazes at our girl. It's like one of those cartoons. His eyes become little hearts that pop out of their sockets." She put her hands to her eyes and pulsed her fingers outward.

I threw a grape at her. "Shut up."

"Hey, I sit behind him. I have a clear shot at him. Most days I have to mop up after him from all the drooling."

"Stop it."

She shrugged. "I'm just saying. He'd stop a train for you. All you'd have to do is *mention* the party, and you'll have yourself a date."

"I don't know. . . ."

"Jack, help me out here. Tell her."

At the mention of Jack's name, I realized he'd grown awfully quiet. "Tell her what?" he said, frowning. He obviously wasn't too interested in the conversation.

"What would a guy want to hear from the girl he secretly crushed on?"

Jack stared hard at the table, and I couldn't be sure, but it looked like the tips of his ears turned bright red.

"How would I know?"

Jules sighed loudly. "Well, I know the girls never give you the chance to secretly pine. One piney look from you and the clothes start dropping, and then they're all 'Ooooh, your place or mine?'" Jules flipped her hair dramatically. "But imagine for a moment that you're not another species. And you were crushing on our dear Becks. What would you want her to say to you?"

I played along and watched Jack. He finally lifted his gaze to meet mine. He had the strangest expression on his face. He seemed . . . embarrassed. And maybe a little bit angry. Or he might've just been really annoyed with the conversation.

"I have no idea. Crushing on Becks would be like crushing on my sister. I can't imagine it."

This time it was my face that turned red.

Jack looked away, as if he were suddenly interested in the group of people next to us. Jules stared at Jack, her eyes narrowed, and a strange little grin appeared on one side of her mouth. I didn't think it was very empathetic of her, considering I was mortified at what Jack had just said.

She looked to me, then announced, "I've gotta go. Return a book I borrowed."

Great. Now she was abandoning me. Before I could compose myself enough to realize I didn't want to be left alone with Jack, Jules was gone.

And I was alone with Jack.

Who was tapping his spork on the table and studying the faux-wood grain so hard you'd think he had a test on the pattern next period.

I was still humiliated, but I couldn't figure out if it was because what Jack had said was really rude, or if I was so offended because of how I felt about him.

"I'm not your sister."

"I know."

". . ."

". . ."

"Is it so hard to believe someone would like me?"

Jack finally looked at me. "Of course not, Becks. It's just . . . I didn't . . ."

His voice trailed off as something behind me caught his attention. If it were possible for his dark eyes to get any darker, Jack's totally did.

I turned around. There was Andrew Hanks. Standing awkwardly behind me, a chemistry book in his hand.

"Hi, Nikki."

"Hi, Andrew." I gave him my widest smile. If that whole thing with Jack hadn't happened, I probably would've dialed down the enthusiasm. "What's up?"

He shoved the chemistry book toward me, almost hitting my chest with it. "I wondered if you could maybe go over today's lab with me? I just ran into Jules, and she told me you understood this stuff."

Jack snorted from behind me. I shot him a glare, and he mumbled, "Sorry."

I turned back to Andrew. "Sure. Have a seat. Do you two know each other? Jack, this is Andrew. Andrew, this is—"

"I know who he is," Jack said in place of a greeting.

Andrew sat slowly, looking from me to Jack. "If I'm interrupting . . ."

"Not at all!" I said.

"Please, do sit!" Jack said, matching my exuberance and swinging his arm graciously in front of him. Then he feigned instant boredom and turned to observe the rest of the courtyard while he finished his lunch. Why was he so angry? I looked at Andrew. Maybe the two of them had some history I didn't know about.

Andrew placed his notebook open on the table. Both pages were filled with scribbles and eraser marks. "I've tried to get the answer three different ways, but I'm coming up with nothing."

I studied his notes, followed the equation, and mentally pictured how I'd accomplished the same problem. "Here," I said, pointing to one part of his equation. "You're using the wrong value for Avogadro's number. It's six-point-oh-two-two times ten to the twenty-third. You have six-point-*two-oh*."

Jack interjected. "It's only, like, the first thing you should've learned on the first day of Chem."

I breathed through my nose. Jack was already in advanced chemistry, and just like everything else, he excelled at it. His dad was a chemical engineer, so Jack had probably had the number memorized from infancy.

I stared at Jack. "Not everyone grew up with bedtime stories like 'The Exciting History of Avogadro's Number.'"

This time it was Andrew's turn to snort. Jack handed him his bottle of water. "Here. Wash it down."

The rest of the lunch was more of the same, but later in the day Andrew did ask me to go to Paxton's party. Before, I might have turned him down for a quiet evening at home with a good book.

But now I said yes.

NOW

The Everneath. The Ring of Wind.

"Man, Jack sounds like a real tool," Cole said.

"You don't understand," I said, kicking a rock off the trail. I felt a little guilty for sharing a story that could give Cole the opportunity to put down Jack, but I remembered the whole thing through a different perspective. Because I knew now that Jack was struggling with his feelings for me at the time. I could forgive him a lot for that.

"My tether's back," I said.

Right then Ashe came up to us. "Wanderers. A few paths away. We've got to move."

Wanderers. Again. At the mention of them, I realized how tired I'd become.

"Why don't you just kick *them*?" I said, stifling a yawn.

"Kicking only works on humans," Cole said. "Let's go."

Of course kicking only worked on humans. How convenient. I kicked the ground, and for a brief moment I acted unconsciously instead of intentionally. I quickly turned to move, and I got a little to close to the wall of wind. A particularly strong gust caught the *ever yours* note out of my hand and sucked it away and inside the wall.

I didn't think. I jumped after it.

The wind lifted me off my feet. Jostled me above the ground like a rag doll. I tried to breathe in, but the wind tunnel was so powerful that I couldn't catch any air inside my mouth. My hair whipped viciously at my face.

The torrent slowed for a second, as if the wall were taking in a breath, and I sank. I caught a glimpse of the others. It was just a quick glance, but I could see Cole trying to jump in after me. Max was holding him back. As I was about to hit the ground, the gale blasted all around me again, throwing my limbs in different directions. My left arm twisted behind me. I thought it would rip off.

I screamed, but the sound got lost. The more I struggled, the more I imagined my tendons ripping. So I stopped. Went limp.

Jack, I thought. I couldn't compose my thoughts into a last message except to say his name. *Jack.*

I started to sink, but the cyclone was catching its breath again. If I was going to do anything, it would have to be now; but what could I do? I reached out toward the pathway. I could see Cole struggling against Max. Reaching for me. I saw his hand, but it wasn't near enough. I couldn't stretch out past the wind.

The reprieve was over. A fresh gust tossed me higher. I wasn't sure how much longer I could survive. The wind would tear me to pieces, and I would never touch ground again.

A blast of air rotated me around so that my feet were heading into the wall. A flash of an idea hit me. The water wall had a solid middle. Maybe this wall did too. I straightened my entire body and put my arms out wide, spreading my fingers so that if the wind was going to move me in any direction, it would be farther into the wall. The same blast of air pushed me in. I pointed my toes. Tried to elongate my body as much as possible.

And then I felt my toes brush against something solid deep inside the wind wall. Before the gusts could carry me away again, I flexed my feet, bent my knees, and shot them toward the solid thing. My feet hit it; and with no force to counteract, I went sailing out of the wind wall.

At the wall's highest point.

Cole must have seen me shoot out from the wall. He dived

toward me, cushioning my impact with the ground. We landed in a heap.

I shivered. It was more like a spasm. My arms and legs were shaking with the relief of being released from their contortions.

Cole scrambled to a sitting position and put his arms around me, holding me as I shook. Max stood a few feet away. His eye was red and swollen.

"What happened?" I asked, squinting at his face.

Cole glanced at Max. "I wanted to jump in after you. Max disagreed with the appropriateness of that reaction. And then his face ran into my fist."

Max was panting. "You wouldn't have been able to save her by jumping in."

"Well, now we'll never know, will we?" Cole smirked at Max, who grinned good-naturedly. Whatever tension was between them had passed, although now I had an idea of what Cole meant when he said he brought Max along to keep him from doing anything stupid.

But as I stared at them, the meaning behind their faces began to fade away. I glanced down at my empty hand.

"My token," I said weakly. "It's gone."

TWENTY-THREE

NOW

The Everneath. The Ring of Wind.

Nik, you don't need the token."

I heard Cole's words, and I immediately knew he was lying. I needed the note more than ever in the Ring of Wind. I sat on the ground, my knees pulled up to my chest, my head buried in my hands. My brain felt as if it were made of cloud. It drifted around in my head and out of my ears in puffy white wisps.

"Can you see it?" I said, my voice muffled by my knees.

"See what?"

"My brain," I said. "It's vapor."

I heard someone sigh and then a deeper voice. "She's gone, Cole. It was the wind."

My toes bounced up and down, and I started to rock back and forth. "I lost something," I said. "I can't find it."

Someone grabbed my shoulders. "Look at me, Nik." I thought I responded, but he shook harder. "Look at me!"

I raised my head to see dark eyes and blond hair. Cole. His voice came out in an urgent growl. "You don't need the token.

You have your memories. Tell me a story about Jack. Now!"

Jack. I knew him, of course. I loved him. But I couldn't think of anything to say. His face floated in the clouds inside my head, with no clues that would ground it to a memory, no tether to our history.

I shook my head. Cole grunted and turned his head as if looking for an answer. The man behind him—Ashe—paced back and forth. Cole met my gaze.

"Nik. Remember your first projection here? There were all those pictures of Jack, all those memories. Remember the pictures of the burned marshmallow? There were like fifty of them."

Burned marshmallow. Burned marshmallow. I grasped on to the picture. Mentally set it next to the picture of Jack in my head. Burned marshmallow. What was significant about it?

I couldn't think of anything except for how much I hated burned marshmallows.

I hated them.

Raising my head, I felt the light of hope show in my face.

"I remember."

SOPHOMORE YEAR
The Surface. Millcreek Canyon.

It was Jack's idea to drive his father's old 1979 Scout up the canyon to roast s'mores. The last day of September felt more like a summer heat wave than a fall chill, and Jack was convinced it was our last chance to have a cookout.

Jack and Will sat in the front; Jules and I sat in the back-seat, waving our arms in the air and screaming loudly like you do when your truck doesn't have a roof.

It was good to be with Jack now that we had buffers in Jules and Will. Things had been strangely tense between us ever since I went to the party with Andrew. More than anything, I wanted our friendship to return to normal.

We pulled into the Church Fork campfire site and had our pick of fire pits. Jack parked the Scout in front of one of the highest places, and then we started up the trail to Grandeur Peak, a spectacular hike that would reward us with a three-hundred-and-sixty-degree view of the valley.

"Race to the top," Jack said.

Jules put her hand on her hip. "It's an hour-long hike. And you're in football shape."

"Excuses," Jack said.

Jules looked as if she was about to argue, and then she took off running. "C'mon, Becks!"

I sprinted after her, laughing.

Jack and Will must have given us a head start, because it took them three whole minutes to catch up.

Jack went in front of me and turned around, jogging backward.

"Show-off," I said, panting.

He grinned. "The view's much better this way."

My cheeks got hot, and not just because of the exercise. But Jack was always saying things like that. He said the same things to Jules too.

I'm not special. I had to remind myself of this over and over, especially lately, because my hopeless crush—the one my mom told me I would grow out of, the one that haunted my dreams—wasn't going away. It felt as if I were running toward a cliff and I could see the edge; but I couldn't stop running, even though I knew that if I jumped off, it would end badly.

"If you're not going to try," I said, and made a push to pass him. The sudden competition sparked him into action, and he turned around and did his turbo thing.

When he was out of sight, I eased up. "Go ahead, Jules," I said. She was a long-distance track runner, so I knew she was just going slow for my benefit. She also couldn't pass up a good race.

"You sure you're okay?" she said.

"Yeah. I'll have more fun if I don't think I'm holding any-one back."

"Okay. I'll see you up there."

"Please beat at least one of the boys," I said.

She waved over her shoulder and took off.

Around the next bend, a small stream intersected the trail. I didn't want to get my feet wet when there was still so much of the hike left, so I leaped to one of the stones in the middle. Only it was covered in moss, and my foot slipped.

I heard a pop as my ankle turned, and I fell into the stream, butt first. Tears sprang to my eyes. I reached down to my ankle.

It felt as if someone had just shoved a billiard ball inside of it. I didn't care about the couple of inches of water I was sitting in. I was too focused on the pain.

"Crap," I said through clenched teeth. I scooted crab-leg style, holding my bad ankle up in the air until I was out of the stream and sitting on a log. The ankle started to swell.

I looked ahead up the trail. "Jules!" I called.

There was no answer.

"Jules!" I screamed louder.

Nothing.

I waited for a few minutes, then stood and tried to put weight on the bad ankle. Pain shot through my leg all the way up to my knee.

Okay, so I obviously wasn't going to get down on my own. I pulled out my phone. No signal.

I did some mental calculations. Maybe forty-five minutes for the three of them to reach the top and then a half hour for them to get back down. But they'd wait for me for a while before they gave up and figured out something was wrong.

It'll be okay, I thought, even though I knew my ankle would be twice as swollen by the time they reached me. But there was nothing I could do. . . .

At that moment Jack rounded the corner, almost at a flat-out sprint, interrupting my internal dialogue.

"Becks! Are you okay?"

It took me a second to get over my surprise. "I'm fine. I just twisted my stupid, stupid ankle."

"Well, don't blame the ankle." He crouched in front of me and examined it, pushing up the leg of my jeans to get a closer look. It gave me chills, and I tried to pull it down a bit.

"How did you know to turn back?" I said.

With his head still down, he said, "I waited for you."

"But it's a race. Why did you wait for me?"

He lifted his head so that his eyes met mine. "I always wait for you." He took a deep breath, my ankle still in his hands. "I'm always waiting for you."

In an embarrassingly breathless voice that didn't sound like my own, I said, "Because I'm so slow?"

He smiled. "Yes. But not in the way that you think."

My heartbeat started racing. It ran right out of my chest and up into the sky, where it exploded in fireworks. At least that's how it felt.

He was waiting for me. Right now. Waiting for me to say something. Wasn't he?

Maybe he was messing with me. And if he was serious, would I be dumped in two weeks? Suddenly that cliff was closer than it had ever been. He'd left the decision open. I could jump off if I wanted to. Or we could pretend the cliff wasn't even there. I could choose to believe that Jack was talking about how I was slow at running.

I turned my face away, trying to hide all the emotions Jack always brought out.

He lowered his head and pulled my hem back down around my ankle. "I think you'll survive."

My heart was beating so fast that I thought my survival was not necessarily a foregone conclusion. Or maybe he was talking about my ankle.

The silence at that point felt heavy. He sat back on his heels and watched me. He was waiting for me again.

"Um." My voice sounded weird. "So how are we going to get down?"

He gave me a wry smile and helped me up. "You're going to walk."

It took us forty-five minutes to cover a distance that had taken me fifteen minutes to climb. But we made it.

He got my leg elevated on the cooler and put a bag of ice on it. Then he built a fire with the practiced hands of a Boy Scout, and we roasted marshmallows while we waited for Will and Jules to finish.

The sun started to set, earlier than we had anticipated. But it was fall. At one point I caught Jack staring at me, the shadows from the flames dancing across his face.

I put a hand to my hair. "Do I look that bad?"

He smiled. "You never care much about your appearance—"

"Hey!" I said, mock offended.

"That's not what I mean." He seemed flustered. Very un-Jack-like. "I just mean . . . What *do* I mean?"

"Are you asking me?"

He nodded, now completely at a loss.

I tilted my head, thrilled to see that even Jack could get flustered. "Maybe you mean, 'Hey Becks, you have such natural beauty, even without effort you shine like the stars.'"

He stared at me and nodded slowly. Which was not the reaction I'd been expecting. For the first time since I'd known Jack, he looked . . . vulnerable. And I was the person who could hurt him. What was going on?

He looked at me with an intense expression, as if each word out of his mouth was paid for with a hundred push-ups. And finally he was too tired to go on. "You're my best friend."

"That was your point? Well, Jack," I said, leaning toward him. "You sure took the long way to get there."

"Am I your best friend?"

"Of course," I said without hesitation.

"Good," he said. His face finally relaxed a little.

"But you know what?" I said, leaning toward him.

His face tightened up. "What?"

"Your marshmallow is on fire."

He looked down at the end of his wire hanger to where his marshmallow had become a flaming ball of black goo. With a smile, he brought it close to his lips and blew it out.

Just like that, his characteristic smirk was back. "Perfect. Exactly how I like them." He gingerly pulled the charred remains off the end of the stick.

"That looks disgusting," I said.

His smile became deranged, and he brought the black ashes to his mouth and took a giant bite. Flakes of marshmallow ash dusted his mouth and cheeks.

He closed his eyes. "Mmmmmm."

I snorted.

The fire had died down, the sun had long ago set, and Jack and I were in a little circle of light. I wanted everything inside that circle to be the only things that existed. Just for a little while.

I hope you're still waiting for me, Jack.

NOW

The Everneath. The Ring of Wind.

I looked down at my feet. My tether was back. It was strong and tangible.

"It worked!" I said to Cole. But he didn't answer. I looked back to where he should've been, but he wasn't there. He was gone.

Frantic, I turned in circles, searching for any sign of him. "Cole!" I shouted his name over and over, but all I could hear was the wind.

We'd been together the whole time, hadn't we? Was he playing some sort of sick joke?

"Cole, this isn't funny," I said, my voice shaking. "Please. Don't do this to me."

There was no reply. If anything, the wind got louder.

What if he was in trouble? I tried to replay the last few minutes in my head, but the memory was shaky. Flashes of images passed through my mind. We were walking together; I was telling my story. Had I lost my balance? Did I fall into the wall again? The moment I asked myself those questions, I was flooded with images of me falling into the wall and being taken up by the wind and blown into the sky.

But were they real? Or were they created by my mind?

I had to get moving. Sitting here, trying to sort out what had happened, would make me crazy.

Retracing my steps might've helped, but by this point I was so turned around that I couldn't remember which way I'd come from. My tether was pointing straight ahead, so I decided to go the exact opposite way. Maybe that would take me back.

I ran. If something had purposely separated us, it couldn't be good. Using my tether as a guide, but in the opposite direction, I sprinted around corners, through hidden archways in the maze that took me from one corridor to the next, frantic.

What if I couldn't find him? What if I was trapped here forever in one of those endless loops Cole had told me about?

I leaped through one more archway and froze. There was somebody there, standing with his back to me. It wasn't one of us, and he looked as if he had too much meat on his bones to be a Wanderer. He had shaggy brown hair. And broad shoulders.

He turned around, and his big brown eyes went wide. "Becks?"

TWENTY-FOUR

NOW

The Everneath. The Ring of Wind.

*T*ears sprang up in my eyes, and I tried to catch my breath. "Jack?"

The edges of my vision started to blur. The blood drained from my face, and my head filled with air. Jack raced toward me and caught me just as I started to pass out.

"Stay with me, Becks."

I fought to keep my eyes open. "You said those exact words. When you left me."

"I know," he said. His strong arms were around me, keeping me upright, and he brushed the hair from my eyes. "I remember everything. Like it was yesterday."

I brought a hand up to his face and ran it over his cheeks, his forehead, his neck. He was so real. His face was rounder than I'd last seen it in my dreams.

I ran my fingers down his arms, tracing the ropey muscles there. He was beautiful. "Jack." His name coming off of my lips was the sound of a wish fulfilled, a longing satisfied. "How are you here? Did you escape?"

He smiled. "I've been waiting for you. For so long."

He dropped his head and kissed me, and I felt that kiss everywhere. My knees went weak. In fact, my entire body went weak, and a strange darkness began to creep in behind my eyes. His lips were hard against mine. They allowed for no space, and too soon my lungs were screaming for air.

It felt as if I were kissing a black hole.

I pulled away. "Wait," I said. "I have to catch my breath."

"Sorry," he said. "It's been way too long."

He leaned in to kiss me again, and I turned my head. He placed his hands on either side of my face and turned it back. "Wait—"

But his lips on my lips cut off any other words. I pushed against his chest as hard as I could, and he released me as I fell to the ground.

"I'm so sorry, Becks!" he said, as if he couldn't believe what he'd just done. "My mind . . . it's not right here."

I pushed myself off the ground and brushed my jeans, and that's when I noticed my tether. It was pointing behind me. But I was facing Jack.

I jerked my head up and stared at his face. There was something in his eyes, something that made them blacker than they were before. His pupils looked too big. They took over his entire irises.

Jack . . . *my* Jack . . . was supposed to be in the Tunnels.

This wasn't Jack.

He held out his hand. "C'mon, Becks. I figured a way out of here." At my hesitation, he raised his hands. "I promise no more kissing until after we get back home."

This wasn't Jack.

But it looked like him. Every inch of his skin, every expression on his face, every callus on his hand. The way his eyes twinkled when he smiled. His devious dimples. The little divot in his forehead. It could've been him. I could make myself believe it was him. I didn't even have to try. My brain was telling me to go with him, even though my instincts were fighting it.

I stayed where I was. "You go first," I said. "I'll follow you."

His eyes narrowed the slightest bit, but he turned around. "Stay close, Becks."

He took a step forward. For just one moment a voice in my head said, *You had him in your hands, and you threw him away.* Did that mean the boy in front of me now? Or the one I couldn't hold on to when the Tunnels came for me?

This is a trap, I thought. *This isn't Jack.* I turned and ran. Through the archway shortcut, around corners. I took every turn that was available, sometimes backtracking in the direction from which I'd come.

All the time, I could hear faux-Jack's screams. Calling out my name. Begging me not to abandon him again. Even though I knew it wasn't him, his frantic voice grabbed at my heart as if it had fingers. I couldn't help feeling as if I was failing him again.

* * *

I ran for a long time, and finally around one corner I smacked right into someone. It was Max.

"Nikki!" he said, looking the happiest he ever had to see me. He didn't embrace me or anything, but he let out a huge sigh of relief.

"Where's Cole? And Ashe?"

He shook his head. "I don't know. I just saw the weirdest thing. . . . It wasn't real."

"Did you see Jack?" I asked.

He gave me a confused look. "No. It was my baby sister. But she's . . ." His face crumpled, and he looked as if he was about to cry. "She wanted me to follow her."

"They weren't real," I said.

"I felt her hand in mine!"

False images of people we loved. Enticing us to go with them. "They're like Sirens," I said.

"Sirens?" Max said.

I nodded. "Like from *The Odyssey*. Only in the story, they'd used music to lure sailors and trap them. But there's no music allowed here, so they used something else to entice us."

"Who did you see?"

"Jack," I said. "And if you saw your sister, that means the images are specific to each person." My pulse quickened. "We have to find the others. Let's split up."

"What?! No, that's an awful idea," Max said.

"Cole and Ashe are probably trapped right now. We have to get to them before they leave with their Sirens. We have the best chance of finding at least one of them if we split up.

Now!" I turned him in the direction of my tether. "You go this way, I'll go backward. Try to cover as much ground as you can."

I shoved him forward, and he was gone.

Then I turned around and ran as fast as my legs would allow, trying not to think about my encounter with the Siren. It had felt so real. His skin, his big hands, his lips.

Actually, it was his lips that had given him away. They didn't feel right. In fact, they felt as if they were sucking life out of me, taking away my reasoning capabilities. But if the Siren hadn't kissed me, how long would it have taken me to figure out that it wasn't Jack?

I was talking myself in circles. Cole was out there, with a Siren that looked like who knew what, and what if he followed it? Ashe was missing too, but at this moment the only person I wanted to find was Cole.

I followed my tether. Maybe I had backtracked enough from my original position that the tether would take me past the last place I'd seen Cole.

If I didn't find him, hopefully Max would.

I rounded a corner and found a dead end. But standing right in front of the barrier was Cole. He wasn't alone.

There was someone in his arms, but because his back was to me, I could only catch a glimpse of dark hair. Who was it?

I opened my mouth to call to him, but then I heard him speak.

"It's okay. You're okay now." He stroked the girl's hair. "I found you, Nik. You're safe."

Nik? The girl pulled away from him to smile, and I saw my face. My face!

"Cole!" I screamed his name, and it sounded like a screech. They both turned toward the sound.

The girl's face crumpled. "There she is again!" she said. "She's following me."

"Cole, that's not me," I said.

The Siren grabbed on to Cole even tighter. "She even sounds like me!"

"Don't worry," Cole said. "She can't hurt you."

Oh brother. I took a step forward, and they both flinched. I held out my hands, palms down. "The girl in your arms isn't me," I said.

Cole frowned. "I've been with her the entire time. Whereas you just showed up."

"You haven't been with her the whole time. Think back over the last hour. I was telling you the story about Jack and the marshmallow—"

"The one where I twisted my ankle?" the Siren said, her tone accusatory. "That was *my* story."

Cole held her even tighter, and he narrowed his eyes at me.

"Please, Cole," I said. "They make us see what we want to see. I just saw Jack."

"Jack's in the Tunnels!" the Siren screamed. Then she turned to Cole. "We have to get out of here. All you have to do is know right here in your heart"—she put her finger on Cole's chest—"that I'm me."

Crap. That was something I would totally do. Cole seemed mesmerized, and he stared at her as if I wasn't even there. He put his fingers on her chin and brought her face closer. "I know you're you, Nik."

She leaned her body even closer to his, and it occurred to me that he would want this version of me more. This Nik clung to him and told him that she needed him. This Nik trusted him. This Nik acted as if all she needed was Cole by her side. Her tether pointed to him, and only him.

Her *tether*! It was pointing directly toward him.

"Cole! Look," I said, pointing at her feet. "It's not me."

He followed my gaze and looked at the tether. I saw his shoulders sink infinitesimally. Then he faced me and dropped his gaze to my own tether, which was now pointed away from him and out of the dead end.

His eyes met mine. "You're the fake," he said, his voice barely above a whisper.

I shook my head, but he turned away and started walking toward the dead end with the fake me. A small archway opened up in the wall of wind.

"Cole!"

He didn't turn.

What to do? With my own Siren, I couldn't see the truth until I kissed him.

I didn't give myself a second to think. Cole was about to duck under the archway. I sprinted toward him, and when I was a couple yards away, I leaped into the air and tackled him. He must have been shocked, because he didn't react fast enough to throw me to the side. We fell to the ground.

I turned him over and leaned down.

And I put my lips on his.

It only lasted for a split second, because he reflexively pushed me back, but not completely. Instead of throwing me off him, he held my face directly above his and searched everywhere, from my forehead to my chin. I let him turn my head right and left. I needed him to know it was me.

Then he brought my lips to his and kissed me.

And something strange happened. Whereas when I'd kissed the Siren, my body had weakened, now it was as if a power surge of energy was coursing through my veins and the fibers of my muscles. And it was all emanating from the kiss with Cole.

He ran his fingers through my hair and to the back of my head and pulled me in closer, and I let him, because the power surge reached the tips of my fingers and my toes and I was sure I would be able to do anything—face anything—if I just had more of his power.

His hands moved down my back, pulling, always pulling me closer. I was lost in Cole's underworld, transported to another place and time where anything was possible. All of my memories, the ones I'd been struggling to hold on to, came rushing back.

And a new memory. Of a girl, sitting quietly at a table in a club, hunched over a soda. She had long, dark hair and pale skin. I squeezed my eyes shut to focus on the memory, and that's when I realized that it wasn't my memory.

The girl at the table was me.

I was seeing myself through someone else's eyes.

Cole's eyes. For the first time ever, I realized the tenderness with which he had viewed me. He noticed every glance of my eyes. Every hint of a smile. Every prelude to a frown. He paid particular attention to the curve of my fingers around my drink. The well-bitten fingernails. The nervous tapping.

I had no idea I tapped my fingers like that.

I felt what he felt. If he'd had wings, he would've wrapped them around me protectively. He was surprised at how quickly he'd become attached to a human.

"I would never kiss you!" The Siren's screech brought me back to the Everneath, and I drew away from Cole.

He had a devilish grin on his face, and he turned toward the Siren. "I know. But the real Nik would—if it was to save my life." He looked back at me. "Hey, Nik."

"Thank goodness," I said. I rolled off of him and sighed.

The Siren opened her mouth wide and wailed. The sound was so strong I thought it would burst my eardrums. I covered my ears. Cole did the same.

She started flickering, oscillating between the image of me and that of a black, scaly creature. She finally settled on the creature. And in a flash she leaped toward Cole, crashing into his body. She opened her mouth wide, unhinging her jaw like a snake, revealing rows of sharp black teeth. She dipped her head and clamped down on Cole's neck.

Cole screamed.

"Cole!" I scrambled to my feet and looked around us, but there was nothing I could use for a weapon. Then I remembered the knife in the sheath at Cole's ankle.

I reached for his leg, trying to avoid contact with the creature, and shoved my hand up his jeans leg. The hem got caught on the knife sheath, but with a little extra force I tore it past. Maybe it was the adrenaline. I grabbed the handle of the knife and ripped it out, brought it high above the middle of the creature's back, aimed for a crack between the scales on her skin, and plunged downward.

The knife sank deep into her back and she let out a shriek. A stream of dark blood spurted from the wound. Her body seized, went still, then seized again and twitched. Her blood sprayed my face and I recoiled.

She made a wailing sound that faded into a sob, and then she went still.

"Cole!" I grabbed what looked like her shoulder and shoved her off of Cole.

He was covered in blood. I had no idea how much was his and how much was the Siren's.

I tore off the sleeve of my shirt at the seam and held it against his neck. "Cole! Can you hear me?"

He opened his eyes and nodded. The move was barely perceptible. "Is it bad?"

I pulled the cloth away, but he was still bleeding, so I put it back and applied even more pressure.

"No," I said. "Not bad at all. You're going to be fine."

He smiled and reached up to my cheek and ran a thumb across it. "You can't lie with blood on your face."

I took his hand from my cheek and placed it on his chest. He closed his eyes and stopped moving. I put my hand an inch away from his mouth to feel for breath. He was pushing out air at least.

I sighed and shifted my position so that I was sitting by his head. I patted his chest softly. "You're going to be fine," I said.

I was talking to myself.

I don't know how long we sat like that before his eyes fluttered open. He sat up and immediately got woozy.

"Whoa," I said. "Take it easy."

He lay back down, and I checked his wound. It had stopped bleeding, but I tied my shirtsleeve around his neck anyway. With that kind of wound, a strong breeze could open it up again.

"I'm okay now, Nik."

"Good. But we're going to stay here for a little while." When he tried to protest, I said, "Staying in one place is the best chance for the others to find us."

Cole furrowed his brow. "You haven't seen them?"

I shook my head. "Only Max. His Siren appeared as his sister, but he figured it out quickly. I don't know how. We split up, hoping to find you and Ashe."

He looked worried. Neither of us considered for a moment just leaving them behind and continuing on.

"Are you okay?"

He nodded. "Do your kisses have this effect on everyone?"

"It was the Siren—" I stopped. He was obviously kidding. But I flashed back to the kiss again.

That kiss. Now that we were so far away from the danger, the thought of the kiss brought heat to my cheeks. The kiss had given me a glimpse into Cole's memories, as well as an intense power surge. I was sure it helped me kill the Siren. But afterward, Cole seemed tired. And when the Siren tackled him, he hadn't put up much of a fight.

"Why was that kiss so weird?" I said. "Did it make you weak?"

He smiled. "Everliving kisses. They're never what they seem, are they? Kisses in the Everneath work in the opposite way as kisses on the Surface. Up there, you have more energy, so a kiss means energy transfers from you to me. Down here, with the Everneath draining you constantly, I have more. So energy flows from me to you. With a kiss, you were feeding off me for a change."

I raised my eyebrows. "Seriously?"

He nodded. "Everything's upside down here."

"But . . . what about the Wanderers? How come they drain me?"

"You need to stop thinking of Wanderers as true Everlivings. They aren't anymore. All they are is hunger, and you will always have more energy than they do. They have nothing to give. But I do."

"I saw a memory. Of yours," I said quietly.

He brought his knees up to his chest and rested his chin on top, displacing the makeshift bandage. "I'm sure you did."

I moved the bandage back into place. He didn't ask me which memory I saw.

"You saved me back there," he said.

I thought about the Siren. "At first I wasn't sure you wanted saving from her."

"She did have her fine points." He smiled, and I was relieved that he was making light of the situation.

I'd been thinking about it. To get someone to follow them, a Siren would most likely appear as that person's deepest desire. The thing they wanted most. Cole's had become me, only it wasn't me as the queen, which I assumed would've been what Cole wanted most. It wasn't even me as an Everliving.

It was me, simply as me.

Maybe the Siren wasn't what we most desired above all else. Maybe it was what we most desired at that moment.

I didn't know. And seeing Cole's face, the fatigue under his eyes, the worried lines around his mouth, I didn't want to ask him.

"When did you know that the Siren wasn't me?" I said. "Was it the kiss?"

He gave me a sad smile. "It was when I saw that her tether pointed to me."

"But . . . you were about to go with her?"

"A moment of weakness. Destroyed by a kiss." He was looking deep into my eyes. "Why did you kiss me?"

I blushed. "Because my Siren was Jack. He kissed me, and I knew it wasn't him. I figured that if I did the same with you, you'd know I was real."

"You reached that particular conclusion fairly quickly."

"No—I didn't—I—" I stammered. Imagined the kiss again. I was lost in it. But I could never admit that.

He leaned closer. "Tell me you didn't feel something, Nik."

"I don't know what I felt," I blurted. How was I supposed to know when the rush of energy masked everything else?

Cole didn't pull away. "Just so you know . . . my tether always points to you."

Ashe had told me the same thing, and now I could see it in Cole's eyes, the tilt of his head, every decision he made. My face was behind it all. I knew it now. And I'd used it to bring him down here. What was I doing to him?

That kiss. It wasn't just about the energy. It was about the memories. It was our connection to each other, again. A connection that only comes with spending a century together. Would it ever be broken?

I opened my mouth to say something, but Max appeared from around a turn, out of breath. He closed his eyes in relief that he'd found us.

"I couldn't find Ashe. He's gone."

"What do you mean he's gone?" Cole said, standing up.

Max shook his head and gasped for breath. "I couldn't find him."

Cole's face drained of any color it had left. Max looked like he was about to be sick. It hit me then just how dangerous this maze was. I'd known it from the beginning, but in the course of a couple of hours, I'd had my mind erased, my body nearly torn apart by wind; Cole had been attacked by a Siren; and now Ashe was gone.

I thought about how quickly things could change. How fast the wind had messed with our minds.

Everything felt heavier now.

Cole looked at his watch. "We need to kick Nikki," he said.

"What?" It couldn't be time yet, could it? But then I thought of all we'd been through. It had felt like three days.

"It's been a day. You need to sleep." He turned away from me, and I caught a glimpse of his expression. It was grim. With his back to me, he said, "We'll keep looking for Ashe while you're gone. Max, do it."

"But—" The word was all I could get out before Max's foot was in my gut, and then I was gone.

Seconds later I was on the floor of the Shop-n-Go again. It was dark. I was alone, and on the Surface.

TWENTY-FIVE

NOW

The Surface. The Shop-n-Go.

Half an hour later, I was curled up in the storage closet next to the mop and a stepladder, with three PARK CITY: ABOVE THE REST T-shirts balled up under my head.

There was no way I was going to contact Will when I hadn't found Jack yet. I couldn't face telling him about everything that had happened, especially the part about the Jack-Siren.

Because it hurt. Thinking he was so close. Feeling as if he were in my arms again.

I hated the maze. Yes, we'd made it to the next ring; but every time I reached the Surface without Jack, it felt like another failure.

I pulled the foil blanket I'd stolen from the camping section of the store up and under my chin and closed my eyes. For once I was grateful that every convenience store in Park City had a camping section.

I closed my eyes. Sleep couldn't come fast enough.

I dream.

But Jack isn't there. At least he isn't there the way he's been there for the past months.

Instead, I dream about the first time he told me he loved me. We are in his uncle's cabin, sitting by the fire and sipping hot chocolate. The dream feels forced, as if I'm half awake and consciously dragging my sleeping brain through my memories.

I relish in the sweet memory; but I feel a tug at my heart, warning me of a bigger problem.

The Jack from the Tunnels is gone. I search for him, trying to find my way to my house and my bed so he can find me.

But he doesn't. I am alone.

My eyelids finally abandoned their fight, and I woke up. Jack wasn't there. No matter how much I'd tried to force him, the real Jack wasn't in my dream. I'd been so worried about how much more he might have forgotten, but I didn't think it was possible that he wouldn't be there at all.

I threw an ammonia bottle against the wall. I was not losing Jack. I would not lose him.

The bottle rolled back to me. I picked it up and threw it harder. This time it cracked, and yellow ammonia pooled around it.

The sound of glass shattering mirrored the feeling in my heart, and I had the sudden urge to break everything within my reach. I wanted to throw the door open and run through the Shop-n-Go tossing bottles and smashing counters. For a second

I even imagined throwing Ezra's chair through a window.

I put my head in my hands. If I didn't do something to distract myself, I'd tear the place apart. That's when I realized a soft light was coming from underneath the storage-room door.

It was morning.

I had to talk to someone. There was no way I could face Will one more time, still a failure. My father was out of the question. If I were to show up again after disappearing from Dr. Hill's office, only to disappear again once Cole found me . . .

The smell of the ammonia became overpowering in that small room. I had to get out of there. Really, there was only one other person I could talk to. Mrs. Jenkins. Maybe she'd come across something new. Maybe she would just let me smash things. Maybe she would want to smash them too, and curse the day she'd ever learned about the Everneath.

I opened the closet door a couple of inches and looked out. The sun was peeking in through the glass windows, and Ezra was sitting at the counter, earbuds in his ears, hunched over the paper.

I threw the door open and went up to the counter where Ezra was working on a crossword puzzle. He looked up.

"I need to borrow your phone," I said.

He handed it to me as if a girl emerging from his storage closet at dawn was no big deal. I called Mrs. Jenkins to come pick me up.

* * *

Mrs. Jenkins sat quietly on her couch as I gave her a quick account of the past few days. When I'd finished, she leaned back.

"So at some point soon, Cole's hand will appear and take you back under?"

I nodded. "And I feel like we're running out of time. Jack . . . he didn't show up in my dream last night. . . ." My voice cracked. We were both quiet as I took a deep breath. "I'm running out of time."

"You never had time to begin with. I wish I knew what to tell you."

"That's the problem, isn't it? We're flying with our blinders on. Nobody's ever tried to do this. Nobody's ever been in this situation before."

At that, I glanced at the urn on her mantelpiece. "Adonia," I said. "I guess she's come the closest. Were there any stories passed down from her? Any details about her that would help me?"

Mrs. Jenkins looked at the urn too and shook her head slowly. "I can't think of anything that would help. She didn't make it the full six months of her Return to the Surface. She was killed by the queen before the Tunnels even came for her."

"I know that part, but how did she end up going to the Feed in the first place? If she didn't love her Everliving, why did she ever choose to go?"

"Oh, I don't know that she didn't love Ashe. At first. But she was still obsessed with the true love of her life, a soldier whom she believed had died in battle—"

"Wait!" I interrupted. "Did you say Ashe?"

She nodded. "That was the name of her Everliving."

"Ashe," I repeated. "Ashe was the one who betrayed Adonia. Turned her over to the queen."

She nodded again, confused.

"I met an Ashe," I said, my voice barely above a whisper. "He helped us. He's a friend of Cole's."

She squinted curiously. "Did he have dark hair and dark eyes?"

I shook my head. "No. He was really gray. Everywhere. It's like he was made up of smoke or something. Cole said he didn't used to look like that until he missed the last Feed. But Ashe is a common enough name, right?"

The look on her face told me she didn't think it was a coincidence. "Ashe is still alive. Of course that makes sense. But Adonia's story is very old. It's strange to think he's still . . . there."

I couldn't figure out how to feel about this new bit of information. My stomach started to churn thinking about it, but I wasn't sure why. Mrs. Jenkins's obvious unease with the news wasn't helping matters.

Ashe took Adonia to the Feed as his Forfeit, just as Cole took me. Adonia survived, as I did. But how? Who was her anchor?

"You said her soldier died *before* the Feed?" I asked.

"No. That was the awful part. He was captured by the

other side, and everyone believed he was dead. But he wasn't. He was a prisoner of war."

I nodded. That's how Adonia survived. With an anchor, just like I did. Did she know he was still alive? Is that why she chose to Return to the Surface?

But her Everliving betrayed her. Instead of letting Adonia have her final six months on the Surface, Ashe turned her over to the queen. The story didn't have anything to do with me.

Did it?

And did Cole know what Ashe had done? Did he know Ashe had essentially killed his Forfeit?

Did he know Adonia?

"Mrs. Jenkins, do you have any more information about her? Anything that would tell us what exactly made her so special? Special enough for the queen to kill?"

She set down her teacup. "Everything I have on Adonia, and all of the Daughters of Persephone, is in the basement. I doubt we'll find anything. I've been through it so many times. But we can try."

I followed her down the stairs and paused when I reached the bottom. The entire basement was filled with stacks and stacks of books and papers and boxes. New-looking moving boxes butted up against ancient-looking wooden crates.

How were we supposed to find anything?

Mrs. Jenkins navigated the mess as if she had memorized it. She held up a framed picture box with two small circular paintings inside of it. They looked like cameos. I'd seen similar ones in period movies set in the late eighteen hundreds.

"This is Adonia," she said. "And this was her soldier, Nathanial. She kept this cameo with her always. They fell in love in England, but he went missing during a colonial battle. In India, I think. He'd been gone for months when Adonia met Ashe. She was a wreck." She held up the cameo of the soldier for me to see. "When Nathanial was found, he asked his rescuers to send the cameo to her, along with a medal he'd been awarded and a few of his other possessions." She handed me the frame and started thumbing through some of the papers in a box at her feet.

The painting of Adonia was beautiful. She had blond hair and blue eyes, and skin the color of porcelain. I pictured the current queen, with her fiery red hair, hunting Adonia down and draining her so completely that all that was left of her was a jar of ashes.

"If Adonia had become queen and had granted her ancestral line eternal life, would you even have been born?"

She looked up. "The queen can only grant eternal life to those who have passed on. The Everliving can't have children. We are descended from Adonia's sister." I shrugged and nodded, and she went on with her search. She flipped through a series of grids with dots mapped out on it. Some of the dots connected into shapes that I recognized.

"Are those constellations?" I asked.

Mrs. Jenkins nodded and continued rifling through the box. "Adonia had a passion for astronomy."

I thought back to Ashe's house and the telescope in the corner. He'd said it had sentimental value. Was it Adonia's?

Mrs. Jenkins straightened up. "Here it is," she said, holding out a metal object in her hand. "Nathanial's medal."

She handed me a worn brass medal that weighed heavy in my hand. It was two swords crossed together inside a wreath. The tips and handles of the swords poked out beyond the wreath, giving the medal a distinct, pointy shape.

"It's beautiful."

"I don't know what it's called, but I think it'd be worth a lot today—" Her voice cut off in surprise. "Is that . . . ?" I followed her gaze to the floor, where a ghostly, tattooed hand appeared.

I glanced back up at Mrs. Jenkins. "It's Cole. But I'm not done asking you questions."

"Don't go," she said. The worry in her eyes told me she was concerned about my interaction with Ashe too.

"I have to," I said. "I have to find Jack. Besides, Ashe is missing." I found myself whispering, even though I was pretty sure Cole couldn't hear us.

His hand made a rolling gesture, as if to say *Get going.*

"If I don't go now . . ."

She nodded. "I know. I'll try to . . . see what I can find out. I'll go through my things here. I can look . . ." She shrugged.

"Thank you." I walked over to the hand. "But I think that if I come back without Jack again, it will be too late."

She didn't protest.

"Can I ask you something?" I said.

"Yes."

"Why are you helping me?"

She gave me a soft smile. "Living without earthly attachments has . . . begun to lose its charm."

I smiled too. I knew that feeling. "I'll be back."

"Here," she said, pressing the medal into the palm of my hand. "Take this. May it bring you luck."

The hurried nature of our parting seemed to make us promise things to each other that we probably wouldn't have promised otherwise. Or maybe Mrs. Jenkins was beginning to like me.

Or maybe she still hoped that I would one day be queen and that I would remember her.

Nothing in either world was as it seemed.

As I grabbed Cole's hand, I had a moment to consider the symbolism of the whole thing. Cole was dragging me down to the Everneath. Over and over. And I was letting it happen. In fact, I was begging him to do it.

I landed on the ground, the debris-filled walls of wind surrounding me and reaching into the sky.

"Sleep well, Nik?" Cole said, stretching as if he was working out the kinks he'd just gotten by reaching to the Surface to get me.

His question weighed heavy on my heart since Jack hadn't appeared in my dreams. But I didn't want Cole to know. If he found out, then maybe he would give up—and I couldn't give up until I was inside the Tunnels. Until I had Jack's hand in my hand. Until I could give him my tether and help him find his way out, like Ariadne did for Theseus.

Jack wasn't dead. He wasn't. He couldn't be. But his absence last night had left a dark specter on my soul, like some Grim Reaper coming too early to claim something I wasn't about to give up. The ominous shadow entreated me to abandon my hope. I closed my eyes, willing it away. No. There was some other reason he wasn't there last night, something beyond his control. But if Cole and Max knew about it, they might think our continued trek was useless. Especially Max. He was always ready to quit.

"You okay?" he said since I hadn't answered him.

I nodded.

"What's that?" He pointed to my hand, at Nathanial's medal that Mrs. Jenkins had given to me.

My discovery at Mrs. Jenkins's house came rushing back. Ashe. Adonia. Betrayal.

"How well do you know Ashe?" I asked.

Cole seemed surprised at my question. "Well enough."

"And you trust him?"

Cole raised an eyebrow. "Implicitly. Where is this going?"

I thought about it. I wasn't quite sure how I wanted to handle this yet; I wasn't even sure exactly what it meant.

At my hesitation, Cole said, "Look, Nik. We can talk about it on the way. But right now, we have to get moving. I think we're almost to the Ring of Fire."

"How do you know?"

He lifted his head to the sky. "Smoke on the horizon. Let's

get your tether and go. Tell a story, and make it a good one."

Suddenly every other worry faded away, and I wanted nothing more than to get closer to Jack. Ashe wasn't even here, so what did it matter if I trusted him or not?

Jack hadn't shown up in my dream, and that was all that mattered. I needed to get my tether back, and fast; and there was one short, sweet story that I knew could succeed the fastest.

I grabbed Cole's hands in mine. "Did I ever tell you about the very first time Jack kissed me?"

SOPHOMORE YEAR
The Surface. Park City High School.

The hallway was filled with students, but they all faded into the background. Jack had just confronted me about my feelings for him. In my mind, nobody else existed anymore.

"Tell me, friend," Jack said, his fingertips grazing mine as people shuffled past us in the hallway. "Is there more for us?"

I looked at my feet. "There's everything for us."

He didn't answer. The bell was about to ring. I could tell because the hallway began to clear out, and yet Jack remained quiet.

Despite the butterflies that had expanded out of my stomach and now filled my entire body, I ventured a look at Jack.

He had the funniest expression. He smiled in a knowing way, as if he had suddenly gotten a glimpse at our entire future and it was amazing. I wasn't sure he would ever move from that spot.

I tugged on his hand and said, "We should—"

"Yes," he interrupted.

His fingers closed around mine, and he pulled me down the hall.

"Um, we're going the wrong way," I said. "My English class is that way." I pointed behind us.

He didn't let up. With his fingers in a death grip around my hand, as if at any moment we would be ripped apart, he led me around the corner, down a side hall, and finally into a dark nook that held a drinking fountain.

The walk to this point had given me exactly enough time to wonder what I had just agreed to. What I had just done to jeopardize the most important friendship in my life.

He faced me, and I backed against the wall.

"Wait," I said.

"What?" He immediately dropped my hands and stiffened, as if we had been discovered doing something illegal.

I let out a shaky breath. "I just . . . Your friendship is everything to me."

He smiled and took a step closer. "I feel the same way."

I put my hand against his chest. "But . . ."

"But?" He raised an eyebrow.

"But . . ." I couldn't find the words. I couldn't figure out how to express my concerns; and I'd waited for this moment for so long, I wasn't sure I wanted to. "But . . ."

His lips turned up in a sly smile. "Becks, can we move on from 'but'?"

I bit my lip and tried again. "We could go back."

"Back to where?"

"Back to ten minutes ago. Back to before you said anything."

His smile fell, and he pulled away a little bit. "You don't want this." It was a statement, not a question.

I leaned my head back until it rested on the brick wall. How could I explain that it was all I ever wanted? It was all I'd been able to think about for months now.

I looked at his face again. His bright eyes had become dull; his shoulders, which could've carried the world two minutes ago, now slumped.

What was I thinking? I was thinking too much. That was the problem. That was always the problem.

Before I could think anymore, I grabbed his shirt and pulled him toward me. I kissed him. Lightly. Quickly.

I sank back, but he gathered me close to him again, and then his lips were on mine. He pulled me tighter against him, his hands pushing against my back; but he wasn't satisfied with our nearness until he pushed me right up against the wall.

I was clawing at him just as much. My fingers tangled in his hair, then grabbed at his shirt, pulling him closer. His kiss became deeper; his lips urged my mouth open.

I didn't care that we'd caught a few stares from students passing by. I didn't care that the bell to begin class rang. I didn't care that everything between us had changed.

All I cared about was the fact that no matter how hard I tried, I couldn't get any closer to Jack.

NOW

The Everneath. The Ring of Wind.

When I finished my story, Cole's face was blank. He wasn't looking at me. Instead, he was looking at my tether, which was stronger than it had ever appeared before.

We all stared at my tether. Which is why none of us noticed the Wanderer at our backs.

"Run!" Max said.

We took off running, following my tether.

"Why weren't you watching?" Cole shouted at Max.

"I took my eyes off our backs for two seconds!"

We darted right, then left, then right again; and then a wave of hot air struck us, searing my face with its intensity. I slowed for a moment, but Cole shoved me ahead.

"Keep going!" he commanded.

One more turn, and the dirt-colored walls of wind gave way to the strangest sight I'd ever seen.

We'd reached the Ring of Fire.

TWENTY-SIX

NOW
The Everneath. The Ring of Wind.

The final ring before the bull's-eye. The only thing standing between me and Jack.

And it was a furnace, with burning walls as high as the Grand Canyon.

My toe caught on a divot in the dirt, and I went flying to the ground. Within a split second, the Wanderer had caught up to us. But then he stopped, mesmerized by the walls of fire. His eyes traveled upward as the flames reached into the sky, dancing and crackling toward the middle of the pathway. It was as if he'd forgotten we were even there.

Cole had his hand on my arm, ready to help me up; but at the Wanderer's reaction, he paused and watched.

Keeping his eyes on the burning inferno surrounding him, the Wanderer turned to the nearest wall, took two steps toward it, and then jumped in.

I flinched as I heard a grotesque sizzling sound; then the

flames engulfed him completely, and we couldn't see anything else.

He was gone.

I looked up at Cole with my mouth open, panting. "What happened? Why would he do that?"

Cole stared at the flames, his eyes wide. "It's the fire," he said in a breathless voice. "It attracts despair." Even though he was saying the words, he was staring at the spot where the Wanderer had burned as if he couldn't believe it.

Max stood nearby. "Coming straight from the Ring of Wind, it must've taken the Wanderer by surprise. He couldn't fight it."

Cole nodded. "It's a good reminder. We have to be ready to feel the effects of the fire."

I looked from Cole to Max and back to Cole again. "You mean . . . the Wanderer felt so much despair that he just voluntarily jumped into a wall of flames?"

Nobody answered me.

"How does fire do that?"

Cole finally tore his gaze from the wall. "It's Everneath fire, which means it's linked to emotion. Fires destroy things completely. Even the things that survive it are still changed on an elemental level. They are brittle and broken and ready to snap. In this way, fire is so similar to despair. If unchecked, despair will consume every other emotion, leaving them all only fragile shells. Fire in the Everneath draws out the fire of despair inside of you."

"We have to move," Max said.

I looked at the narrow pathway, trying to forget the sizzling sound of skin burning. The flames shot out from the walls at random intervals. There would be no way to anticipate a sudden flare bursting from one side to the other. I couldn't see how we could avoid getting burned, no matter how hard we tried to stay in the middle.

The little spark of energy I had left turned to ash in the face of the fire. There was no way we wouldn't burn.

My shoulders sank. The adrenaline that had kept me going up until this point was gone. Drained.

Cole stood beside me as if he could read my thoughts. "We stay in the middle, Nik." His face was a sober mask. "We can do this. We just have to stay focused."

I closed my eyes. "How?"

"Same as we've been doing this whole time. We follow your tether."

My tether. My gaze went from the tether at my feet to the scorching pathway ahead of us. I was going to lead us down it, knowing the whole time that Jack hadn't shown up in my dreams last night. Would Cole follow if he knew the truth? Or would he say it was a lost cause?

I allowed myself only a moment of guilt that I was keeping the secret from Cole. Maybe Jack wasn't dead. But Cole would never attempt the Ring of Fire on a "maybe."

"Which way, Nik?" Cole asked. I looked at his face. He trusted me now, I thought. He would expect me to tell him the truth.

I glanced at my tether. "That way," I said, pointing down

one of the fiery corridors.

Cole nodded. "Let's move."

The going was slow. Max stayed in front, I was in the middle, and Cole brought up the rear. Our steps were careful. One wayward mistake and our shirts would get singed.

At first I was good at dodging the sparks that flew our way and staying in the middle. But the extra effort took its toll on me. After a particularly narrow section, I blinked a little too long and stepped to the side.

I heard the sizzle before I felt it. Somewhere near the right side of my face. Cole tackled me to the ground, escaped out of his leather jacket, ripped off his shirt, and smothered the flames on my arm. The whole thing took place in about a second.

When the flames were out, we sat there panting.

And then the pain hit.

I screamed and tried to rip off my sleeve, but Cole grabbed my wrist and pinned it against my side. "You'll rip the skin off too," he said.

I strained my neck, trying to see the damage; but the angle made it difficult. The fire had gotten my upper shoulder and neck.

"Is it bad?" I asked through clenched teeth.

"No." But the tightness around his eyes told a different story. "You feel the pain, right?"

I nodded, unable to get a normal sound out.

"That's good. If the burn was really deep, it would've destroyed your neurons, and your brain wouldn't get the message that it hurts."

I blew out a few breaths. "My brain definitely got the message," I said with a whimper.

"Good."

He helped me up, guiding me toward the center so I could avoid the flames that seemed to be reaching for me now, as if they were attracted to the burn. Cole put on his jacket and threw his shirt into the flames. Again I tried to crane my neck to get a good look at the damage.

"Stop looking at it," Cole commanded. "Focus on walking."

I turned to face him, and he raised an eyebrow at my appearance. "What is it?" I said.

He bit his lip. "It's okay. I always thought you should have short hair."

My hand flew up to the side of my head. I felt brittle, curly strands that fell away as I touched them.

Cole looked at me anxiously, probably wondering what my reaction would be.

I gave a halfhearted laugh, which dissolved into tears. I turned away. Seriously? It was the hair I was crying over?

No. The hair was just the breaking point.

I sniffed. And then I sank to the ground. The movement was the exact opposite of what I was telling my muscles to do. My brain was screaming at them to walk, but I couldn't move any farther.

Cole immediately crouched down and put a hand on my shoulder. "It'll grow back, Nik."

"It's not about the hair." I shoved the palms of my hands into my eyes, plugging the tears.

He put his arm around me, careful to avoid the burn, and let my head fall on his shoulder. "I know you're tired. I'm tired too. You don't have to think about making it through the labyrinth or conquering another ring. All you have to think about is putting one foot in front of the other."

"I'm trying," I said with a shaky voice. "It's my stupid legs. They won't . . . w-w-work." Now I was stuttering. What was my problem? It was *Jack* we were trying to save, and Cole was giving *me* a pep talk?

And yet here we were. My arm felt as if a pit bull had sunk in its teeth and refused to let go. My legs felt like two barrels of cement, and Cole could make me bald simply by blowing on my hair.

But my exhaustion went even further than that. "Cole, is this the despair?"

He sighed. "Don't think about it."

"I can't *not* think about it." The words were harsh and sharp.

Cole winced at the acid in my voice, and I noticed the evidence of the fire's work on his face. The darkness in his eyes. The accentuated shadows under his cheekbones. The defeat in his posture.

Max had signs of it too, in the frown lines that ran deeper than usual.

But neither of them was incapacitated by it. I wondered

how bad I looked, with half of my hair and the smoke still rising from my arm.

"Well, that's just great. How are we supposed to rally against all this despair?" I said.

Cole's lip twitched microscopically. "Now, Nik. That's the despair talking. Don't think about it."

"But—"

"Did I ever tell you about *how* I became an Everliving?" he interrupted.

"No," I said. "You never wanted to talk about it."

"Did I ever tell you I was a Viking?"

I lifted my head off his shoulder and wiped underneath my eye. "No."

"You're going to love this story." He smiled despite the strain on his face and hoisted me up to a standing position, which I wouldn't have thought was possible until I was actually standing. "This story has everything. Intrigue. Tension."

"Romance," Max interjected.

Cole rolled his eyes. And with his hand on my good shoulder, he turned me around and pointed me in the right direction, then gave my back a gentle nudge and got me going again.

"And it all started centuries ago, with a little blond boy skipping through the fields of Norway."

I turned and gave him a quizzical look, but he waved his hand in a *Watch where you're walking* sort of way.

"Yes, Nik. This jackass—who according to you has no morals—was once a little boy." His tone was light, and it was working. I was putting one foot in front of the other.

"How does a Viking get mixed up in the Everneath?" I said, my voice sounding noticeably stronger.

But he was quiet for a long time. I glanced backward to see him rolling a small, flat rock between his fingers as he used to do with his guitar pick. I realized he was probably struggling to carry on just as I was. Max called over his shoulder, "Just tell her, Cole."

Cole threw the rock, pinging it off of Max's head. Max gave an exhausted laugh and rubbed the spot the rock had hit. "It's nothing to be embarrassed about."

"Why would you be embarrassed?" I said.

Max answered. "He came over for a girl." He sounded as if he were ten years old when he said it.

I stopped. "What?"

Cole kept walking, making no attempt to slow down. I started up again.

"You were in love?" I said.

"Yes," Max answered, and at the same time Cole said, "No."

I smiled. "This is getting good. I'm totally focusing." And it was true. I was. The pain in my shoulder seemed duller and the cement in my legs more manageable. "Keep going."

"He fell for her hard," Max said. "She came up in a skimpy little Viking outfit—"

"Shut up, Max!" Cole said, exasperated but grinning. "I'll tell the story."

"Good," Max said.

"Her name was Gynna, and she wasn't wearing a skimpy little Viking outfit. There's no such thing as a skimpy little Viking outfit. Vikings are cold. Anyway, I was working as an apprentice to one of the merchants in my village when she showed up one day. And it went on from there."

He was quiet again, and it sounded as if he was finished. But I wanted more. "That's not a good story. That's girl meets boy. I want the meat."

"There is no meat."

I whipped around, and Cole nearly ran into me. I put a finger on his chest. "For a split second there I forgot about the blistering pain in my shoulder and the fireballs licking at my feet. Unless you want to make a permanent home in the Ring of Fire, you'd better keep talking."

A smile played at the edges of his lips. "Whatever you say."

I turned around and started walking again, and Cole continued. "Gynna came to our storefront. She looked lost. She had a bag full of money, all sorts of coins from all over the world. Coins I had never seen. Master Olnaf ordered me to take her to the back room, where we kept all of our reference books, to try to document each of her coins. We spent a lot of days in that room."

"Is that a euphemism?" I looked back.

He raised an eyebrow. "If by 'euphemism' you mean we spent hours and hours researching the origins of ancient coins, then yes, it's a euphemism. Anyway, she seemed interested in me. She was the first person to ask me questions about my life, my family, my dreams. And every time she was near me, my worries seemed to disappear. Now, of course, I know she was able to siphon off the worst of my emotions. But at the time I was fooled into thinking it was friendship."

"You mean love," Max interjected.

I glanced back and caught Cole glaring at Max. "Yes. I was in love with her. And when she asked me to follow her to the Everneath, I didn't hesitate. I had no family. My parents were dead, and my brothers had been shipped off to different parts of the country."

"So she took you to Feed on you?" I never would've imagined that Cole had been through a Feed.

"No. She took me for the sole purpose of bringing me over. To become an Everliving. But it wasn't long before I realized why she had done it."

"And why was that?"

"She wanted out."

I paused. "Out? Out of what? Out of the Everneath? Couldn't she just go to the Surface?"

"She wanted out of . . . immortality."

"What do you mean?"

He exhaled. "She didn't want to live like this anymore. She wanted to break her own heart."

"Well then, why didn't she? Didn't she have a pick, or something, like you?"

"Yes, but simply breaking her Surface heart wouldn't kill

her. Everlivings have two hearts."

I stopped dead in my tracks and stared at him. "*Two* hearts?" Was that why the Wanderer had used that odd phrase *Surface heart*? "You mean you have more than one heart?"

"Yes, that's traditionally what the number two means. When we become Everliving, our hearts split in two, creating a Surface one, which we carry with us, and an Everneath one, which goes straight to a vault held in the High Court. They are two halves of a whole heart."

"So . . . that night at your condo . . . when we tried to . . ."

"Kill me by breaking my heart? I remember. No, even if you had broken my pick, you wouldn't have killed me. All you would have done is made it impossible for me to travel back and forth between the Everneath and the Surface."

"Why didn't you tell me?"

"Why would I?" For a moment, a sad smile appeared on his face. "It was obvious you thought you were killing me. And you didn't hesitate. I was hoping, someday, you might feel guilty about that, by the way. But maybe I have misplaced faith in your humanity."

I looked into his eyes. I'd always thought I'd missed my chance to kill him. And now to find out I hadn't even been close?

And to ask myself the tougher question: Would I do it again? If I had the chance to kill him . . . would I?

If it came down to Jack's life or Cole's, there'd be no question.

"I'm sorry," I said. Sorry that I had been so willing to kill him, and sorry too that I would do it again if it would save Jack. Hopefully it would never come to that.

Max called from some ways ahead. "Guys, we need to keep moving."

We started walking again. Cole was quiet, so I said, "Tell me more about Gynna. And her hearts."

"The Surface heart allows passage between the worlds. The Everneath heart holds our world together. If you imagine the Tunnels as the power source of the Everneath, then you can imagine the vault of hearts as the keystone. If an Everliving wants to give up her immortality, she has to bring a new heart to the High Court to replace the one she wants to break. It's like if an employee at a factory leaves, there's a loss of productivity. The Shades don't like losses of productivity."

It finally all clicked. "So she used your heart to replace hers. So she could leave. So she wouldn't end up a Wanderer."

"Yep. You see, it's not really a love story. But I guess there is an element of betrayal in it."

"I'm sorry," I said, and I meant it. "What happened to her?"

"Who?"

"Gynna."

"Oh, she was gone before I knew what hit me. She took her Everneath heart and left."

"Gone where, to the Surface?"

He nodded.

"Did she break both of her own hearts?"

He finally looked me in the eye. "I don't know. I never saw her again. I assume she grew old and died. So I guess the joke's on her."

He said it without an ounce of mirth, his voice caustic.

"She was crazy," Max added. "She didn't grasp the benefits of being an Everliving."

"What exactly *are* the benefits?" I said.

"Seriously?" Max let his mouth hang open for a dramatic moment. He started ticking off his fingers. "Eternal life. Eternal *youth*. A fountain in the center of every Common that makes you forget all of your worries."

I remembered that fountain. I'd seen it at the slaughter.

Max went on. "Plenty of time to hone our musical skills. A paved road to rock stardom."

"A paved road how?" I asked.

"All we need is a room and a captive audience . . . ," he said.

My stomach sank as I remembered what it felt like watching them perform. "You mean an audience whose emotions you can easily manipulate."

"Exactly. There's nothing like that breakout moment, when some influential guy in a suit looks at you and thinks he's found the next Beatles." Max looked away wistfully. Cole walked next to me in silence. His head was down. I'd never heard him talk about being an Everliving like Max was talking now.

"Is that why you spend all of your time on the Surface? Because music isn't allowed in the Everneath?"

Max answered. "Yep. That's what makes us different. And it's worth it. We've had that 'breakout'"—Max made air quotes—"moment on the Surface several times now, in different generations; right, Cole?"

Cole gave half a smile. "Right. But you're forgetting the best part of immortality."

"What?" I asked.

"The absence of that one part of your body that makes all the dumb-ass decisions. The beating heart. The place where emotions reside." He said it with equal parts disdain and awe.

We were quiet. Cole seemed as if he was done talking, so I turned to Max.

"So why did you come over?" I said to Max.

He turned around and started walking backward. He spread his arms out wide. "For love!" He had to jerk his hands back in when they got too close to the flames.

Cole broke out in spasms of laughter.

"What is it?"

Cole looked at me. "*I* brought him over. Ages ago."

"I meant for love of music," Max said with a grin.

"Careful how loud you say that," Cole said, but he was still smiling.

"Why do the Shades hate music?" I asked.

"Because they can't control it," Cole said. "Music is full of emotion, so it's unstable. They're wary of energy they can't control."

"At least, that's Cole's theory," Max said. "Nobody really

knows. They only know what happens if the 'no music' rule is broken. . . ."

Max turned back around and jogged forward to scout ahead. We walked for a while in silence, the conversation having counteracted the despair just enough to keep our momentum going.

My mind kept going back to Cole's story about Gynna. I wanted to say something to Cole, but I'd already told him I was sorry, and I didn't know what else to say.

The truth was, I was in a strange place. I felt sorry for Cole despite all the pain he'd caused me. I didn't like it. For so long I'd been content and sure in my hatred of Cole. But now to learn how he'd been betrayed . . .

Actually, betrayal seemed to be a theme with the Everliving. I reached into my pocket and felt Nathanial's medal in there. Cole seemed to be in a sharing mood now. Maybe it was the right time to ask him about Adonia.

"Cole?"

"Nikki?" he replied.

"You know Ashe . . ." I paused as I figured out the question I wanted to ask. I wasn't sure I wanted to reveal that I knew Ashe had his Forfeit killed. But I wanted to find out Cole's place in it all.

"Yes, I seem to recall him."

"Do you think he escaped the Siren somehow?"

Cole sighed. "I don't know. I hope so."

"You said you did something for him. And that he owes you."

"Yes." He wasn't offering anything.

"Well, what did you do that he would owe you?"

He was quiet for a moment. I could feel Max's eyes on us. "I helped him find something he had lost."

My breath caught in my throat. *Something he had lost.* Something, or someone. Adonia.

"What did he lose?"

Cole hesitated. "It doesn't matter now, Nik."

It mattered to me. "This thing he lost, was it a person?"

Cole grabbed my elbow and jerked me back. "What did you say?" He stared at me, apprehensive.

I stood my ground. "Was her name Adonia?"

At the mention of her name, Cole closed his eyes. "How do you know?"

"I visited Mrs. Jenkins. Adonia was her ancestor. She has her ashes in an urn above her fireplace."

Cole opened his eyes and watched me. "It was a long time ago."

"You hunted her down? And turned her location over to Ashe?"

"It was a unique circumstance."

"You were a different person then?" I said, not even trying to mask the sarcasm. "You'd never do it again?"

"I *didn't* do it again!" The quiet after his outburst was intense. Cole backed away from me. "You'll notice *you're* not in a jar on someone's fireplace," he said.

"Were you there?"

"Was I where?"

"Were you there when the queen found Adonia?"

He shut his eyes again. "No. But I hunted her down. Told Ashe where he could find her. And he told the queen."

"And you knew she'd be killed."

He opened his eyes. "Yes," he said simply. "But, Nik." He stepped forward and put his hands on my good shoulder. "I didn't do it to you."

Staring at him right then, I didn't put voice to the word in my head. *Yet.* He hadn't betrayed me to the queen *yet.*

TWENTY-SEVEN

NOW

The Everneath. The Ring of Fire.

Silence filled the next few minutes as we traversed the fiery corridors, dodging the occasional rogue flare. I kept a steady pace until we came to yet another archway. The others passed through without hesitation, but something about it made me stop. An uneasy feeling gripped me as I looked up at it. We'd already been through several archways, but this one was different. The flames at the top formed strange shapes. Mostly round ones, with stems sticking out.

As I passed underneath, I finally realized what the shapes looked like: fruit. Grapes, apples, cherries, all formed out of flames. I realized how long it had been since I'd eaten anything, and yet I'd never felt hungry. Mrs. Jenkins told me not to eat, but she didn't have to worry. Until now, eating had been the last thing on my mind. But as the archway faded behind us, I felt a new hole in my stomach.

I tried to think of something else. I focused on the story

of Ashe and Adonia. How was I supposed to feel about it all, knowing Cole's role in her death? He didn't do it to me. But he could. Would that possibility be hanging over my head for my entire life?

His actions had resulted in someone else's death. But that was a way of life here. And Adonia was headed to the Tunnels anyway. Was I excusing his behavior because my feelings for him had changed? With everything we'd been through down here, it was hard to remember that for so long Cole had been an adversary. His history with Adonia simply reminded me of what Cole's role was supposed to be.

But I couldn't help thinking again that despite his protests, he would've made an excellent hero in somebody else's story.

We didn't say anything else about Adonia or Ashe. In fact, we didn't speak much at all, until suddenly Max stopped.

"I'm hungry," he said.

"Me too," Cole said.

I looked from Max to Cole, confused. I thought of my own empty stomach and how I'd become acutely aware of it only after passing under the archway with the fruit. But the hunger wasn't strong enough to make me stop. "Do you mean . . . hungry hungry? As in, for food?"

"Fooooood," Cole said, drawing out the word.

"But, I thought you guys didn't need to eat. Down here."

Cole shook his head and gave me a pacifying smile, as if I were a toddler. "Of course we need to eat. And it's been a long time."

Max rubbed his stomach. "Potato chips," he said in a moan.

I looked behind us. We'd been standing in one place for too long, and up until this moment, Cole and Max had been the ones saying we needed to keep moving.

"Let's go, boys," I said. "Remember, we're in a hurry."

They looked at me as if I were speaking in Latin. I pulled on Cole's hand, but he didn't budge.

Did the fruit arch have a stronger effect on them than it did on me? Did I make a wrong turn by going under it? I thought I'd been watching my tether the whole time. But maybe in my obsession with the Ashe-and-Adonia story, I'd missed something.

"Stay here," I said, which was pointless because they looked as if they'd never move again. I ran back toward the arch to see if we'd taken a wrong turn or if there was another way we could go, and that's when I saw them.

Wanderers. More than a few. Walking in single file to avoid the flames.

"Crap," I muttered. I darted back down the path toward Cole and Max. They were in the middle of a fight, each accusing the other of forgetting to pack a snack bag. "Guys, we have to move now. Wanderers are coming."

They didn't even look up. They hadn't even noticed I'd been gone.

"Guys! Move!"

Cole shot me an annoyed look. "Eating should be our number-one priority, don't you think, Nik?"

Exasperated, I put my hands on their backs and shoved them forward. They took maybe two steps before they stopped again.

Whatever was happening, it was affecting them but not me.

"Crap . . . crap," I said, spinning around, trying to think of a way to get them moving. The ground was empty of anything except dirt. My pockets held a cell phone and Nathanial's medal. I hadn't thought to bring an apple I could use to entice them forward.

"Crap!"

The Wanderers hadn't been moving fast, but I knew they had to be right on top of us now.

"Cole! Max! Move!"

By now they were ignoring my existence completely.

I looked down at my feet and realized I hadn't counted one thing in my list of assets.

My projection.

Cole always said my projection was strong enough to be tangible. Maybe if I focused on it, I could make another projection, one that could help us.

I closed my eyes and focused on an object. It couldn't be too complicated. There wasn't enough time.

With every ounce of my energy, I focused on a simple image: a stick.

I felt a tiny whoosh of energy leave my body, and when I opened my eyes, there, lying next to my tether, was a stick.

I crouched down, put my hand around it, and grabbed it. It was real!

I shoved the pointy end into the flames of the wall to my right and left it there until I saw a faint red glow at the end. When I took it out, the end was charred, and the tip glowed red. A tiny flame materialized.

And right then the first of the Wanderers appeared from around a bend.

I faced Cole and Max. "Sorry, guys."

I lightly touched the hot poker to Max's back. He screamed and ran forward. Cole looked at him with an amused smile on his lips, then I did the same thing to Cole's back, angling it under the hem of his jacket. He lurched forward.

We ran this way for several long minutes, and eventually I didn't have to prod them as much. They were sprinting. So fast that I had to work to keep up with them, and even then I was losing them around corners.

"Wait!" I called out; but they didn't hear me, or they ignored me.

I dropped the stick, and it disappeared in a poof. My tether was pointing in the direction I should be going, but it wasn't following where Max and Cole went.

I couldn't lose them. Digging in my feet, I scrambled around turns and juts in the pathway, catching glimpses of Cole's black leather jacket.

"Wait!" I screamed.

Finally, I turned a particularly acute corner and stopped

dead in my tracks. There, in the center of a large chamber surrounded by the fire walls, was an ornate wooden table with a
large bowl of fruit.

Bent over the bowl, shoving apples and bananas into their
mouths, were Cole and Max.

"No!" I screamed, but it was too late. They'd both already
swallowed.

Cole stood upright and looked at me for a split second, recognition of what he had done painted on his face.

"Nik." The word was all he got out before he collapsed to
the ground. Max followed moments later.

I heard noises coming from behind me. The Wanderers.

The only other exit from the chamber was on the opposite
side. I couldn't face the Wanderers by myself. I raced across,
leaped over Cole, and hid in the exit behind the wall of fire.

I said a little prayer. *Please pass us by. Please choose another
way.*

The wait seemed interminable. I convinced myself that too
much time had passed. That the Wanderers had indeed taken
a different route, one that led away from this chamber.

And then the first foot appeared in the entrance, followed
by the face of the Wanderer who had been leading the pack.
He eyed Cole and Max, lying there immobile on the ground,
as if they were fresh meat.

One by one the wanderers filed in, and I got a look at just
how many had been following us.

Twenty. At least.

They swarmed over the lifeless bodies of Cole and Max.

I ducked behind the wall out of sight.

What do I do? What do I do?

I couldn't take them all on by myself. Max and Ashe could barely handle one at a time, and they were much stronger than I was. I looked down at my tether. Could the cattle prod approach work with them?

Again, no. Too many.

Confronting them would never work. I needed to get them away from Cole and Max, and then I could outrun them.

I needed a distraction. But what?

I thought back to everything I knew about Wanderers. They were missing their Surface hearts, but it wasn't as if I could tell them I had twenty extras just around the corner. It had to be something that wouldn't require a lot of thought on their part.

Then I remembered what Cole had told me. Wanderers could make a meal out of Everlivings, but they wouldn't be able to resist the freshest energy from an actual human.

My tether was a manifestation of my energy. When I'd first come to the Everneath, my energy had spilled out all over. I could do that again.

I stepped into the chamber, closed my eyes . . . and focused on everything about Jack that I loved.

Every memory, every quirk of a smile, every wink of his eye, every embrace, every kiss. I jammed them into my head all at once. Every word he'd ever said to me, the first time he'd snuck into my bedroom, the way he'd held me and told me he loved me in his uncle's ski cottage. Everything.

When I opened my eyes, I was surrounded by a cloud of memories: pictures of Jack and me, movies of him under the tree at the cemetery, waiting for me at his locker, spotting me in the crowd from the bench at the football game.

His image was everywhere, swirling around me. It didn't form the canyon in the Fiery Furnace that it had the first time I'd let it all out, probably because I had more control now, or because I didn't have as much energy. But it was enough. Beyond the energy cloud I could see that every Wanderer was turned toward me, and only a split second passed before they lunged for me.

I turned and took off running.

I ran and ran, but my legs were aching. Pure adrenaline kept me going, but I was losing focus. I turned around to see how far ahead of them I was and ran smack into a dead end of fire.

Pain tore into my chest. I recoiled from the wall and again heard that sizzling noise. I'd reacted quickly enough that the burns wouldn't be as severe as the last one, but I still had to pat out the tiny flames that had jumped onto my shirt. How far had I gone? Were Cole and Max dead? Would I ever find them again? Every turn I made was one turn farther away from them. But at least the Wanderers were following me and not feasting on them.

I backtracked and then turned down another corridor, and that's when I saw something reaching up above the wall of fire on my left. It was a dark wall shooting high into the sky. Not made of flames or wind or water, but made of black stone.

I took every turn that led me to the left, and several seconds later I exited the maze and found myself standing on grass in front of the giant black stone wall. I glanced at my tether, but it pointed toward the wall. I looked to either side, trying to figure out which way to run, but maybe fifty yards away in each direction I saw dark figures swirling in the air.

Shades.

I bowed my head. A solid wall in front of me, Shades to the left and right, and a maze of fire behind me filled with Wanderers.

There was nowhere left to run.

I sank to the grass. "I'm sorry, Jack."

TWENTY-EIGHT

NOW

The Everneath. The Ring of Fire.

$\mathcal{I}$ wasn't about to run toward the Shades, so I turned around and faced what I knew was coming out of the maze.

I didn't have to wait long. The herd of Wanderers appeared from the Ring of Fire. There was no escape. I shut my eyes, and before I knew it, they had piled on top of me as if I were the opposing quarterback in a football game.

I couldn't tell which Wanderer was feeding, but I felt my energy leaving my body, as if I were in a giant vacuum that was sucking out everything that made me alive.

The hole I'd felt when just one Wanderer had fed on me was amplified throughout my entire body. A dark cloud appeared behind my eyelids, and I knew it wouldn't be long before I passed out. There were too many.

I heard them growling, groaning with satisfaction as if they were at a buffet. One of them, in the heat of the frenzy, started to gnaw at my shoulder. Another at my fingertips.

When they drained me completely, would they finish me off?

Panicked voices reached my ears. Cole and Max . . . and someone else?

I couldn't tell. Another moment and the pain stopped. Maybe they had reached a point where they had taken away all feeling whatsoever. The neurons no longer shot to my brain. I was left with only my mind, and one last thought.

It was over so quickly. I'd made it through the maze. I'd made it to the bull's-eye. I was so close to Jack. So close. So close to seeing my brother again. And my dad.

But in a split second, I'd failed them all.

The darkness kept me reeling in a blackout haze for a long time. Or maybe it was only seconds. But when I opened my eyes, expecting some sort of afterlife, I caught a glimpse of that same tall black wall. The same flames from the maze.

The Wanderers were no longer on top of me.

A pungent odor hit my nose, like the smell of burned, decaying flesh, and I coughed and then dry heaved.

Once I'd stopped, I saw the blurry outline of a figure holding something with a flame on the end. It looked like a torch. He was waving it toward the ground, lighting things on fire, and then he would wave it in the air. I squeezed my eyes shut and then blinked a few more times. When I opened them, the image came into focus. A familiar face . . .

Ashe! Was it really him? I couldn't believe it. He'd escaped the Siren. He must've found Cole and Max and somehow revived them. He had the torch in one hand and his sword, red with blood, in the other. There was another figure with a torch too. Max. He was on the other side of me. They were standing over bodies of Wanderers, bringing the lit end of their torches down to the bodies and then waving them toward something dark and swirling in the distance.

Right then I realized someone was stroking my face, and soon I became aware of other sensations. Especially the pain in my chest.

"Nik?"

I could see Cole's face in the periphery of my vision. I opened my mouth to speak, but I didn't have any energy to form the words.

"Hey," he said. "I thought I'd lost you."

He glanced toward Max and Ashe. "The Shades are closing in. I'm going to kick you to the Surface." *The Surface?* I shook my head as violently as I could. It was still a weak effort. "Shh. It's the only way. Max and Ashe can keep them at bay for now with the fire. But you have no energy. You have to go to the Surface to recover. And it's almost night. You have to be there for Jack."

I tried to get words to my mouth, but it wasn't working. I tried to grab Cole's hand, but my arms felt as if they were made of cement.

"It's okay, Nik. We're going to try to hide from the Shades overnight. We can go into the maze again. The Shades hate fire. They won't follow. And then in the morning we'll bring you back down and regroup."

But Jack hadn't appeared in my last dream. If he wasn't appearing, no amount of me sleeping could help him. He was out of time. He'd been out of time for a while. Cole couldn't kick me out. Here in the bull's-eye, I knew time ran slower. This was where the Feed caverns were, where a hundred years only equaled six months on the Surface.

Now that we were here, we couldn't go back to Surface time. We couldn't go back in the maze.

I would lose Jack.

I used every last drop of energy I could muster to bring my teeth down to my lips to form an *F* sound. "Feed me." The words were so soft, I couldn't even hear them.

But Cole had been watching my lips. "What?"

I could tell from his confused expression that he knew what I'd said.

"Feed me," I said again. Taking in a deep breath, I put the tip of my tongue on the roof of my mouth to form the next words. "Jack's gone . . . from my dreams. No time."

Realization dawned on Cole's face. "Why didn't you tell me?"

The blackness started to invade my eyesight, and I fought to stay conscious. "No giving up," I said.

Cole looked up desperately at Ashe and Max, flanking us, lighting fires. They wouldn't burn forever.

His eyes met mine again. "If we don't go back into the maze, we'll be surrounded by Shades."

I could only nod.

He lifted my head even closer. "And that might be it. If we can't hide in the maze, it could be our last stand."

I blinked and nodded again.

It hit me what I was demanding of Cole. Here we were, about to face the Shades, and I was asking him to make himself weaker by feeding me. I was asking him to stay and fight instead of run for the relative safety of the maze.

He pressed his lips together, his face showing his resolve, then dipped his head down and put his lips on mine.

That same whoosh of energy that I'd felt when I'd kissed him in the Siren's lair came rushing through me, or, more accurately, from him to me.

He moved his lips against mine, pulling me even closer to him, supporting all of my upper body with his arms.

A scene slipped into my mind. The view from a stage, with fans on the floor below, jumping and dancing, their hands in the air. Only one out of the sea of faces was clear. My face. I was near the back, moving to the music but not as animatedly as the fans around me. Cole watched me, only breaking my gaze to glance down at his guitar strings.

Euphoria overshadowed any other emotion; and I realized I was feeling what Cole was feeling on that night, and part of it was because I was watching him play. It was a rush for him.

Max started yelling and Cole pulled away, and again I was in the Everneath.

"Cole!" Max said. "We need to get back in the maze—"

His voice cut off when he saw us and realized what had just happened.

"We're not going back," Cole said. The color had drained from his face, and his cheeks looked hollower. I wondered if he knew which memory he had just shared.

I felt strong. I disentangled myself from his arms and stood then reached down to pull Cole up after me.

"We're making a stand," I said.

Ashe's eyebrows shot up, but he composed himself quickly and reached into his pocket. "We'll have a better chance with this."

He pulled out a note. My note. My *Ever Yours* token.

"Where did you find it?" I said incredulously.

"In the maze. The wind had carried it over several corridors."

"I can't believe it!" I grabbed the note and pressed it to my palm. "Finally, fate is on our side. We can't fail now."

Cole gave me a tired smile. Ashe and Max looked at me as if I were bonkers.

"Whatever you're going to do, make it fast," Ashe said. The torch in his hand barely held a flame, and several Shades blocked him from the wall of fire. Max's torch had already died out, and the three of us were huddled behind Ashe and his torch, which was now more like a candle.

"Can we fight them?" I asked Cole.

"We can't even grab them," he replied. "They're made up of a different substance entirely."

We backed against the dark stone wall. My tether pointed to the right, but the Shades had formed a semicircle around us. Every way was blocked. Ashe waved the torch wildly, but the Shades were venturing ever closer.

The last remnant of the flame disappeared, and Ashe threw aside the torch, swearing. He pulled the sword out from the sheath at his back.

"Which way do you need to go?" Ashe asked, looking over his shoulder.

"To the right," Cole said.

Ashe eyed the Shades at our right . . . and then he charged. He swung his sword wildly. It cut through the Shades as if they were made of smoke. None of them even flinched away enough to give us room to run.

He threw the sword to the ground, and right then the closest two Shades darted toward him.

I don't know if it was a reflex action or what, but Ashe made a fist and swung toward the place where their faces would be if they had heads.

And he made contact.

The two Shades flew back from the blows from Ashe's fist. They landed on the ground in a heap.

Everyone froze for a split second. Obviously we weren't the only ones shocked that Ashe could fight them.

And then Ashe's fists were flying.

"Go!" he shouted, making an open pocket in the midst of the Shades to our right.

We didn't stop to figure out what had happened. We just

sprinted along the wall, on the wide strip of grass that separated the wall from the Ring of Fire.

My tether grew darker, as if it was urging us forward. "Keep going!"

Up ahead, something shimmered on the horizon. It looked like a small lake.

I started to veer to the right, figuring that the best way to pass it would be between the lake and the stone wall; but as I veered, my tether dimmed, and the pointed end tugged counterclockwise, toward the lake.

Maybe the best way was to the left, between the lake and the Ring of Fire; but when I veered left, the tether dimmed again and tugged clockwise, again pointing to the lake.

"It's pointing to the water!" I said to Cole, who was running beside me.

He shook his head. "Can't be. The Tunnels aren't in a lake."

The closer we got to the body of water, the more my hope plummeted. The side of the lake butted up against the black wall on one side and the Ring of Fire on the other side.

There was no way around it. But I knew what the water did to people here. There was no way I could swim across it. Even Cole couldn't. The water would make us crazy, until we drowned in it.

We slowed to a stop just outside the reach of the lapping water.

Max caught up with us moments later. We turned around. Ashe was booking it toward us, followed by several more

Shades. I couldn't count how many because they swirled together, joining and separating as they pursued us.

There was one exit point from the Ring of Fire right near us. I wondered why my tether wasn't pointing to it.

I motioned to the exit and tugged on Cole's sleeve. Maybe we could take shelter in the maze for a few moments and then come back out past the lake. We took two steps toward the fire.

Cole saw her before I did. I was watching his face, trying to gauge if he had enough energy to last ten seconds in the maze. His eyes widened as he stared ahead. He skidded to a stop, and I turned to follow his gaze.

Stepping out of the maze in high-heeled black boots and glowing white robes was a woman with fire-red hair, pale white skin, and dark, ruby lips.

I told my feet to stop, but it was as if they were working in slow motion. I slid to the ground at her feet. She glared at me, and I scrambled backward, trying to get my clumsy legs to put as much distance between her and me as I could.

It was the queen.

She smiled, showing teeth that were whiter than the summer clouds in Park City.

Cole grabbed my arm and yanked me to him and away from her. The Shades that had been pursuing us went still. I could hear my own blood pulsing in my ears.

Ashe and Max coiled, as if ready to run for it, but then Max thought better of it and lowered his head toward the queen in a subservient bow. Ashe watched him and then did the same. Cole's breaths came out in anxious, shallow pants. We stood there, the lake to our right, the stone wall to our backs, the Shades to our left, and the queen of the Everneath in front of us.

I couldn't tear my eyes away from her face, and I remembered how she had so calmly obliterated that man in the square.

He became red mist. With a nod from her, I would become a cloud of red mist.

Cole squeezed my arm, and I realized I was shaking uncontrollably.

"I heard someone was trying to come through," she said in a voice that was amplified as if she were speaking into a microphone. "I had to see for myself."

Cole pulled me back and stepped in front of me. It was the wrong move.

Her piercing eyes tracked him like a hawk's. "Who are you trying to protect? Show her to me."

I peeked out from behind Cole.

She studied my face. "Ah. The human from the Ouros square. Tell me, human. Why did you come here?"

I didn't answer. I couldn't. My voice was paralyzed in the face of the queen. I had no idea what to say. Telling her about Jack in the Tunnels was out of the question. Who knew what she could do to him?

Then I realized that she had no idea I'd survived the Feed. There was nothing to give me away.

Except my tether.

I glanced down at it. Still pointed directly into the middle of the lake. Cole stood close enough to me to partially absorb the tether and block it from the queen's view.

"Speak, girl. I'm used to having my questions answered."

I couldn't let her see the tether. I ducked my head behind him again and closed the distance between me and Cole so the tether completely disappeared.

I showed my face and forced my mouth to make words. "I wanted to become an Everliving . . . Your Majesty. To be with him." I tilted my head toward Cole. "But he didn't want me. So I tried to get down here by myself, through the Shop-n-Go; but he caught me. He promised he would make me like him, then he betrayed me. I escaped to the maze, and I've been running ever since."

The queen looked from my face to Cole's, then to Max's and Ashe's. Her gaze stayed on Ashe's face for a moment longer than the rest of us, but she quickly turned back to me.

"Then why is he protecting you now?"

Cole spoke up. "Because, Your Majesty, she doesn't deserve to die just for being foolish. I was going to take away her memories and drop her on the Surface."

I glanced at Cole. Good thinking.

The queen narrowed her eyes and then shrugged. "Shades, take them away. We'll feed them to the Everlivings of Ouros."

"Wait!" Cole shouted. "You have to believe us!"

"What does it matter if I believe you? You still face the same fate."

"But I love her!" Cole said.

The queen froze. I held my breath.

She took one step toward Cole. Then one more. "Love doesn't matter here."

She gestured with her arm as if inviting the Shades to come and get us, and that's when I saw something dark on her inner wrist. A tattoo. A symbol of some sort. She held out her arm for a few long moments, so I got a good look at the mark.

Two swords, crossed. Embedded inside a circular wreath.

The tattooed swords. The indictment on love. Something clicked, but before I could do anything about it, Ashe charged the queen, his sword drawn in front of him. He swung it back, like a baseball player would swing a bat, and let it fly right for the queen's chest. It made contact with something, but it wasn't the queen. It was suddenly embedded in the trunk of a tree that had appeared out of nowhere but now stood between Ashe and the queen.

Ashe tried to pull his sword out of the wood, but his efforts were in vain.

With a snap of her fingers, the queen made the tree disappear, and Ashe's sword fell straight to the ground.

Why would he charge the queen? Sure, he had success against the Shades, but did he really think he could take her on? She picked the sword up with two fingers, as if she were too delicate to grab it by the hilt, then she tossed it into the lake.

Strangely, it didn't make a splash. It just disappeared. I stared at the surface of the water. It looked too glassy. Too calm. No ripples from the sword. Nobody else noticed.

The queen stepped closer to Ashe. "I'll save you for last, brave man."

She started to turn away, and the Shades moved toward us.

"Wait!" I called out.

She paused with an eyebrow raised. "What?"

I thought fast. "I'm really a messenger. For you, Your Majesty."

She made a fist, and at the signal, the Shades again were still. "A messenger from whom?" The tone of her voice was skeptical, and I knew I had just one chance. I only hoped I wasn't mistaken about the tattoo on her wrist.

But I felt the medal in my pocket. I wasn't wrong.

"From the person who anchored you."

"And who would that be?"

I took a deep breath, praying that my gamble would pay off. "Nathanial."

TWENTY-NINE

NOW

The Everneath. The Ring of Fire.

*E*verything went quiet. Even the crackle from the flames of the Ring of Fire grew soft. Cole looked at me, shocked. He had no idea what I was doing. I wasn't sure I did either.

I thought back to every conversation I'd had with Mrs. Jenkins, everything I knew about the queen and the High Court.

"Once you reached the High Court, you thought you'd be able to grant your entire ancestral line eternal life. That's the rumor, right? Did it work?"

She watched me with wide eyes, and I thought she would ignore me; but slowly she shook her head.

But even as the queen affirmed that it hadn't worked, she didn't seem convinced. So I pressed on.

"But you haven't given up hope that it's possible, right? You didn't love your Everliving. You didn't choose this life. All you want is what you've lost. The only man you've ever loved. But the magic of the High Court doesn't allow you to raise the dead." I was figuring it out as I was saying the words.

Her face cracked, and suddenly the image of her flickered in and out, oscillating between the tall redhead and a shorter, slighter woman with blond hair and blue eyes.

I took a tentative step forward. "I know who you are, Adonia."

Ashe flinched, and his feet stuttered as if he didn't know whether to run at her or run away from her. "Adonia," he said, breathless. "It can't be."

She turned to glare at Ashe. "Why? Because the queen killed me? When you had me hunted down like a dog?" Her gaze fell on me again. "Nathanial wasn't dead. He wasn't killed in the war. They found him, wounded and disoriented in a run-down hospital two days after I'd left with Ashe. Two days!" She pressed her lips together and looked at Ashe. "He was saying my name. He held on for the entire six months I was in the Feed with you. He never gave up hope. I knew he was alive. For the entire century I was with you, all I could see was his face."

She looked away, her mouth open, her entire body trembling as if she couldn't contain the pain. I knew that feeling.

"So you Returned to the Surface for him," I said.

She nodded, still with a faraway look in her eyes. "We were reunited for one whole day before he succumbed to his wounds." She looked down and blinked. "He died in my arms. It's like he was waiting to see me so he could say good-bye."

Everything went quiet. Even the crackling from the fire

walls dampened, as if in reverence to the grieving queen.

When she raised her head again there was fire behind her eyes, and it was directed at Ashe. "I was grieving for my love. I was trying to make amends to my family. I was ready to face the Tunnels, but that wasn't enough for you. You wanted to see me torn apart!"

"But . . ." Ashe looked at Cole helplessly. Cole seemed just as lost as he was. "But if you're here, that means you killed the queen. You took her place. And you never told me."

She looked taken aback. "You betrayed me. So I betrayed you. The last thing I wanted was for you to get anything out of it."

As they spoke, I glanced at the water behind me and slowly stepped away from Cole. My tether appeared fully, still pointing to the lake. But I no longer thought it was just a lake.

"I loved you," Ashe said. "I only did what I did because you broke my heart."

"You broke *me*," Adonia hissed.

The conversation sounded familiar. Cole and I had had it many times. And yet here we were, standing next to each other, not facing off against each other. And closer to saving Jack than we'd ever been.

I grabbed his hand, and he squeezed mine. Then I started to inch backward, toward the lake. He gave me a confused look.

"Trust me." I mouthed the words.

Had we reached that point? Where we trusted each other implicitly? If I jumped into the unknown, would he follow?

The queen had moved toward Ashe, following him step

by step away from the lake. After all they had been through, the two of them still couldn't resist the attachment that once bound them together as Forfeit and Everliving.

Ashe's voice was calming. "Donia. Be with me. You can't bring Nathanial back to life. I'm here, and he's not. Let's be together."

I froze. Ashe had said the wrong thing. At the mention of Nathanial's name, Adonia whipped around and stared at me.

"But this one said she had a message. For me. From Nathanial."

Cole's grip tightened on my hand. I cursed myself for saying I had a message.

I took a breath. "I came here for love. You understand that, don't you?" It was the most honest thing I could think to say.

She got a wild look in her eyes. "If I can't have love, neither can you. Now, tell me the message before I make another tree, but this time out of your friend."

Adonia dropped her projection of the redhead and reverted back to her true self. Her face became maniacal. I knew she wouldn't settle for anything less than the hope of being reunited with Nathanial. It was a hope I couldn't give her. Her blue eyes bore into me, and yet she looked as angelic as she had in the cameo.

The cameo. *The cameo!* I remembered what Nathanial looked like in the cameo. Now I needed to buy some time.

"You have no message," she accused.

I pulled the medal out of my pocket. "I have this."

She stared at Nathanial's medal for a few seconds and then

snatched it out of my hand to examine it. I used that moment to close my eyes and shut out everything around me. The queen, Ashe, Max, Cole, the Shades. I only allowed for one image in my head, and that image was from the cameo of Nathanial. In my mind, I gave the portrait flesh and blood. I took a deep breath and breathed life into him. I dressed him in uniform, stood him up straight, and then I opened his eyes.

I placed him as far away from us as I could.

"Look!" Max called out.

I opened my eyes. Max was pointing behind the queen, and everyone turned to see. There, maybe a football-field length away, stood a man in an army-green uniform.

The queen took two hesitant steps forward, then she was running. The Shades followed her close behind. Even Ashe took off after her.

I turned to Cole, who was staring at the soldier with a stunned expression.

"We don't have much time. We have to jump."

He furrowed his eyebrows. "Where?"

"Into the lake. Did you see how the sword didn't make a splash? It's not a lake, I don't think."

Cole considered this for a split second and then turned to Max. "Go home, dude."

"I'm not leaving you," Max said.

"When they turn around, let them see you run into the maze, as if you were following us. They'll think we're in the maze. Then go to the Surface and hide out. I'll find you."

Max looked unsure. By this time the queen would be close enough to realize that the soldier's face lacked real definition. We had only moments.

"Do it!" Cole commanded. "She'll never think anyone willingly went into the lake."

"Okay."

Cole and I turned toward the water. "Ready?" I asked.

"We have no idea what we're jumping into."

"I know. But I don't have anything to lose."

"I do!" His voice was gruff, and full of more emotion than I'd ever heard from him before. I looked into his eyes. He was holding on to something as dear to him as his own life. I knew that. I'd seen it in his memories. "You have to know . . . if I lost you . . . Why can't you see that would be the end of me?"

I knew exactly how he felt. Because I felt the same way about Jack. I was asking Cole to risk his life, again and again, for the boy I loved. And it wasn't him.

I eased his grip from my arm and clasped his hand in my own. "I'm going. But I understand if this is where you have to leave me."

He brought my hand up to his lips. "Never. We jump. If something happens, it will happen to both of us."

We coiled our legs and jumped.

I was right. The water didn't splash. We went right through it, into a free fall.

THIRTY

NOW

The Everneath. The Tunnels.

$\mathscr{I}$fell for a long time. Well, fell or floated. I wasn't sure. All I knew was that once we passed the threshold of the water, there was no light. There was no sound except my pulse thrumming in my ears. There was no feeling except the rough skin of Cole's hand enveloping mine. After a while there was no up and no down anymore.

We'd been falling for minutes. Hours. Maybe we would never stop.

"Cole—" I started to say when suddenly the wall slammed into my back. I had no air to scream. My lungs smashed against my ribs. My head felt as if it had exploded against a cement slab. I imagined my brain in a gooey mess coming out of my ears.

But it was still dark. I couldn't have seen that. Now I was cold, and when I opened my mouth, water rushed in.

"Nik!" Cole's voice came from beside me. I wondered when he had let go of my hand, but then he was pulling me upward.

I couldn't feel my hand. "It's water! We landed in water! Nik!"

Maybe I wasn't dead. But I couldn't breathe. Something was squeezing my lungs together.

I tried to cough, but I couldn't even manage that. My arms flailed. I tried to grab something for support: the ground, a wall, Cole's face, anything that would help me get air. I could hear water splashing all around us.

"Whoa, Nik. Settle down."

He didn't understand. I couldn't breathe!

"Step down. Reach your foot down. It's not that deep."

Why didn't he understand that the depth of the water was the least of my concerns at the moment? Air. Air. *Air.*

My foot grazed something slippery. The ground. Large rocks. I pressed against them and regained my balance. All at once, the invisible vise around my lungs loosened. I gasped. Sputtered. So loud it sounded like a horse with colic.

"You okay?" Cole said. I realized he hadn't been yelling the whole time. In fact, he was whispering.

I nodded. "I couldn't breathe."

"Shhh. It's okay."

"Easy for you to say."

He chuckled as I gasped in precious gallons of air. I blinked the tears out of my eyes. It was still too dark to see. My eyes should've adjusted by now.

"Where are we?"

"Good question," Cole said.

"How come you"—I gasped—"recovered so quickly?"

"I dove."

"What?"

"I don't know how I knew. I think I heard lapping water or something right before we hit. So I twisted around and dove. Whereas you went flat as a pancake on your back."

"You could've told me."

"Yeah, because there was plenty of time for that," he said sarcastically. As Cole was talking, he pulled me forward, and I realized that whatever water we were in, it was getting shallower as we went.

"Once we're out of the water, we can check. And see if you feel anything."

I nodded, even though he surely couldn't see me. I couldn't get over how dark it was. My eyes would've adjusted by now, but there was nothing to adjust to. There was absolutely no light. The air I was breathing felt heavy and stale. I wondered if light could even survive down here.

The water now barely covered my feet. "We're out," Cole said.

I shivered. We still held hands. If we were separated, I wasn't sure I'd ever be able to find him again. My other arm was outstretched in front of me. I assumed Cole was doing the same. We took a couple of steps forward, the ground shifting beneath my shoes as if I were walking on wet sand at a beach. But not fine sand.

"Stop," Cole said.

"What is it?"

"I feel a wall."

"Your arms are longer than mine."

I inched forward until I felt the same wall, craggy and rough beneath my fingers.

"Okay, Nik. It's down to you again. Which way?"

I didn't have to close my eyes and concentrate. The pull toward Jack—at least I hoped it was toward Jack—was constant in my chest. A dull ache that never went away. It had only become more pronounced down here. Even as I grew weary, my connection to him was there.

"This way," I said, tugging Cole toward the right. We felt along the wall; and as we did, the sound of lapping water retreated farther and farther in the distance.

Wherever we were going, it was leading us farther away from the body of water in which we'd landed.

"How are your lungs?" Cole asked.

I was sure my whole body must be one big bruise. But as I was about to answer, I realized Cole's voice sounded different. As if it were no longer bouncing off a small, enclosed space but rather a larger, cavernous place, which made me nervous. In a large, dark space, there were so many places to hide. So many ways to convince myself we weren't alone.

"Do you hear that echo?" I asked.

"Yes," Cole said. "We're in a bigger cave."

"Come away from the wall," I said.

"Why?"

"Just do it!" I couldn't explain why I was suddenly so adamant about not touching the wall. The pull from my chest was drawing me away, and more toward the center of whatever place we were in. But even without the pull, I didn't want either of us touching the wall anymore.

"Nik, it will be easier if we can feel our way—"

"Just trust me on this, Cole. Please?"

He didn't say anything, but I imagined him nodding. Without the wall for guidance, our steps became more tentative. I carefully placed one foot in front of the other, slowly increasing the weight. The ground was uneven and full of sharp rocks. Underneath our voices, there was a constant sound in the background. A sort of shushing, as if somewhere in the distance people were shuffling through newspapers. It was unnerving.

"We need a light," I said.

"You could always project one like you did that Nathanial guy."

I closed my eyes and pictured a candle.

"Nik, I was kidding. Please don't tell me you're trying."

"Shhh."

"The Nathanial image would've taken everything you had. Plus, we're in the Tunnels now, and they'll drain you fast."

I could already feel them working on my energy. But I focused everything I could on a tiny little candle flame. And just when I thought I couldn't hold the focus anymore, a tiny blaze appeared. It burned bright in the dark.

We looked all around us . . . and froze.

At first glance the walls seemed to be moving. But I quickly realized it wasn't the walls themselves. It was what was inside the walls. Sticking out of the clay and dirt were hundreds . . . thousands of hands. Smashed together. Fingers interlocking with fingers. Stretching out. Grabbing at . . . nothing.

My little flame hung there in the air, illuminating Cole's face. "What the hell?" he said.

He turned around. More hands. Hundreds. Thousands.

Both of us instinctively backed toward the center of the tunnel, circling with our backs to each other. The hands went as far as I could see to where they disappeared farther down the tunnel. I focused on one of the hands. It was opening and closing, as if looking for something to grab on to. The hand just below it was skinnier, with a distinctly gray pallor. The bones in the pointer finger nearly poked out of the skin. That hand, the sickly looking one, lay limp.

Lots of the hands were limp.

Others were fresh and pink, and those were the ones that were creating the illusion of the walls moving. They reached and grabbed; fingers tangled with other fingers; some grabbed the limp hands as if all they wanted was something to hold on to.

Cole leaned his head back, and I felt him shiver against me.

Oh no. I followed his gaze to the ceiling. It was full of hands. Reaching down toward us. These hands seemed livelier, as if the pull of gravity to the ground gave them extra energy. I ducked down. The nearest fingertips were at least a couple of feet out of reach, but I couldn't help it.

Cole held my arm. "It's okay, Nik. They're just hands." It sounded as if he was trying to convince himself.

"Yeah. Thousands of them. Sticking out of walls. *Moving.* Sure, everything's okay. For the Tunnels of hell." I gave a nervous laugh. I'd cracked. My brain was officially on its side. My tiny candle flame crumbled and seemed to turn to dust. The Tunnels were quick to eat my energy.

"Nothing's changed, Nik. You still have your tether to Jack, right? You can still feel it?"

I closed my eyes and focused on the pull in my chest. I nodded.

"Okay. You're going to lead us to Jack. I'll be right behind you."

I didn't know what was worse: seeing the hands all around us or wandering in the dark and *knowing* they were all around us.

And I couldn't ignore the shushing sound that I now knew was flesh rubbing against flesh a thousand times over.

Focus on the tether. Focus on the connection. Find Jack.

I really wanted that connection to point me in the direction from which we'd come, but instead it led me deeper into the blackness.

We started walking. Slowly. Heel to toe. The constant thrum of skin rubbing against skin—thousands of fingers chafing against one another—made my skin prickle. Cole seemed to sense this, because he kept talking.

"What's the first thing you're going to say to Jack?" Cole asked.

"I don't know. I've only ever thought about getting to him. I haven't even thought of the after."

"What if he's changed?"

"I don't care," I said resolutely. "But how do you mean?"

"Well, what if he's . . . old? He's been down here for years. What if he's ninety?" Cole's voice sounded very pleased at the notion.

"I wouldn't care," I said.

"Oh, you wouldn't care if you brought Jack all the way home from the Tunnels only to end up sending him off to a rest home? You'd be fine spoon-feeding him mashed peas as long as the two of you were together?"

I grimaced. "Believe it or not, I would. As long as I had him back."

"Kinky." Cole smirked.

But his words were getting lost in my head. Everything felt heavy. I tripped and fell to the ground, and it took me a very long moment to get back up.

"You okay, Nik?"

"I'm tired," I said, and I could hear just how true it was in my voice.

"It's the Tunnels. Try to focus on something else." His voice was full of concern, even though he tried to mask it.

"Like what?"

"Did I ever tell you what it was like to be aboard a Viking ship?"

I grimaced. "No."

"Did you know that the Vikings used birds—ravens, specifically—to navigate the waters? They would release the ravens, who always started out flying back toward the way they had come. But eventually the ravens would fly a different way, and the Vikings would change course to follow."

"Huh. Fascinating," I mumbled, trying not to slow down my gait even though my first instinct was to stop entirely, sit on the ground, and curl up into a ball.

"Isn't it, though?"

I knew Cole was trying to distract me, and I was grateful. It surprised me how much I liked him at this moment, until I realized that in every aspect of this seemingly hopeless trip, Cole had surprised me. I wondered for a moment how all this would change him, how he could continue feeding on humans after all of the noble things he'd done for me.

"Cole, what's going to happen to you when we get through this?"

"What do you mean?"

"I mean . . ." What *did* I mean? "Will things change? For you? Jack will be back. I'll be home, with my family. Life will sort of go on."

"Are you worried about me, Nik?"

I smiled in the dark. "Of course. Won't the queen come after you?"

"Possibly," he said. "But in the last few centuries, I've become very good at staying hidden and changing identities. She's not as powerful on the Surface anyway."

"But what will you do?"

Cole didn't say anything for a moment. I wished I could see his expression, but I felt as if the only energy left inside of me was my tether. There was nothing more. No way to make light.

When he spoke again, his voice was sad. "Don't worry about me. I have plans."

"What plans? What do you want to do with your life?"

"Same thing I've always wanted. Find that special some-one . . ." I could hear the smirk behind his voice. "Take over the world."

Before I could ask him how he planned to do this, he said, "Did you know that Viking helmets never had horns?"

He was obviously uncomfortable with the conversation, so I let him off the hook for now, mostly because talking took up so much energy. "Nuh-uh," I said.

"It's true. It was just a myth."

"Well, you know how I feel about myths—" My voice stopped right there.

"Nik?"

"Shhhh!" I felt pressure inside my chest. More than ever before. It took my breath away. My connection to Jack. He was close. So close. "I feel him, Cole."

And then a tiny miracle happened. When we turned the next corner, we could see. A crack in the ceiling of the tunnel reached all the way to the surface, and a small, dull light illu-minated the walls.

"He's here," I said.

Cole moved to my side. "Which hand?"

"I don't know." I started grabbing hands. The same hands that had grossed me out only minutes ago. I grabbed one, turned it over, discarded it as soon as I could eliminate it. Hand after hand I wrenched toward my face, picking the larg-est ones. Jack's hands were large. One hand didn't have the right calluses. Another, the knuckles were all wrong.

I moved down the wall. Cole grunted. "It'll take forever this way. Think of your tether!"

I closed my eyes and willed it to guide my hand. I took another breath, and grabbed the nearest hand.

The hand squeezed me back.

I opened my eyes. The knuckles were big and . . . boy. The grip was wide. I spread out the fingers, opening the hand, and placed mine on top, palm to palm.

His fingers curled over the tops of mine.

Jack's fingers.

I'd know them anywhere.

"Jack," I said. I kissed his fingers and put the *Ever Yours* note in his palm, wrapping his fingers around it. I kissed his fingers again and put the tip of his thumb on my lips while I spoke. "I'm here. I'll guide you home. And then I'll never let you go again."

I held his hand to my cheek for a moment.

"Um . . . Nik?" Cole's voice sounded different than usual. Lower. Gravelly. Broken. He'd only uttered two words, but that was all it took for me to feel his uncertainty right now. He was happy for me, but his heart was breaking.

I wouldn't have been there without him. I wouldn't have Jack's hand in mine. I turned to him. "Cole. Know this now. I will never forget what you've done for me. Never. Do you hear me?"

He nodded, but I could see he was crumbling, as if finding Jack would put an end to everything he wanted. Because it would. I placed my hands on either side of his face and brought his lips to mine in a light kiss.

It was fast. The power rush as quick as a gasp. The transferred memory was only a still picture. Me and Jack, standing on Cole's balcony. The Tunnels behind me. It was a frozen moment in time, but I still felt the pain *he* had felt on that night—the night we'd tried to kill him.

I pulled back. His face showed me what that kiss meant to him. It was everything. Even though the kiss was no longer than a second, he had to sit down. I couldn't help the wave of sympathy I felt for him then.

"You rest. I'm going to start digging." I reached for Jack's hand again. There was no time to find something resembling a shovel. I used my fingers, scraping away the dirt from around his hand. As I tore at the dirt, the hands around Jack's seemed to move away, almost as if they were giving me space. It was working.

His hand was in mine. I was giving him a ball of twine, just as Ariadne had done for Theseus. I would be his guide. His lamppost in this dark world. His candlelight. Just as he'd always been for me.

I dug harder. My fingernails felt as if they were tearing off.

"It's working!" I said to Cole over my shoulder.

"Let me take over."

"Do you feel well enough?"

"I'm much better now."

I kept my eyes on Jack's hand as I stepped away, which

is why I didn't see it coming until it was too late. Cole's foot, swinging back, hard and unmoving. His eyes were set with a steadfast determination until his gaze met mine.

And there was a moment. A fleeting second when everything seemed to stand still. His foot frozen in midair. His eyes wide. Did I see a flicker of hesitation?

Maybe. But it didn't matter. The frozen moment ended. Cole's foot crashed into me, and I was in the air. I reached out for Jack's hand, and my fingertips grazed his just as the wall of hands disappeared behind me in a swirl of haze.

It wasn't until my fate was sealed and my course for the Surface was set that I finally found my voice.

"Cole. Please."

But there was no one to hear me. I repeated it over and over, begging Cole to undo what he'd done. Soon the words became as much a part of me as breathing; and when the darkness dissipated, I was lying on the Shop-n-Go floor, Ezra standing over me.

"Cole. Please."

He crouched down. "Cole's not here."

I rolled over onto my side and crumpled into myself. "I lost him."

"Cole?"

I shook my head. "Jack."

THIRTY-ONE

NOW
The Surface. At the Shop-n-Go.

What happened? *What* happened?

Ezra stood still above me. He'd given up trying to get me to talk.

"Will should be here soon," he said.

"Thanks for calling him," I said. I wasn't really surprised that Ezra had called Will for me. Ezra had never acted as if he had something against me. I looked up at him from my position on the floor. "Why did he kick me out?"

"Who?"

"Cole," I said. "Why did he kick me out when we were so close?"

Ezra shook his head. "I don't know. It's above my pay grade." He grabbed a bag of Cheetos and ripped it open, offering me some.

I took one and bit off the end. It was the first taste of food I'd had in what felt like weeks. Mrs. Jenkins's warning came back to me. *Don't eat while you're there.* I hadn't broken her rule, and yet I had failed.

"Why do you help them?" I said to Ezra. "You're human. Are you hoping they'll bring you over or something?"

Ezra gave me a wry smile. "I do it for the money. It's a job. A job where I get paid a little bit better than other clerks. And all I have to do is keep quiet."

I closed my eyes and sighed. It was nice for a moment to hear about someone doing something for a boring reason like money. Not eternal life.

When I opened my eyes, Ezra put a hand on my shoulder. I stared at the hard floor. That floor that I'd slipped through so many times. If worse came to worst, maybe I could go again. "Do you have . . . any part of Cole? Or any of them?"

"No. They're careful. And they'd kill me."

The bells jangled, and footsteps made their way to the back.

"Nikki!" Will rounded the corner and scooped me up in his arms.

I buried my head in his chest. "I had him, Will. I had him in my hand. And I lost him."

As Will helped me out of the store and into his car, the tears came. Fast and hard. I wondered how many more times I could fail Jack before it was too late.

Will offered to drive me home, but I wasn't sure I was ready to face my father yet. I'd been missing for twenty-four hours since I'd disappeared from Dr. Hill's bathroom. I hoped it just looked as if I'd slipped out through the window or something.

As we drove to the city park, I told the whole story to Will. How we had made it so far . . . How we were so close . . .

And how, then, Cole had kicked me.

Will leaned back into his seat. "Maybe Cole sensed some sort of danger."

"But he would've said something to me first." I shook my head. "And we were alone. I would've seen Shades. Or at least felt them."

"Maybe it was something other than Shades. I mean, he's come with you so far. There'd be no reason for him to risk so much only to kick you at the end. It wouldn't make sense. Why would he have gone with you in the first place?"

"I don't know."

Will took my hand. "No. I'm sure he was protecting you from something. You'll see a hand soon. I'd bet on it." But he didn't sound convinced. Maybe he wasn't willing to face my failure.

I nodded. "That has to be it." I guess you never give up on the people you love. Which reminded me. "Can I borrow your phone?"

Will handed it over, and I called my dad. When he realized it was me on the phone, he said a few lines with such practiced perfection that I suspected he'd tried them out in a mirror a few times.

"Nikki. I don't care where you've been. I don't care why you left. Just come home. We'll deal with the rest later."

When I got home, I expected an interrogation from my dad, but it didn't happen. There were no threats of emergency therapy sessions. No mention of my escape from Dr. Hill's office. No mention of my appearance, although I'd hidden what was left of my hair under a baseball hat borrowed from Will, and my hoodie was zipped up, covering the burns.

There was only the smell of takeout from Café Trang. Stir-fried veggies and crispy chicken over steamed rice, in white boxes on the kitchen table.

Dad and Tommy had started without me. Maybe that's why the interrogation hadn't begun. Tommy held a heaping spoonful of chicken and rice halfway between his plate and his mouth. My dad was navigating the kung pao chicken with a pair of chopsticks. He had tried to teach me how to use chopsticks when I was twelve, but I never got past the kiddie sticks with the rubber band and the rolled-up paper as the fulcrum.

When he saw me, his face relaxed and he blinked at the sudden moisture in his eyes. "Nikki." He spoke my name quietly, but the two syllables were filled with love. "Come help yourself." He gestured to an empty plate on the table. "Hungry?"

"Yeah." I sat down, and he scooped a spoonful of chicken onto my plate. I watched his face, looking for some sort of hint as to what he was thinking, but there was nothing. "Dad, aren't we going to talk about what happened at Dr. Hill's office?"

He sighed. "No. Not tonight."

"But—"

"Just let it be, Nikki." He leaned toward me, staring into my eyes. "Dr. Hill wants you in a treatment center. Especially after yesterday. But you said to give you forty-eight hours." He searched my face again. "I'm not sure what the next step is. I told myself that if you didn't come home tonight, I would consider the in-patient treatment. But you came back." He looked down. "I didn't react well the last time. I shouldn't have put Valium in your water. Dr. Hill said that I had broken our trust, and she wouldn't be surprised if you didn't come back after that. But you did. So for the next few days, let's both take a step back from our mistakes. Let's regroup. Let it simmer. And then we'll reevaluate."

I smiled at his word choice. It sounded exactly like something he would say in a meeting with his top advisers.

But I would take it. My dad was offering me grace, which was more than I deserved. "Thanks, Dad."

"And, Nik, if you're going to lie to me, there's no need to make up fanciful stories about alternate realities. I'd rather you just didn't tell me anything."

"Okay."

That night I slept.

There was no sign of Jack.

The next morning, I put the hat on again and then told my dad I was going to get some coffee, but instead I drove up to Cole's condo. I knocked on the door. Pounded. The lights were off, and there was no noise coming from inside.

I sat on the porch with my back against the door. I sat there for three hours. Nobody came. Not Gavin, not Oliver. Not even Max. Hadn't he come back to the Surface after he disappeared in the maze?

I couldn't stay any longer. I couldn't test my dad's anxiety levels.

When I walked back through the doorway, carrying a coffee for him, he couldn't mask the relief on his face.

I handed him the coffee and then went to my room. Stared at the floor. Waited for Cole's hand.

Twenty-four hours. Cole had never let it go this long without taking me back under.

I kept replaying the events in my head. We had made good progress digging out Jack. We had been alone in the Tunnels. Hadn't we? There had to be more to the situation. There was something I wasn't grasping.

Or maybe it was something I didn't want to face. Did Cole betray me? Did he hate Jack so much that when it came down to the moment of his salvation, he couldn't see it through?

Was he hiding from me now, in shame?

Was he watching me from the Everneath?

"Cole," I said, my voice sounding loud and crazy in my quiet bedroom. "If you're watching me, it's okay that you freaked. Just take me back. Take me back, and we'll pretend it didn't happen. We're so close."

I got off the bed and crouched by the carpet, staring at the fibers until I thought I'd go blind.

Twenty minutes later, I was still waiting.

Nothing.

That night, I slept. It was a sleep full of darkness. Empty of any sounds or images.

It was a lonely sleep.

How had this happened?

How had I gotten so close . . . wrapped my fingers around his again . . . and failed? All I could do was sit on the side of my bed and stare at the floor.

How had I lost him again? The dam around my heart was gone, and my emotions coursed through me in waves. One moment it was as if I were back in the Tunnels, with everything drained except for the memory of the touch of his fingers. Then I would remember his face, his kiss . . . and it would all flow through me again.

But there were too many holes in me. Too many places the Wanderers had ripped apart. Too many leaks the Tunnels had made. I couldn't keep myself together this time. If Cole didn't come for me soon, no amount of glue would ever fix me.

I shook my head and knocked it against the wall a couple of times. I hadn't lost him. He wasn't gone. Cole would come back. His hand would appear, and I would grab it, and he would drag me back to the Tunnels and explain what happened.

He was only waiting for when it was safe again.

I closed my eyes and buried my face in my knees. Time was passing slowly, or maybe it was flying by, and all I could do was sit in a ball on my bed.

Rocking back and forth.

My dad knocked on my door. "Nikki? I'm headed to work."

Pause.

"Are you okay?"

I mustered my cheeriest voice. "Yep. Just reading. Have a good day!"

He probably didn't buy it, but he left. Maybe he was just relieved I was home.

Sometimes I could almost picture myself, as if I were out of my own body and watching myself from the corner.

The girl on the bed looked wide-eyed. Wild haired. And a little bit crazy. Her nails were bitten down to nubs. The right side of her head was missing most of its hair.

But if I was sane enough to recognize how crazy I looked, was I really crazy?

Oh boy. I needed to get out. But where to go?

Will had left me several messages, none of which I answered. Maybe he assumed I was already back in the Tunnels. I couldn't face telling him the truth. I was still on the Surface. And I was beginning to think Cole would never come back.

Then I remembered Mrs. Jenkins. She'd said she would look in some of the old books she had in the basement. Maybe if I told her what had happened, she would have an idea of why Cole kicked me out. What he was scared of. And what I should do now.

Someone had to know what I should do now. I would do anything, if someone would just tell me what to do.

"Get up," I whispered to myself, my lips against my kneecaps. I had wallowed long enough. I owed it to Jack. I imagined him speaking to me. "Get up, Becks. Get up now."

Finally, in one last push to get myself off the bed, I dug my teeth into my knee. Hard enough and long enough to draw blood.

A tiny drop formed at the site, growing bigger until it began to run down my leg. I watched it go, gravity pulling it down my shin, my ankle, all the way to my foot. When it was about an inch away from reaching the quilt, I sprang off the bed.

I could wallow for days at a time on my bed, but I wasn't about to spill blood on the sheets.

My reasoning sounded ridiculous even to me. But I was standing. And headed to the shower.

Two full mugs of coffee later, I drove to Mrs. Jenkins's house.

There was no answer on my first knock. I stepped back and glanced at the windows. There were no lights.

She was always home, wasn't she?

I walked around the side of the house to the garage. There, parked in front, was an old Honda Civic. The same one that was usually parked there.

Had someone picked her up? I didn't think she had any friends.

I started toward the front again when an outline of a figure caught my eye through the translucent curtain. A silhouette of someone . . . Mrs. Jenkins, I would guess from the outline, sitting on the couch.

Why was she ignoring my knocks?

Peering in the window, trying to get a clearer look, I knocked again. But the person didn't move.

"Mrs. Jenkins! It's Nikki," I called out. Still no movement. I went to the front of the house and pounded on the door; and surprisingly, it creaked open, as if it hadn't been closed all the way.

I pushed it farther open.

"Mrs. Jenkins? It's Nikki. Are you okay?"

There was no response. I looked around. The place felt . . . different. Quiet. I shook my head. *Seriously, Becks, get a grip.*

"Mrs. Jenkins? I'm coming in."

I made the familiar walk past the foyer and into the living room. Mrs. Jenkins was sitting on the couch, her back to me. I knew it was her, because her silver-gray hair was pulled into the same loose ponytail.

Papers were scattered on the coffee table in front of her. Maybe she had found something in the basement. Something that could help me.

"Hello?" I said.

My voice seemed loud. Too loud. And then suddenly my breathing was too loud.

I tiptoed toward the side of the couch; and as I rounded the corner, everything seemed to freeze.

It was Mrs. Jenkins sitting there. Only it looked nothing

like her. Her skin hung loosely from her skeletal frame. Her eyes were sunken back and dried out, and her head looked as if someone had papier-mâchéd a skull with gray paper and attached a wig on top. Her fingers were wrapped around the handle of one of her teacups, the saucer balanced precariously on her lap.

"Mrs. Jenkins?" a soft voice said. It took me a moment to realize it was me. I would never have consciously tried to speak to her considering the way she looked.

I don't know why, but I went to take the teacup out of her hand. In that instant, her body deflated even more, as if the rest of the air holding her shape had escaped.

Mrs. Jenkins was dead. Deader than I'd ever seen anyone.

People don't just spontaneously . . . shrivel up. She had been fine two days ago. That was when I last visited, wasn't it? When she'd given me Nathanial's medal? Someone did this to her. Someone strong. Someone who could still be around.

Instinctively, I backed up and ran into the end table, toppling it over onto the tiles, one of the figurines smashing on the floor.

I had to get out of here. Whatever had happened to her, it wasn't caused by another human being.

An immortal, perhaps. But not a human.

I set down the teacup and started to wipe it off in case of fingerprints, which I quickly realized was a ridiculous thing to be worried about. My fingerprints weren't on record or anything. And I'd done nothing wrong.

The sound of a car's engine outside made me freeze. The ignition cut off, and a door slammed.

"Crap," I breathed.

I looked at the books and papers on her coffee table. This might be my last chance to grab them. Without thinking, I scooped up as many as I could into my arms, then I bolted out of the living room and toward the front door, threw it open . . . and ran headfirst into someone with a familiar beige jacket. The papers went everywhere.

It was Detective Jackson.

Our eyes met, and for a moment I considered running. But I didn't do anything wrong. I told myself over and over that I didn't do anything wrong.

Detective Jackson grabbed me by the shoulders. I hadn't realized I'd been saying the words out loud. "Nikki, are you okay?"

"Call 911."

THIRTY-TWO

NOW
The Surface. Mrs. Jenkins's house.

$\mathcal{D}$etective Jackson looked behind me, into the house, then said, "Stay here."

I nodded, and as I sank to the step, he charged inside. I gathered the papers and stacked them neatly, lining them up perfectly, as if that would help everything that had happened make sense. Then I held them against my chest.

The street was quiet. Empty. I felt exposed sitting there on the porch, but I had no idea what, exactly, I should be scared of.

Mrs. Jenkins. Dead. Not just dead. Drained. Was there any other explanation? No. I'd never seen anything like it. But I'd heard about something like it.

It sounded like the way everyone thought Adonia had died: all of the energy sucked out of her so fast that there was nothing but a shell left. Had the same thing happened to Mrs. Jenkins? But who could do something like that?

"I didn't do anything wrong," I said again. But I couldn't help feeling responsible. "Cole," I said out loud. "What's happening?"

Nobody answered.

Detective Jackson came out of the house and sat down next to me.

"Did you call 911?" I asked.

He sighed. "I called the police. There's really nothing an ambulance can do at this point."

We sat in silence for a few minutes.

"What have you got there?" he asked, noting the papers and book in my arms.

Everything that I had taken had an old look to it. The parchment was dyed and rough around the edges. The book's spine was cracked in a hundred places, and the title had long ago been worn away.

I thought quickly. "Just some stuff I was bringing to show her. She was into antiques."

The wail of sirens sounded in the distance. Maybe that's why he didn't ask me anything more about it. The police station was nearby down the canyon, so the mountain walls carried the sound.

"Am I in trouble?" I asked.

"Did you kill her?"

I jerked my head up. "No!"

He put a hand on my shoulder, and I realized he was smiling. "I know. I followed you from your house. Besides the fact that I don't think you have it in you to take a life, you also didn't have the time. She's been gone for a while, it looks like. I don't think you had anything to do with . . . what happened here."

"What *did* happen?"

"I don't know."

The sirens got louder, and a few moments later the first patrol car came into view. Detective Jackson looked at me. "We'll face them together."

"I thought you hated me."

"Nikki, I'm investigating the disappearance of a boy, and you were the last one to see him. But it's an investigation. Not a vendetta."

I answered their questions. Explained how I found her. How the door was open. Detective Jackson backed up my story, especially the timeline, which wouldn't have allowed for any involvement in possible foul play. For once it was lucky the detective had been following me.

I heard the police officers giving their theories. Mrs. Jenkins was a quiet woman. Private. She'd probably been dead for weeks, considering how decomposed her body was.

I knew she hadn't even been dead for days. I'd only seen her two days ago.

But nobody knew that. Not even the detective.

I didn't tell my dad about what had happened. If the police had any more questions, he'd find out then. But I didn't think they would. They had already explained away what had happened.

Now I was left with only my own thoughts as to the truth

about what happened. But what was the truth?

Someone had drained Mrs. Jenkins, to the point where her body looked like a centuries-old mummy. But who was powerful enough to do it? The queen, probably. But could other Everlivings do it? Destroy somebody so completely?

Could Shades do it?

Did she die with the false hope that one day she would be granted eternal life by a future queen?

I couldn't think about it anymore. My body was shutting down. I put the book and papers that I'd taken from Mrs. Jenkins's house on my desk and then collapsed on my bed, curling up and tucking the quilt underneath my chin. My brain couldn't take any more. Just when my father and Dr. Hill were giving me space, for the first time in my life, I felt as if I were snapping.

I folded my knees to my chest, pressed my head farther into my pillow, and closed my eyes. I must've fallen asleep, because Jack's voice came to me.

NOW

In my dream.

I can hear him, but I can't see him.

"Hi." The voice sounds as if it comes from right next to me, from his usual place beside me on my bed.

I hold my breath. He sounds so real. I don't know why I can't see him. Is he still alive? Am I dreaming of being in the Tunnels with him?

"Aren't you going to say anything?" he says.

How can I tell him how close I was, only to have failed? Better not to say anything. If this is really him and not just a regular dream about him, I don't want him to lose hope. Even though my own hope was obliterated.

"I've missed you," Jack says. "So much. I don't know how I got here."

"I know," I say. *Has he forgotten how he took my place?* "You're there because of me."

"You don't sound surprised."

I grimace. "Surprised at what?"

"That I'm here."

"You're always here."

"I am?"

"Of course."

"What do I say?" *He sounds curious.*

"Stuff."

"Like what?"

"You always say you miss me."

He gives a soft laugh. "That's obvious. What else?"

"You talk about the time Jules told you I liked you."

"And?"

My words flow out. "You tell me that you love me. You tell me that you'll never leave."

"Can you at least face me, Becks?" he says.

I open my eyes to discover I am facing the wall next to my bed. Which is weird, because in my dreams I am always automatically facing the center, to see Jack.

That's why it's dark.

What the . . . ?

NOW

The Surface. My bedroom.

I turned over and faced him. And gasped.

Jack wasn't back in my dreams. He was here. He was alive. And he was covered in what looked like a thick layer of soot. Nasty red gashes blanketed his face, and they continued down his arms and legs. His clothes were mere rags, covered in soot and blood.

His eyes were barely open, dark slits on his swollen face. His feet hung off the edge of the bed, and for a brief second I thought he seemed too big to be my Jack.

I moved to touch his face but held my hand just above where I would've made contact if he'd been real.

"What happened to you?" My breaths came hard and fast. "Are you hurting? Are you dead?"

He smiled. "Dead? I've never felt more alive." He opened his hand, and inside it was a note. Our note. *Ever Yours.*

Without thinking, I went to reach for it. And grabbed it.

I froze. The paper was in my hand. I'd taken it. The note

was real. It was tangible, and it was *in my hand*. I dropped it and grabbed Jack's hand. His real hand.

I looked at his eyes. "What . . . ?" I saw the window in the corner of my room. It was ajar. As if someone had just come in.

I tried to speak, but the breaths were coming too fast.

"Put your head between your knees." He urged my head down, and traced his fingers up and down my spine. He was quiet as I slowed my breathing. "There. You okay now?"

I sat up gradually. There was no way I was going to lose consciousness. There was no way I was going to let him out of my sight. "No, I am not okay. Is it really you?"

Jack nodded.

"How?"

"I'm not sure. I was buried alive. Then I felt your hand. You gave me the note. And you kissed my fingertips."

He smiled because as he was saying those words, I was already kissing his fingertips.

"I held on. Waiting for you to come back. Eventually the note started to pull away, as if it were attached to a string or something; and I thought it meant you were leaving. But I wouldn't let go. It pulled away, and I followed. It was the digging-out part that felt like it took days. I dug and scratched until I was out of the wall. I couldn't see anything, but the note was still pulling away. I was so tired. So weak. But I held on to the note, and the next thing I knew, I was in the air. At least it felt that way. I couldn't see."

It sounded almost like a kick, but he was being pulled out

of the Everneath instead of being pushed.

He blinked a few times and squinted. "I still can't see very well. I wish I could see your face."

I took his hand and rested my cheek in the palm. "You can."

He leaned in close; and when he was only a couple of inches away, I felt the whoosh of my energy going out of me and into him. He must've been so empty. I knew, because when I'd returned so drained after the Feed, I'd stolen energy from him in the same way.

"I'm sorry," Jack said. He tried to pull back, but I wouldn't let him.

"Kiss me."

"But—"

"No arguing." He didn't move, so I basically tackled him. And then our lips were smashed together. We kissed until the initial rush of emotions from me to him had calmed, and then we kissed some more.

Then I was grabbing at him and digging my fingers into his shoulders. His back. Knotting them in his hair. Keeping him here, and keeping him real. He kissed me back with a similar fierceness, and I thought about how no dream could feel this tangible.

And it was a long time before we remembered where we were. We slept with our fingers and legs tangled together.

THIRTY-THREE

NOW

The Surface. My bedroom.

The next morning I watched him sleep. The fluttering of his eyelids. The twitches of his lips, as if he was dreaming of kissing me.

The swelling in his face had gone down some, but many of the cuts on his body still bled. I was so focused on having him back and in my arms, I hadn't been very good at tending to his wounds.

I inched away from him and tried to creep out of bed, but in a lightning-quick move, his hand wrapped around my wrist.

"You're not going anywhere," he said.

"But your cuts—"

He pulled me to him, interrupting my words with his lips so fast that it literally took my breath away.

The sun had risen high in the sky before we stopped again. Finally, I insisted that he had to eat something and we had to get him cleaned up. There were people who were just as invested in Jack as I was, and they needed to know he was back. Will. Jack's mom. Jules. Even my family.

My dad was at work, and Tommy was fishing with a friend, so we had the place to ourselves. I let Jack rest while I threw a frozen pepperoni pizza into the microwave.

It had been cooking for thirty seconds when I heard a commotion coming from my bedroom. I raced down the hallway to find Jack leaning against the wall.

"I don't think I was quite ready for the whole upright thing."

I put his arm around my shoulders and noticed again how much he'd changed. He wasn't only taller. He was bigger too. I nearly disappeared under his arm. I shook my head. Maybe I was remembering his dimensions wrong.

He regained his balance; and when the pizza was finished cooking, he ate it. The entire thing. While standing.

I sat on the kitchen counter, watching him. It was so good to see him eat. It was so normal.

But I noticed the size thing again as his hands folded the slices of pizza in half. They seemed bigger. Everything about him seemed large, from the muscles that wrapped his arms like ropes to the broadness of his shoulders.

"You're bigger," I said.

He raised an eyebrow, midbite. He'd given me the same face many times when he thought I'd said something funny. The only difference now was that his eyes weren't focused on my face. He still couldn't see me clearly.

"You are," I said. "Look at you."

"It's been a long time since I've looked at me."

"Well, you should." I held up my hand. "But not right now. You're sort of a mess."

He touched his face. "Are all the features where they're supposed to be?"

I pursed my lips. "Yes. But it looks like you've been swimming in ashes. And it smells like it too."

He dropped the piece of pizza on the cardboard box, unfinished, and came to stand in front of me. Putting his hands on either side of my legs, he leaned toward me. "You always said you liked that campfire smell."

I still had to look up to meet his gaze. I wasn't imagining it. "You're taller too, I think."

His eyes fluttered, and he stumbled backward. I jumped off the counter and put his arm over my shoulders. "Whoa. Are you okay?"

He nodded but didn't answer.

"Let's get you lying down."

I took him to my room, where he collapsed on my bed. After only a few moments, his eyes were closed and his breathing even. I stood up, but he grabbed my arm.

"Don't go."

I smiled. "I'm not. I'm just going to get a wet cloth. So I can try and clean up the mess that is your face."

His grip on my arm loosened. "Okay. But come right back." When he let go, his fingers left white marks on my arm. I couldn't believe how strong he was. When I'd pictured him in the Tunnels for years, I'd imagined him growing weaker. But right now, except for the almost fainting, he seemed stronger than he'd ever been.

And larger.

I couldn't imagine why. It wasn't from anything that had happened on the Surface. He came back this way. What had happened in the Tunnels?

I shook my head at how many more unanswered questions we'd probably have. At least now we had time to figure it out. Grabbing a washcloth, a towel, soap, and a bowl of hot water, I hurried back into the room. His eyes were still closed. I sat on the edge of the bed, dipped the cloth into the water, and started with his forehead. After a few scrubs his features were visible.

"Hi, you," I said.

He smiled. "Hi."

"I still can't believe you're here. Yesterday I was convinced nothing would ever be right again. But here you are."

"What happened yesterday?"

I shook my head, hesitant to tell him about Mrs. Jenkins's horrifying death. "Nothing we need to get into right now. But there is one pressing matter."

"What's that?"

"Your mom. She hired a detective to track you down. You have to see her. Let her know you're okay."

"We'll go together."

I thought about my last encounter with his mom. At Jack's graduation. It seemed so long ago, but the memory would be fresh in her mind. "You should probably go alone. I think she'd rather see you . . . without me."

"I'm not leaving you."

"I promise, it would be better—"

He grabbed my hand, so fast I could hardly see the movement. "I'm. Not. Leaving. You."

I winced. "Okay. Just . . . let up a bit." I started to pull his fingers away from my hand so the circulation could return.

"Sorry, Becks."

I smiled. "Like I said. You're bigger now."

I called Will and told him to make sure his mom was home. I wouldn't tell him anything else, except to say I'd be right over.

Once we were out front, Jack started toward his family's door, and I leaned against my car.

"C'mon, Becks."

He held out his hand to me. I shook my head. "Your family deserves this moment. Alone. Please trust me. I'll be right here."

He looked unsure, but he knocked anyway. The door swung open, and then Will was tackling his little brother. Jack was always taller, but now he seemed to have at least half a foot on Will.

Mrs. Caputo came onto the front porch and embraced her lost son, tears streaming down her face.

Will raised his hand to me, and I waved back. The three of them stood in a circle, their arms linked with one another's. The scene was incredibly tender. I didn't know what Jack would tell his mom about where he'd been. That was up to him.

I walked down the street and around the corner. They deserved this time together without me there.

I wound through the neighborhoods, contemplating the events of the past two days. How had it happened? How had it worked out like this?

Yesterday I had thought my world was splitting at the seams. But now . . . Yes, Mrs. Jenkins was still dead. But I didn't have anything to do with that. Maybe she was dead because of her association with the Daughters of Persephone. But that wasn't my fault. I wasn't a threat to the queen. I was human, and I wasn't going back to the Everneath anytime soon.

And what about Cole? Where did he go? Had he planned this?

If he had, then where was he? Did he know how it had all turned out? No. If he did, he would've been back in my room, gloating over how much he had sacrificed for me and demanding some sort of payback.

Wouldn't he?

What if his absence was a sign of something more sinister? The last time I saw him was in the Tunnels. Not the friendliest environment. What if something had happened to him after I'd left?

There were too many questions. But only one answer I cared about right now. Jack was back. And I would never let him go again.

When I rounded the final corner heading to the Caputo

home, Jack came loping toward me. His sunglasses were perched on his nose. His old Giants T-shirt stretched tight across his chest.

He threw his arms around me and picked me up in a tight embrace. "You said you'd stay right there."

My feet were dangling in the air. I buried my face against his neck. His hair was damp. "You showered."

He kissed my neck. "I had to get rid of the ashy smell."

"What did you tell your mom?"

He set me down and frowned. "I told her I've been away. It was hard to explain, so I didn't even try. I have no idea what to say that will . . . satisfy her."

I brushed his hair off his forehead. "I know exactly what you mean."

"Where do we go now?"

We walked toward my car. "There's someone else we need to see right away."

Jules was sitting on her bar stool next to the Scentsy candle shop in the center of the walkway at the mall. When she saw Jack, her face broke out in a giant smile, and then she burst into tears.

I stood back so Jack could be with her, but Jules grabbed my hand and pulled me close. And then the three of us were hugging. And crying.

THIRTY-FOUR

NOW

The Surface. My bedroom.

That night, after a visit with my dad and then dinner with his own family, Jack sneaked into my room, although I don't know how much sneaking was involved. There was no way his mother thought he wouldn't.

We were on our sides on my bed, facing each other, as we had done every night. Only now we could touch. Hand to hand. Palm to palm. Skin to skin. I couldn't get over him.

"How did you find your way out?" I asked. "Once you were free of the Tunnels. Where did you land?"

"It's all a blur, really. I was so out of it. It's like I was sling-shotted out from the Tunnels, and then I ended up on the floor of the Shop-n-Go."

He shook his head as if it all sounded so ludicrous.

"That's the weak spot," I said. "Between the Everneath and the Surface."

He stroked my hair. "It was late at night. I couldn't open my eyes. I could barely walk. I didn't know where I was going;

I only knew I had to find you."

I smiled. "You found me."

He kissed my head. "I found you."

I nestled in closer to him. He smelled like Jack, and I breathed in deeply. I looked at his face again, traced the lines again.

I touched his eyebrow. The steel post that had been there was gone, and in its place was a gash. It must've been ripped out at some point.

He brushed some hair out of my eyes. "How did you do it, Becks? How did you find me?"

I grimaced. "It's a really long story. Cole helped me. He transported me there. Helped me the whole way." I thought about explaining the tether from my heart to his, but that was a story for another time.

"Cole helped you?"

I nodded, wincing as I remembered the strange, confusing ending to our journey.

"What is it?" he asked.

"It doesn't matter. You're here."

"I'm here."

"That's all that matters."

He brought my face up to meet his and then easily pulled me so I was on top of him. We were kissing again. But we were both exhausted.

The entire night was spent kissing and dozing and kissing some more. I couldn't imagine anything better.

* * *

I woke up with a start and a gasp. I wiped my forehead. It was dripping with sweat. What had woken me?

It was just a nightmare, I told myself. *Just a nightmare.*

But something wasn't right. I glanced down at Jack next to me. He was sleeping peacefully, snoring a little. I sighed. As long as he was here, I could take anything.

I looked around the room, trying to find the source of whatever had changed. But I couldn't see anything. Everything seemed the same.

I tried to lie back down, but before I knew it I was up and wandering the room. My breath came out in shallow puffs. I put my hand on my chest in an effort to calm my breathing, but it didn't feel right. Was I still dreaming?

I heard a scrape at my window. Someone was opening it. I moved to wake up Jack, but before I could, Cole came through. Dove in, more like. But quietly, and agilely, like a cat.

We locked eyes, my hand still over my heart.

At first I felt relief at seeing his face, before anger took over. "What the hell happened back there? You kicked me!" Then I took a few deep, calming breaths, and in a complete turnaround, I threw my arms around him. "Where have you been?"

Cole hugged me back, but his arms felt stiff; his back went rigid. I released him and looked at his face. "What's wrong?"

He smiled. "Nothing. I'm good. I'll explain it all." His voice drifted off as his eyes darted around my room. "First, I need you to tell me if there's anything strange about your room. Anything here that wasn't here before."

I frowned and shook my head. "What are you talking about?"

He grabbed my shoulders. "It's important, Nik. Look around and tell me if there's anything out of place. Any new object that you don't recognize."

His eyes were wild.

"You're scaring me," I said.

"Everything will be okay once you find it."

Apprehensive, I looked all around for whatever he was talking about, frantically searching every surface for something foreign. The darkness made it difficult to see, but even so I thought everything seemed fine. But when my gaze got to my desk, I froze. There, next to my laptop, was a small gold object about the size of a pocket watch. I'd never seen it before.

Cole followed my gaze.

He held up his hand, warning me not to move.

"What's going on?" I whispered.

"I'll explain," he said, his hand still up. He was creeping sideways, toward the desk. "Just give me . . . a . . . minute. . . ." He snatched the object as if it were a mouse about to run away.

Once he had it in his hands, the tension in his body disappeared. He opened it, checked out the contents, and then gave me a smile that could only be described as triumphant.

"Cole, please. Talk to me." I don't know why I was worried. I had Jack. We'd both made it out alive. "What's wrong? It worked. We saved Jack."

His eyebrows shot up. "What?"

He was surprised? "Look." I pointed to my bed, where Jack was buried deep under the covers and sleeping soundlessly. His exhaustion was otherworldly, and I wasn't worried that we would wake him.

Cole frowned. "How did he . . . ?"

"It was the token. The note. I'd left it in his hand."

"But I told you to hang on to it."

I shook my head in confusion. "Yes, but if I had, he wouldn't be here."

"How *is* he here?"

"He climbed out using the note. I know it sounds crazy, but . . ." Cole's face told me the news was entirely unwelcome. "Wait. I thought you would know this. Why don't you know this? What happened to you in the Tunnels?"

He gave me a look. "Nik, I never wanted to save Jack."

"I know. But you helped me anyway. You were my hero."

He shook his head. "I told you. There are no heroes."

How could he believe that now? What loathing ran so deep inside him that would block out anything good? I stepped closer. "I don't care what you think of yourself. I think you're a hero."

"Then you're blind."

I flinched. He seemed so unfeeling. So distant. I'd thought we were past the point where I had to convince him of his worth. I closed the distance between us and put my hands on either side of his face. "Tell me what's going on."

He sighed and leaned his head down toward me. "I don't

want to yet. I have this one moment . . . and only this one final moment . . . to enjoy how you see me. It's in your eyes. I've done what I thought was impossible. I made you love me, but not in the way I needed. You love me as your friend."

I nodded, still lost. "After what you've done, you *are* a friend."

He leaned in, bringing his lips close to mine. Surprised, I pulled back and glanced at Jack to make sure he was still sleeping. "Cole, don't," I said.

Cole pressed his lips together. "Only ever a friend."

"You know how it is," I said, glancing at Jack again. "You know how it's always been."

"I know. That's why I did what I did." He released me and pulled away.

"Please tell me what you're talking about."

He took my hand and brought it to his lips, kissing it briefly before pressing it against my own chest. "Feel," he commanded.

I felt. Nothing. I felt nothing.

Where my heart should be, there was nothing. Blinking rapidly, my eyes darted around the room as if I'd misplaced something.

Cole backed up toward the window, and when he was at the farthest point away from me, he folded his arms.

"Isn't it amazing how well the Everneath knows what's inside you? It takes three full days, but my world can transform your Surface heart into something that epitomizes you, right down to your very soul. And when you get your heart, you realize that object is so appropriate—so *right*—it could never have been anything else. The whole process is quite extraordinary. The power of the Everneath makes it happen, but it's always seemed magical to me."

There was a heaviness in my chest that I couldn't explain. "Why are you telling me this?" I said in a low voice.

He brought his hand forward, showing the metal object he had grabbed from my desk. "You've completed your first step to becoming an Everliving. Your Surface heart is a compass. Your Everneath heart is vaulted."

I couldn't move. I was paralyzed.

My heart. *My heart.* It was gone. It wasn't beating under my hand. That's what was different.

My mouth dropped open, and I fought for breath. "You did this to me?"

"Actually, you did it to yourself. It was your choice to feed on an Everliving. *In* the Everneath. *Three* times, Nik. You chose it. All three times. In fact, that was the hardest part of this whole thing. The rules for creating an Everliving are very specific. The mortal has to *ask* to be fed by the Everliving. There was no way I could offer to feed you or even suggest that feeding you was a possibility. I have to admit, there were times on our little journey when I wondered if I'd ever get the chance to show you how feeding you would energize you. Was it too much to hope you would initiate a kiss? You gave me mouth-to-mouth, but unfortunately I wasn't awake for it. I decided to find another chance to drown or get knocked out, but there weren't a whole lot of opportunities.

"Then I saw you with your Siren. I only caught a glimpse,

but I saw you kiss him. I thought, Maybe, just maybe . . . I ran back to my Siren—yes, Nik, I'd already figured out she wasn't you—and I waited for you to find us. And voilà. The magical kiss to save me from the Siren."

"I saved your life," I said, incredulous.

"Yes. After I put myself in jeopardy. See, once you had a taste of what a kiss from me could do, I finally allowed myself to hope. There had to be at least two more times when you would be weak enough to beg for another kiss."

I racked my brain, trying to remember.

Cole smiled. "The second time was when the Wanderers attacked you. The third time was in the Tunnels."

It didn't make sense. None of it made any sense. Cole had gone to the Everneath to help me, hadn't he? I thought of the ultimatum I'd given him, when I threatened to ingest his hair and go back by myself.

"I had to beg you to come with me," I said.

"If I had instigated the whole 'let's go to the Everneath and search for Jack' scenario, you never would've trusted me. You would've always been looking for my ulterior motives. And I needed your trust. Your unquestioning, implicit trust."

"But Max warned me to stay away from you! Why would he do that if being with you was part of the plan?"

"We knew if Max looked too eager, you would get suspicious."

I shook my head. He'd played me. He knew me so well, and he'd played me. That was the real reason Ashe had followed Cole. Why Max had never gotten so frustrated that he abandoned us. They were in on it.

I glanced quickly at Jack and then lowered my voice. "Mrs. Jenkins warned me not to eat."

Cole frowned. "Yes. Mrs. Jenkins was the wild card. I had no idea how much she really knew. She knew enough to warn you not to eat in the Everneath, but she didn't know what was really meant by 'eating.'"

"She's dead."

Cole's face remained blank. "I know."

"Did you kill her?"

Cole smiled wryly. "No."

I let out a small sigh of relief.

"Max did. With the help of the rest of the band."

My mouth dropped open. "But . . . why?"

"She knew about you. She was a loose end."

I put my hand on my stomach and sank to the ground. Cole watched, but he didn't make a move to comfort me. I put my head in my hands. "No. This can't be right. Tell me this is a dream."

"It's a dream come true," Cole said with a smirk. Then his face became serious. "You're safe, Nik. Nobody knows about you except the band now. The queen doesn't know you survived the Feed. She doesn't know a threat even exists. We've made you safe."

"You've made me one of you!" I hissed.

"I know. I'm sorry." He stood next to the windowsill, knees slightly bent, coiled and ready to spring.

He was leaving. "Wait!"

"What?"

"Give me my heart. Please. It doesn't matter if I break it since my second heart is in a vault in the Everneath, right? So give it to me."

Cole looked from his closed fist to my face. He slipped the compass into his pocket. "Sorry, Nik. I'm really sorry. But there are certain . . . perks for the Everliving who holds your heart. And I hold yours. Now we're even."

"How?"

His face went soft. "You've always held mine."

He swung one leg over the side of the window.

"I trusted you," I said, my voice shaky with anger and exhaustion.

"I know," Cole said simply. He jumped out the window and leaned his head in for one last moment. "And now I have all of eternity to earn your forgiveness."

When Jack opened his eyes the next morning, I was sitting with my back against the wall, watching him. He looked at the bed next to him, put a hand on the pillow, and turned.

When he caught my gaze, his eyebrows furrowed.

"Becks. Are you okay?"

I nodded.

He stretched his arms above his head. "What time is it?"

"It's eight thirty."

He looked at me again. "What's wrong?"

I tried to smile. "Nothing."

He grimaced. "Do you honestly think I'm gonna buy that? Tell me what's going on."

There was no avoiding it. What I had planned, Jack would find out eventually. It would be better if he knew now. Then maybe he could help me.

I pushed off the floor and returned to sit by him in the bed. I took his hand in both of mine.

"You know the Everneath?"

He smiled and gave a small laugh. "Uh, yeah, I think I'm familiar with it."

"Good. Because I'm going to destroy it."

His smile faded.

"I'm taking the whole. Damn. Thing. Down. Are you with me?"

He brought my hand up to his lips and kissed the space between my thumb and fingers. "Always. Forever."

ACKNOWLEDGMENTS

Thank you to my agent, Michael Bourret, who deserves to be knighted for his hard work and patience on my behalf.

Thank you to the rest of the DGLM staff, especially Lauren Abramo, who has my back on every other continent.

Thank you to my amazing editor, Kristin Daly Rens, who worked tirelessly on draft after draft after draft of *Everbound*, always pushing me a little bit further to make the book shine and ensure that the world of the Everneath came alive. Now you know this world better than I do! I hope you liked the healthy dose of Cole.

Thank you to the rest of the HarperCollins team, especially Sara Sargent, Caroline Sun, Emilie Polster, countless "smoke" designers, mapmakers, and all the other people behind the scenes.

Thanks to the SIX: Bree Despain, Emily Wing Smith, Kimberly Webb Reid, Valynne Maetani Nagamatsu, and Sara Bolton, a.k.a. the best critique group a girl could ask for. Without you all and our weekly writing days, the Everneath would've been a bland, boring world.

Thank you to all of my friends who have supported me

on this crazy ride. If I named you all, I know I'd leave someone out.

Thank you to my mom and dad. Despite everything going on, you read my pages like you have nothing else to do in the world.

Thank you to my family: the Erin and Dave Gubler family, the Jacksons, the Johnsons, the other Johnsons, the Ellingsons, and the Otts. Together, you are responsible for at least half of my book sales.

Thank you to my boys, Carter and Beckham. You have been so patient, even though you think I live in my study.

Thank you to Sam. No words.